READY
TO
FALL

MARCELLA PIXLEY is a teacher and the author of two previous books for teens. She lives in Westford, Massachusetts with her husband and two sons.

READY
TO
FALL

Marcella Pixley

PUSHKIN PRESS

Pushkin Press
71–75 Shelton Street
London, WC2H 9JQ

Ready to Fall was first published
in the United States, 2017

First published by Pushkin Press in 2018

1 3 5 7 9 8 6 4 2

ISBN 13: 978 1 78269 151 8

Offset by Tetragon, London
Printed and bound by CPI Group
(UK) Ltd, Croydon CR0 4YY

www.pushkinpress.com

To Stanley and Jacqueline Fleischman,
who read every draft,
and
to the kids in Writers' Guild,
my zany menagerie of kindred spirits

PROMISES

When Mommy finally comes home it's almost bedtime.

I'm sitting on the top stair wearing my green railroad pajamas. Grandma is sitting next to me, our knees close together.

Daddy opens the door and they come in.

She walks into the house first, with slow shuffling steps. Daddy holds her around the waist very, very gently, almost not touching her.

He is carrying a white plastic bag with her things in it.

The dark winter sky gasps behind them.

Daddy closes the door.

He puts down the white plastic bag.

He takes Mommy's coat from her shoulders and drapes it over the arm of the couch.

Mommy is wearing her Vassar sweatshirt that zips up the front. She is wearing yoga pants and slippers. She is also wearing a plastic hospital identification bracelet.

Daddy takes Mommy by the elbow and leads her to the rocking chair, which is waiting for her like a grandma with purple velvet arms. This is our favorite chair in the entire house because it is where we used to rock and cuddle and drink milk when we were new. I almost remember it. My head in the crook of her arm the way it is in my favorite baby picture. I am one day old. Just a furry black head. Max.

Daddy helps Mommy into the chair.

She leans back and closes her eyes and doesn't rock or move at all, which is very strange because Mommy is usually moving all the time.

Daddy lets her sit there a minute. He hangs up their coats. Then he closes the closet door, goes to the white plastic bag, opens it, and places things on the coffee table one at a time. There are pamphlets and bandages and boxes and medicine bottles and tubes of ointment. Then he comes back and kisses Mommy on the head and they both stay like that for a while, his cheek resting on the top of her head, not saying anything, just being there together.

Grandma holds my hand and hushes me so I won't interrupt them.

Don't go down yet, she says. Let them settle in first.

But I haven't seen Mommy for two days and one night

4

and I'm not about to stay up here. I want to tell her a joke about a boy and a dragon.

I yank my hand out of Grandma's and crash down the stairs in my pajamas feet like a green hurricane, with Grandma close behind me step by step, holding on to the banister saying, Here we come. Welcome home, honey. Oh, look at you.

I am tumbling and twirling down, stomping and slobbering like the Tasmanian Devil, growly and monster-crazy, whooping and leaping off the last three stairs all at once, so I land with a thump and slide in my pajamas feet toward Mommy, who is not rocking in the rocking chair. She opens her eyes and smiles at me. Her eyes are still as blue as they were before she left, and her smile is still filled with the same pretty white teeth. I think she is going to tell me a joke. But instead she holds out her arms.

Baby boy, she says.

It is the same voice she had before she left.

But she looks smaller than Mommy.

I stand in front of her and don't know what to do.

I want to jump in her lap and scrunch up under her chin and kiss her cheeks and put my fingers in her hair and rock like I used to when I was a very little Max-Max. But Daddy told me it might hurt to have me press, so I need to be very careful with Mommy and not hug too tight.

How about an air hug, Daddy suggests.

Yes, says Grandma. An air hug would be just right.

Mommy holds out her arms and closes her eyes and kisses the air.

I hold out my arms and close my eyes and kiss the air too.

Not good enough, I whisper.

Not good enough at all, Mommy says, laughing. Come over here. Let me take a look at you. It's okay. Come on up.

I tiptoe to the rocking chair. She smiles and nods, which is the same as permission, so I climb up on Mommy's lap and hug her really gently around the neck with both my arms.

Good job, honey, says Grandma.

Mommy kisses my nose and my chin and she tickles my back with her fingers up and down like dancing spiders and then she blows a slurpy raspberry in my neck and I growl like a monster.

I forget what Daddy said and lean in a little too far.

Mommy pulls back.

Okay, she says. Her voice is tight. Time to climb down now.

Daddy lifts me off.

There you go, champ, he says. Give Mommy some space now.

Grandma takes one of my hands.

He's been such a good boy, Grandma tells them.

Mommy's eyes go all soft and watery.

I'm so glad you were here, she says.

Oh sweetheart, says Grandma, I'm just glad I could be here for you. I wish I could do more. You know that, don't you?

I know, says Mommy. But tell me, was he really okay? Did he get upset at night?

Grandma swings my hand back and forth and then kisses my fist.

He was just fine, she says. Her voice is light and cheerful because she is pretending I was not upset so Mommy won't feel bad about leaving us.

Mommy looks doubtful, so Grandma finally admits that I cried at bedtime. But we told stories, didn't we, Max? And the stories helped calm him.

Grandma told me a story about a magic toy store, I say. You want to know what toy I picked at the magic toy store?

What did you pick? Mommy asks.

A magic jack-in-the-box that when you wind him up and wind him up, he finally pops, zoing, out of the box, he zoings up and then he keeps on zoinging higher and higher and higher until he reaches up to the moon.

Holy moly, says Mommy. Grandma sure is a great storyteller, isn't she?

I nod. I want to keep on telling, but Mommy looks small.

7

She is putting her head back in the chair and closing her eyes again.

Listen, Max, says Daddy. Why don't you go upstairs for a while and let Mommy and Daddy talk with Grandma.

I want to be with Mommy, I say.

I know, Daddy says. But we need some alone time with Grandma. You've had her all to yourself for two whole days. And now it's our turn, okay?

I don't say anything.

You know what I really want, Maxy? Mommy asks me.

Her eyes are still closed.

I really want you to draw me a special feel-better picture of something that will make me laugh. Would you do that for me? Would you go up to your room and get your sketch pad and imagine me something funny with lots of colors?

Mommy opens her eyes. Even though they are the same blue they've always been, they are full of something new. Something that hurts.

My lip is quivering like a big baby.

Hey, she says. Hey, come here.

I come over.

Mommy kisses me on the forehead.

Go on, son, says Daddy. Be a strong boy.

He looks me in the eyes.

Being strong means you're not allowed to show them you're scared.

Okay, I say.

Promise? says Daddy.

I promise.

Okay, says Daddy, I promise too.

We do pinkie swears.

Daddy rubs his eyes. I don't think he will be able to keep his promise.

Go on upstairs, says Grandma. I'll be up in a few minutes to tuck you in.

Can you tell me the magic train story again? I ask.

Anything you want, says Grandma.

So I march back up the stairs to my room like a soldier wearing boots.

I am a strong boy. I am the strongest boy in the house.

I take out my colored pencils and my sketch pad. I find orange and purple.

I draw a purple dragon with a little orange boy riding on its back.

I want to know which color is Mommy's favorite, because I will use that color for the fire coming out of the dragon's mouth. If Mommy says her favorite color is green, then the fire will be green, but if Mommy says her favorite color is blue, the fire will be blue.

I go to the top of the stairs.

Daddy and Grandma are talking.

They are talking in soft voices so I won't hear them, but I do.

I crouch behind the banister and listen.

I hear lots of words I don't know like prognosis *and re-cuperate.*

Give it to me straight, says Grandma.

Daddy tells it straight. His voice is flat like the kind of line you make with a ruler that stretches all the way across the page without any lumps.

Okay, says Daddy. After the first five years she has an eighty-one percent chance of survival. Then after that, the odds go up to something like ninety. That's pretty good odds. Plus the surgeon said the tumor was con-tained. It had not spread to the lymph nodes and they think they got the whole thing. So we have reason to be optimistic.

Mommy is crying.

It is not a quiet, hiccupping, sniffling cry like I make when I don't want anyone to hear me. This is a cry that comes from Mommy's heart, which used to be covered with breasts that fed me milk, but is now only covered by stitches and gauze and bandages, which are all thinner than breasts, which is why I can hear the cry coming so loud from beneath her Vassar sweatshirt, breaking out of her chest like a huge bird and rising into the house, its great wings casting shadows on each of us.

Oh, honey, says Grandma.

Grandma and Daddy go over to her. They put their hands around her shoulders and lean in their heads. They hold her while she cries.

I want to run down there so they can hold me too, but I pinkie-swear promised I'd be strong, so instead of running into their arms, I scramble as fast as I can from the banister back into my room, slipping and sliding down the hallway on my pajamas feet with my mouth pinched tight so nothing comes out. I jump into my bed and scrunch myself up in the corner and put my blanket over my head like a tent and cry into my hands under the blankets, holding on to my sobs so no one can hear, keeping all the howls inside my mouth with my fingers, all alone in my room until Grandma comes up the stairs and finds me.

Max. Max. Oh sweetheart.

Grandma takes the blanket off my head and takes my hands away from my mouth and gathers me into her arms so I can press my face against her shoulder, and she rubs my back and holds me and whispers into my hair that it's okay, it's okay, and she rocks me and rocks me and rocks me until my head droops against her shoulder and she holds me and kisses me and lowers me down onto the pillow that feels like a cloud.

I wonder if in heaven the angels sleep on pillows made of clouds. I hope so. I hope they have someone nice to tuck them in. I wonder if God has warm lips like Grandma. I hope he sits on the edges of their beds when they are too scared to go to sleep. And then when they have finally stopped crying, I hope he closes the door slow and quiet so the light in the hallway makes a triangle across the pillow and they can curl up in the light and pray that everything is going to be all right.

FUNERAL ON RYE WITH MUSTARD

THE BELL RINGS AND I OPEN THE DOOR. WOULD YOU look at that? It's Great-Tanta Sarah. She's flown in from Florida, rented a car, and picked Grandma up from Green Meadows Assisted Living Facility. They are both dressed to the nines. Great-Tanta Sarah is going all Old-World on us. She's wearing a black woolen dress even though it's the middle of August, she has a black lace doily on her head, and she's carrying a leaning tower of deli platters from Barry's down the street because let's face it, nothing in this godforsaken world tastes better with grief than a little corned beef on rye. Except maybe some chopped liver and a pickle on the side. Great-Tanta Sarah stretches up to kiss my unshaven cheek and bustles past me into the house. She wants to make herself busy. Grandma reaches for my hands just like she used to when I was little. She swings them back and forth with gnarled fingers.

"Look at you," she whispers with tears in her eyes.

She hugs me as hard as she can, but it feels like being hugged by a sparrow.

"It's the wrong order of things," she rasps into my shoulder. "Last year I buried Marty. And now I'm going to bury my Anna."

The top of her head smells like salt.

"They don't prepare you for this. No one prepares you."

"I know," I say.

But who am I kidding? I don't know a goddamned thing.

When the cancer came back, it was in her brain.

After ten years of remission, no one could have guessed it would come to this.

In the last few weeks, her left eye bulged out so far she would joke, *The better to see you with, my dear.* Which was almost funny. What was funnier was the fact that she referred to the tumor behind her eye as *he*, and occasionally gave us blow-by-blow reports of what he was doing. *He's watching football. He's scratching his armpits. He's sitting on the couch with a bottle of beer and a half-finished cigarette.* He was a lousy tenant. But what can you do? *Inoperable* means you better say goodbye. And we did.

In the limousine on our way to the synagogue, I lean my forehead against the glass and watch the sunlight stream through the trees.

Dad grabs my hand. "Be strong for me, okay, Max?"

"Yeah," I say. "Okay."

"What's going to happen to him when I'm gone?" Mom asked toward the end. She was so far gone already, at first we weren't sure if she was talking about me or the tumor. *Who's going to take him in, with his smelly feet and his hairy armpits and all his rottweilers? Who's going to give him a place to stay?* I told her not to worry. We would make sure someone took care of him, and she quieted and sighed, her left eye bulging like a horrible secret.

In the synagogue lobby, Rabbi Birnbaum, who looks like a fish, makes an announcement in his practiced, baleful voice. "As you requested, Mr. Friedman, before the service begins, we'll open the casket in the sanctuary for a short viewing so close family can say goodbye. I'll take you and Max in first to have a private moment with Anna, and when you're ready, the others can join you. Then we'll close the casket, you all will be seated, the rest of the mourners will enter, and the service will begin. Okay?"

"Okay," Dad mutters, brushing the wrinkles from his slacks. "Thank you, Rabbi. Let's go, Max."

But I can't move.

"Come on," says Dad.

"Just a minute," I say.

Last night I stayed awake until three in the morning googling embalmment photos. Black-and-white ones from the turn of the century when they used to pose the dead with their loved ones before burial. One corpse was sitting propped up in a chair with her eyes open, a pale arm around the shoulders of a freaked-out little boy in a black suit. Another was lying in his bed in a cowboy hat, holding a rifle in one hand and a rabbit skin in the other, his head cocked, his mouth half open, smiling like a puppet. But Jews don't believe in embalming corpses. We leave the body pretty much as it was when it died. That means no embalming fluid. No makeup. No wig. Nothing to fool us into thinking they are going to wake up.

One thing on this earth I know for absolute certain is that I do not want to see my mother in that coffin.

I do not want to know what twenty-four hours in a funeral home has done to her face.

The rabbi opens the door to the sanctuary.

There is the casket that Mom picked out. Plain wood. Nothing special. How could she fit into something so small and still? She never sat in one place, and she was always throwing back her head and laughing so hard that you couldn't help but laugh along with her, even when it felt like your life was cracking down the middle. You might think that a person who is dying would stop laughing, but this was not the case with Mom. She laughed right through to the end. Well, not the very end. In the very end, when she was mostly trying to breathe, no one was laughing. Not even her. That last day we sat around her bed and held her hands and stayed quiet so she could concentrate on leaving us. But the day before that, she tried to laugh as much as possible. Dad said she was doing it for us. To help us through. But I think she was doing it a little bit for herself too.

"Tell me a joke, Max," she had said.

And I did. Even though I felt like I was dying too.

The rabbi opens the lid.

She's in there.

From where I'm standing I can see the tip of her nose.

The world spins.

"It's time to say goodbye," says Dad.

He leads me to the casket and we look inside.

"Oh God," says Dad, holding his heart. "Oh my God. Look at her."

I look. My knees buckle. Dad puts his arm around me.

How can this be?

Lying in her bed at home, she was Mom. She was Mom

when she took her last breath. She was Mom when the men came with the stretcher to take her away. But now she's something else entirely. A wax sculpture. A mannequin. All the raucous, snorting, swearing, moving, bigger-than-life attitude snuffed out like a candle.

I put my hands on the edge of her coffin and I look and look.

Her face is white and fallen, but the tumor is still there, bulging behind her eyelid. If Jews believed in embalmment, they would have sucked him out with a straw, vacuumed him from her cranium along with her brain, or maybe they would have sliced him out with a scalpel and thrown him away. But they left him just as he was the moment she died, and here he is now, reaching out to me, the last piece of my mother left on this earth. Her favorite tumor. Starving. Licking his lips as I lean forward.

Who is going to take him in?

Now the rabbi leads the rest of our family into the sanctuary to pay their last respects before the service begins. They cry when they see us standing alone by her casket, two lost men with our hands in our pockets.

They gather around us and tell us how sorry they are, how she was so beautiful, so funny—and we say *Yes she was* and *Thank you* because that's what grown men say when they're strong like Dad wants me to be. They don't say *I wish it was my face in that coffin.* They don't goad my mother's favorite tumor the way I am doing, silently in my mind. *Please. Take me next. My brain is delicious. You can eat it with mustard.* Because this would be a heinous thing to think before your own mother's funeral when you're supposed to be thinking about her. *Psst. Hey there. I promised I would take care of you. You want somewhere to live for a while? My brain is ripe. It will fill your belly. Come eat. And when you're done, bury me next to her so I don't have to be alone.*

The rabbi announces it's time to close the lid and we will open the doors for the service to begin unless anyone wants to say one last goodbye. Dad raises his hand like a schoolboy. He approaches the casket. His back is straight. He stands there looking at her. Then he leans over and kisses her on the lips one last time, a man and his bride.

The family is silent, waiting.

This isn't a fairy tale. She doesn't wake up.

Instead, the prince falls across her body, puts his head on her chest and weeps.

His yarmulke falls to the floor.

The bride is still dead when Great-Tanta Sarah finally comes and pulls my dad away from the casket. She's still dead when the rabbi, who continues to look like a fish, closes the lid, a grim finality. She's still dead when Dad slumps into the pew next to me. The doors to the sanctuary open and all the other mourners start filing in. Congregants. Neighbors. Friends. The hospice nurse. People from Dad's caregiver support group. People from Mom's yoga class. They all look at me with sorry faces. They think I'm strong, just like Dad wants me to be. They have no idea that when they weren't looking, my mother's favorite tumor entered my brain like a thief.

I do not cry during the entire service. I do not cry during the Mourner's Kaddish, the prayer that falls around us like rain. I do not cry during the eulogies or the sermon. And later, at the cemetery, where the sun slants between the stones like the golden wings of an angel, I do not cry when they lower the casket into the grave. One by one, we shovel dirt over her blind, expressionless face. I don't tell anyone that with every thump of dirt, I am imagining my own face in that coffin. I am imagining my own empty eyes, my own skin pale as wax.

Shhh, says the tumor as he coils his tendrils into my cerebral cortex. *Don't tell a soul.*

WELCOME TO THE HOTEL GLIOBLASTOMA

THE WEEK OF SHIVA GOES BY LIKE A SHADOW. I pretend to be strong so no one has any idea how far I've come unhinged. When they ask me how I'm holding up, I say, "I'm doing okay," because that's what they expect me to say. *I'm doing okay* is a much better response than *My mother's favorite tumor is letting his rottweilers use my cerebral cortex as a fire hydrant*, because this would prove what I have begun to suspect lately, which is that I've completely lost my grip on reality. Besides, no one likes a lunatic when they are trying to mourn. Especially at the end of August, when the roses are too hot to hold up their heads.

August turns to September. Labor Day comes and goes. It's time for Dad to go back to the frame shop and for me to start my sophomore year of high school. Dad says it's time for us to begin functioning like regular human beings again. Notice the erroneous simile. *Like* regular human beings. I'm pretty certain that *"regular"* is not a word you could use for me anymore.

The first week of school, I sleepwalk through my classes. Instead of doing homework, I spend my evenings imagining what the tumor looks like winding himself into my cerebral cortex with his long red tendrils. I draw pictures of him leering at me. In many parts of the world, brains are a delicacy. Cow brains, anyway. Human brains, not so much. But the tumor is a culinary risk-taker. He sautés mine with shallots and white wine and feasts upon it with a napkin tucked under his chin.

One week passes into the next. I settle in to school. Dad has a few jobs. He photographs a bar mitzvah. A wedding. A family reunion. At the shop he develops a few prints and sells a few frames. It's not fine art, but it pays the bills. The green leaves on the maple tree outside my bedroom window blush at the tips. Every morning, Dad urges me awake, kisses me on the forehead, a heartbreaking and tender gesture, even though I pretend I hate to be kissed. Later, he hands me a bagel and pushes me out the door. *I'll be home when you get home, okay?* And I say *Okay*, because that's what you say when the guy who loves you is doing his best. I grab my sketchbook and my skateboard, and I set off down the road to the high school, a tall black figure dissolving into the distance.

At school I slump in my chair with my sketchbook, my black hood pulled over my face, lanky legs crossed at the ankles, and red Converse All Star sneakers tapping against each other. I sketch corpses. Some with their eyes open. Some with their eyes closed. I imagine Dad closing my eyes after I die. That's why I can't answer when Mr. Mancini, who doesn't tolerate slackers, stands by my shoulder and barks, "Which branch of government is responsible for making laws? Legislative or executive?" The whole class gets quiet. They're wondering if Mr. Mancini will push me to speak today, or yell at me for not paying attention, or just give up, as most of my teachers are doing these days, just give up and move on to the next kid, leaving me at my desk to fester silently.

Shhh, says the tumor, twirling his impossible fingers through the cracks in my brain. *Don't tell a soul.*

The end of September brings the cinnamon of leaves beginning to crisp. Mom always loved it when the heat broke and the cool sun started shining through the branches. There's a picture that Dad took when I was a baby. She is holding me up to see the leaves. I am reaching with my

23

hands, wide-eyed and smiling as though the leaves were jewels, and she is laughing, her long hair falling behind her. Now I'm sitting in the guidance office with my father, but no one is laughing. Dad takes out the letter the school sent about my grades and unfolds it on Ms. Cunningham's desk so we all can see my brilliance.

Honors English—C
Trigonometry—F
Honors French—D
American History—C
Honors Biology—D

"I know it looks alarming," says Ms. Cunningham, "but it makes sense that his grades are suffering after what he's been through. Mr. Friedman, the teachers know it's been a hard time for you and Max."

"He's failing Trigonometry," says Dad. "His highest mark is a C."

"I think we should be asking Max about it," says Ms. Cunningham. "He's the only one who can tell us what's really going on in his head. Max? What do you think of all this? Can you help us understand what's been happening?"

"Nope," I say without looking at either of them.

"Don't be rude, Max," says Dad.

"I'm not being rude," I mutter to the floor. "She asked if I can help you understand what's going on. I said nope."

Nope. Nopity. Nope.

Ms. Cunningham leans forward and tries to make eye contact with me. "Max," she says, "your dad and I are trying to figure out what we should do next, but it's hard if you won't talk with us."

"I'm not much of a talker," I say.

The tumor applauds. He appreciates sarcasm.

"Well, I think it makes sense that you aren't available for academics right now," says Ms. Cunningham. "You're grieving. That's why you're struggling to get your work done. This is a really tough time for you, isn't it?"

"Yes," I say.

"See?" She smiles sadly at my father.

"But a kid doesn't go from getting straight As freshman year to getting Cs, Ds, and Fs sophomore year if there isn't something very, very wrong going on."

"Something very wrong *is* going on," says Ms. Cunningham gently. "His mother died over the summer."

"We can't just let him fall apart," says Dad.

"No one's going to let him fall apart," says Ms. Cunningham. "That's why we sent the letter. It's clear that we need to take some action to help Max get back on track."

"Yes," says Dad emphatically, "now you're talking. Action. Thank you."

25

"Mr. Friedman, is Max having any therapy to help him work through his loss?"

"Well, no, not exactly," says Dad. "But we're in a family bereavement support group. It gives us a chance to talk about our experience with other folks who understand. That's sort of like therapy."

"Does Max share what's on his mind during these sessions?"

Dad looks at me. "He's always been quiet when it comes to emotional stuff. I'm like that too. But his mother—she could talk to anyone about anything. People loved that about her. And she could listen too. Listening is a gift, you know."

"I know," says Ms. Cunningham. "And I can imagine that must make the loss even more difficult. Was Max close to his mom?"

"Yes," says Dad. "They were very close."

I take my sketchbook out of my backpack and start drawing a tumor with vampire fangs and a cape. I draw quickly, shading in lines.

Dad and Ms. Cunningham watch me.

"So here's what we'll do," says Ms. Cunningham. "I'm going to suggest that Max meet with me twice a week for a while so I can help support him through this. I think talking about how he's feeling would help him. What do you think, Max? Would you like to do some counseling with me?"

26

No, I would definitely not like that at all.

I shrug.

"So it's a plan," says Ms. Cunningham.

"And what about his teachers?" asks Dad.

"What do you mean?" asks Ms. Cunningham.

"I mean, what about telling his teachers that it's okay to start pushing him a little bit? His mother wouldn't have wanted him to fail."

"Well," says Ms. Cunningham, "until we start our sessions together, I won't know how much we should push him. Max is fragile right now, Mr. Friedman."

"Please," says Dad. His eyes are wide and desperate. "Please, Ms. Cunningham," he says again, this time much more quietly. "I don't want his teachers to give up on him."

"No one's giving up on Max," says Ms. Cunningham. "Believe me. Things are going to start getting better around here. Just you wait."

THE ROAD TO HELL IS PAVED WITH GOOD INTENTIONS: AND OTHER UNFORTUNATE PLATITUDES

BUT THEY DON'T GET BETTER.

All I can think about is the tumor.

He is the only part of Mom I have left.

At school I sketch ghosts rising from graves.

At home, Dad and I try to make our way together, two men in an empty house, trying to exist in a new, astonished silence. After the ladies from the synagogue stop coming over with noodle kugels and chicken soup, we lapse into bachelorhood. At first, Dad cooks dinner like he's been doing since Mom got sick the second time, but soon we're just heating up frozen pizzas and eating Chef Boyardee ravioli from the can. After dinner, Dad lies down on the couch, exhausted. I go upstairs to draw corpses: wormy-eyed wraiths, shadow lords, dark specters both with and without wings.

I eat my pathetic lunch in Ms. Cunningham's office twice a week so she can help me "get in touch with the grief," a plan that pisses me off, not because I'm missing out on some spectacular social experience in the cafeteria (I've always been pretty much a loner, sitting with my sketchbook drawing while my classmates either ignore me or look on, bemused), but because let's face it, there's no way I'll ever tell Ms. Cunningham what's actually going on inside my defective but delectable brain. She thinks talking about my emotions will eventually help me be more *available* for academics. But most of the time I don't talk at all. I look out the window and watch the blazing orange leaves wave in the wind.

In class, I put my head down on my desk or stare off into space or draw on my wrists in black ink.

Sometimes my teachers surreptitiously push an extra classroom copy of the textbook and a few pieces of white lined paper onto my desk so I will not look so obvious in my apathy.

"Max," says Ms. Cunningham, "I'm wondering if it might be time to start trying to work at school again. We know you're sad. Believe me. It makes a lot of sense that you're sad. Anyone would be. But I've met with your teachers, and I've talked to your dad about it, and we all think it's time

29

for you to try getting back to your normal routine here at school."

I don't say anything. I'm thinking about the tumor.

Mom's cancer started out in her breasts and ended up in her brain.

"Just too beautiful and too brilliant for this earth," she told us toward the end, all teeth and eyes when she smiled. "God's taking back all my best parts."

I know she meant to make us laugh, but it's hard to laugh when you're trying so hard not to cry that you have to bite your lips. Dad kissed the top of her head and said, "Anna, you are just too much perfection in one human being," and then he took a photograph of her, which was, if you ask me, the perfect response.

———————————————

Ms. Cunningham leans over and looks right in my eyes to make sure I'm paying attention to her.

"So, Max. We all think it's important that you start bringing your materials to class, even if you're feeling sad. And that you start paying attention to what your teachers and your classmates are saying. Even if it's overwhelming at first. And when you and I talk together, it's important that you listen to me, and when the teacher assigns homework, it's important that you do it, Max, because the school year goes by so fast, and once you're behind, it's hard to catch up. I don't want to pressure you, but next year you're going to start looking at colleges, and we really don't want failing grades on your report card, especially someone like you, with so much talent and so much promise. We want to send you into your junior year with a good, strong, clean academic record. Okay?"

"Yeah," I say. "Okay."

But it's not okay. It's really not.

Because the tumor is watching NFL with the sound turned all the way up and I have always hated football. Every time his team scores, he jumps up and down on the couch and the rottweilers go wild.

Not surprisingly, I don't bring my stuff the next day or the next day, or the next day either.

US History. Mr. Mancini has been lecturing about the Magna Carta and *Rights of Man* and, true to form, I don't have my spiral notebook or my textbook *United We Stand*, the one with the waving flag and the bald eagle on the front, or the rough draft of my assigned reflection on John Locke's philosophy of natural rights, and instead of turning to talk with my partner about life, liberty, and property, I'm drawing scenes from the zombie apocalypse in my sketchbook and trying not to think about tumors.

And because more than two months have gone by since

the funeral, and because Ms. Cunningham has made a *plan* (scrunch invisible finger quotes around the word *plan*) with my dad and my teachers about consequences for continued bad behavior, Mr. Mancini does not shrug his shoulders and leave me alone like he's been doing. Instead, he gets in my face like he wants to fight.

"Excuse me," says Mr. Mancini. "Where are your materials?"

"In my locker," I say.

Students watch. Only an idiot would mess with Mr. Mancini.

"And why, Mr. Friedman, did you think it was a good idea to attend my class without the materials you need in order to participate?"

I shrug.

"A few minutes ago, I asked you to talk with your table partner about the meaning of John Locke's philosophy of natural rights. Why are you not doing that?"

I shrug.

"We read about John Locke and reflected upon his philosophy for homework. Do you have your homework with you?"

"No," I say.

"Is that in your locker too?"

"No," I say. "I didn't do my homework."

Kids around me shift in their seats.

"And why didn't you do your homework?"

I shrug.

"I expect you to do the homework I assign, Mr. Fried-man. Do you understand?"

I shrug.

"I asked you a question. Do. You. Understand. Answer me with words, please."

"Yes, sir," I say. "I understand."

"Good," says Mr. Mancini. "From now on, I expect you to behave as a full member of this community. That means you read what we read, you write what we write, and you discuss what we discuss. Do you think you are capable of that?"

"No," I tell him.

"Excuse me?" asks Mr. Mancini.

I clear my throat and stand up beside my seat so he will hear me loud and clear.

"I said no, sir. I do not think I am capable of that."

"Then get out," says Mr. Mancini.

There is a beat.

"You want me to go?" I ask.

"Yes," says Mr. Mancini. "Get out of my classroom. Now."

All eyes are on me.

"Where do you want me to go, sir?"

"I don't know," says Mr. Mancini. "But if you're going to

be in my class, I expect you to participate. Otherwise, I want you out of here. Go. Now."

"Okay," I say.

"Don't come back until you're ready to be part of the class."

"Okay," I say through my teeth. "I'm leaving."

I grab my things. I pull my hood low over my eyes and walk out the door.

BROWN-RICE SUSHI

ACCORDING TO OUR FRIEND LYDIE GROSSMAN, GLUTEN is an addictive drug sold cheaply by mass-market food stores to keep the consumer bloated and thus less likely to rebel against the tyrannical culinary monopolies plaguing our society. Along the same lines, white rice has only a tenth of the varied nutrients contained in God's own ultra-wholesome, whole-grain hippie-dippy wild rice, which, by the way, is better for digestion and neuroplasticity. Grains are our friends. You know that, don't you? Besides wild rice, there are other delicious, albeit gassy substitutes, including grains with names that sound like they belong to Iranian rock stars: Freekeh, Kasha, and Quinoa.

Organic vegetables are better than regular vegetables because no one needs the carcinogens they put in those pesticides. Only eat free-range chickens and grass-fed beef. Only eat mercury-free fish and free-trade chocolate. Make your own juice. Whenever possible, add flaxseed or lemongrass. It is better to spend two hundred dollars at Whole Foods than fifty dollars at a regular supermarket, that horrible hegemony of classist dogma.

"Ugh," says Lydie, "I can't believe you're still buying groceries at Stop and Shop."

She says the words *Stop and Shop* as though it were a well-known den of iniquity, and then she wrinkles her nose and makes a worried face.

We met Lydie and her pint-size blond daughters at the Caregiver Family Support Group that was held in the basement of the local JCC every Tuesday and Thursday, but now we know her from the Bereavement Family Support Group, which is down the hall on Wednesdays and Fridays. They don't put the caregiver-support people on the same day as the bereavement-support people because they don't want the caregivers to lose hope or the bereavement people to feel jealous.

Sometimes, after group, Lydie takes us all out for lemongrass-and-ginseng smoothies. Dad and I pretend to like them, but mostly we are just thankful for the company.

Tonight we're home making vegetarian sushi with brown rice because Lydie wants to show us how to make an organic, nontoxic meal with a very small carbon footprint, a plan that makes me think of tiptoeing dinosaurs. She has everything set up on the kitchen counter in bowls. There's a stack of dried seaweed. Then there's a bowl of brown rice, and a plate with radishes, spinach, ginger, and carrots, all cut into slivers. Finally, there are scrambled eggs from her backyard, free-range, feminist yoga hens, Gertrude, Camille, and Gloria.

We join her at the counter, making five of us. First there's Luna and Soleil, Lydie's New Age, freaky, feral, four-year-old, late-in-life twin daughters. There's me and my dad. And then there's Lydie, smelling of patchouli and peppermint with her long gray hair down her back in a braid.

Lydie gives us each a square mat made of thin strips of bamboo. She shows us how to put the square of seaweed on the mat, how to scoop on the brown rice so it only covers half the seaweed, how to pat down the rice with a wooden spoon so it makes a thin layer across the bottom, how to place the vegetables in a pyramid on top of the rice, and when that's finished, how to lay down the pièce de résistance, the eggs, courtesy of the fussy triumvirate of feminist yoga hens, fried to perfection. We roll up the seaweed and rice and veggies and eggs with the bamboo mats, squeeze them so they stick, and then chop them into pieces with a wetted knife. Luna and Soleil are masters at sushi making. They work quietly with their little fingers and their little knives.

"All done," says Lydie. "These look good. Don't you love the color of the carrot and the spinach against the eggs? It's just beautiful."

"Bee-you-tee-full," sings Luna.

"Beautiful," my dad agrees.

"Not as beautiful as steak tips," I say.

Soleil jumps up and down and pants like a hungry dog.

Dad elbows me. "Try it," he says.

We bring an assortment of plates to the table along with a bottle of soy sauce, five tiny dipping bowls, and five pairs of chopsticks. Luna and Soleil climb into their chairs. I sit down. Dad pushes in Lydie's chair for her. Then he sits down as well.

We all look at one another.

No one knows what to say.

Dad clears his throat. "Eat up," he says.

Lydie pours some soy sauce into her dipping bowl, picks up a piece of sushi with her chopsticks, dips it into the soy sauce, and takes a bite.

"Mmm," she says, chewing, eyes closed. "This is fabulous. You must try this, girls. Max. Joe. Come on. It's good."

"Namaste," says Luna, closing her eyes and pressing her palms together like a small blond monk.

Soleil meows.

They dig in.

Luna uses her chopsticks perfectly.

Soleil puts her head down and laps at the sushi like a cat.

Dad picks up a piece with his fingertips, plunges it into the soy sauce, wiggles it around until it's drenched, and then chews and smiles so Lydie will think he likes it. "Wow," says Dad, still chewing. "That's really something."

"You like it?" asks Lydie.

"I do," says Dad. "Very flavorful."

"Now you try it," Lydie says to me.

"I'm not hungry," I tell her.

"What did they serve you for lunch today?" she asks me.

"Pizza."

"It's all the gluten they're giving kids at the public schools," Lydie tells Dad. "Keeps them bloated and docile. Max, you really need this. It'll clean you right out."

I look down at my brown-rice sushi and imagine myself sitting on the toilet excreting it.

"Just try it," says Dad.

I take a piece of sushi from my plate with my chopsticks, dip it in the soy sauce, shove it in my mouth, and chew. It's not so bad, actually. It's crisp. Fresh. Kind of nutty. I love the eggs from the free-range, feminist yoga hens. I love the crunch of the carrots and the texture of the rice. I am about to swallow and tell Lydie all this when something catches my eye. The pattern on my plate, the plate my mother used to love best. There is a strange blue geometric pattern all along the rim. And then inside, a scene. A bridge over a river. A pagoda on a mountain. A path. A tiny woman holding a walking stick. I cough and spit my sushi into the napkin.

Soleil giggles and spits her sushi into her napkin too.

I run to the sink and dump the sushi into the garbage disposal. I flick the switch. The kitchen is filled with a sound like grinding bones.

"Oh, come on," says Dad.

"That's okay," says Lydie. "He doesn't have to like it."

I rinse the plate and look at the little woman. I remember when my mom found this plate in an antique shop. She loved Blue Willow china. All the tiny details. The willow tree, the path, the waterfall, the pagoda. She always wanted to travel, but she never got the chance. I imagine her walking down a path in China with a stick in her hand. A little blue mother.

"It's not just this," says my dad quietly to Lydie. "He doesn't like anything these days. He's been having a terrible time at school."

"I know what you mean," says Lydie. "Soleil is having a really rough time in preschool too. She used to sleep on her own during nap time, but her teacher tells me she suddenly needs to hold on to Luna in order to fall asleep. She climbs onto Luna's mat, grabs her around the waist, and refuses to let go."

When I was little and Dad worked late at the frame shop, Mom would lie down with me to help me fall asleep. She smelled like lemons and honey. I gaze into the plate. All the blue patterns. There's the tiny blue woman on the path. Walking past the mountains. Way down there. So tiny I almost can't see her. I turn on the hot water, drip a few drops of lemon soap, and fill the sink with bubbles. I squint my eyes and trace the willow path with one soapy finger.

"I'm so worried about him," says Dad. "The school's been trying to help, but it just seems like he's getting lost."

I keep my back turned and busy myself with following the path. There are thousands of tiny details. *Hello, all you tiny blue details.*

"Have you thought about transferring him to a smaller school?" asks Lydie.

"The school year's already started," says Dad. "What school's going to accept a sophomore at the end of October?"

"You should check out the Baldwin School," says Lydie. "I work in the office. Some families moved away this fall and they're looking to fill those spots. The teachers are amazing, Joe. Max would love it."

"I've heard good things about it," says Dad.

"It's a pretty special place," says Lydie. "It's very progressive. They value creativity and self-expression. It's primarily a boarding school, but there are day students as well. It's great for artistic kids like Max who are just a little offbeat."

"Max isn't offbeat," says Dad.

I stalk back to the table with my clean plate clutched to my chest like a baby and my hood over my eyes. I place my plate on the table, drop my forehead down onto the cool, smooth surface, and rock my head back and forth because sometimes even a rotting frontal lobe needs some loving. I take deep breaths in and out, rocking the tumor to sleep on this plate that my mother once loved.

"Okay," admits my dad. "Maybe he is a little offbeat."

I rub my cheek against the plate, close my eyes, and sigh. At night I used to curl up with my face resting against Mom's soft hands.

"I'll bet it costs an arm and a leg," says my dad.

"They have financial aid," says Lydie.

"Still," says my dad. "We don't have extra money lying around."

"Maybe someone in your family can help you," says Lydie.

"Maybe," says my dad. "Everyone's been through so much. I just don't know how I'd ask for something like that."

"Yeah," says Lydie. "I get it."

I rest my head against the blue plate and breathe.

Soleil gets out of her chair and moves wordlessly to my side. She takes off my hood, puts her hands in my hair, and starts petting me. She leans her warm little head against my head. Soleil smells like lemons and honey. It is the warm smell of my mother's healthy skin. I put my arms around her and she leans into me. It feels good for just a moment. Just one blessed moment. I close my eyes and hold my breath because if I breathe right now I am going to lose it completely. I am frozen in this moment with honey-lemon skin that smells like my mother and hands on my head and my horrible secret twitching inside my brain like a frenzied bat looking for a window.

BALDWIN

THE ACCEPTANCE LETTER COMES IN A THICK ENVELOPE
with the school crest stamped on the front. Inside is a note
of congratulations from the dean of students, a course cata-
log, and a load of different forms that we have to fill out
ASAP, including an elective-request form, a financial-aid
form, a health form, a family-information form, a booklet of
rules and regulations, and a tour-request postcard to be
filled out and returned immediately.

Dad lets me skip school to go on the tour. Our guide tells
us that her name is Felicia Santacroce, but everyone around
here calls her Fish. She has long pink hair. When I say
pink, I don't mean cherry pink, like the girls at my school
who sometimes dye a lock of their hair with Kool-Aid for a
psyche before a soccer game or something. I'm talking about

hair the color of cotton candy, a pink so wonderfully pink that it's hard to notice the campus, especially since Fish is whirling breathlessly from one place to the next so fast we have to hustle to keep up with her.

Fish whisks us up a brick walkway, past a line of ancient bare trees, up a set of granite steps, and onto the landing of a huge stone building, past clusters of students who move out of the way as they argue amiably about some book they must be reading for class. There, next to the door, is an engraved plaque. She brings us close and then stands back to speak her script while we watch.

"This is Trowbridge Hall," Fish recites dutifully. "Trowbridge is the main building, which houses most of our academic subjects at the Baldwin School. Trowbridge Hall was erected in 1880 by Thomas A. Trowbridge the First. It was originally set up as a seminary for Episcopalian boys who were interested in becoming priests. Every student had to take Greek and Latin. They studied the classics: Ovid, Homer, Plato, and Marcus Aurelius. Carved on this plaque by the front door is our time-honored motto: *Ipsa scientia potestas est,* which means *Knowledge Itself Is Power.* Wise words, don't you agree?"

"I do," says Dad, right on cue.

Fish smiles at him and then goes back to her script.

"In the early 1960s, Baldwin expanded and became known as a progressive school, adopting a more relaxed but

45

still rigorous whole-child approach. Now there's more student freedom. More hands-on learning. More discussions. Less memorization. Now the school is known for its commitment to the arts. Students are encouraged to express themselves through drawing, creative writing, painting, dance. There are several different art studios on campus, music groups, theater programs, and a student radio station that plays awesome alternative rock. Sound good?"

"Sounds great," says Dad. "What do you think, Max?"

"I like it," I say, but my stomach is twisted in knots because it sounds glorious, it sounds fabulous, it sounds perfect, and this makes me nervous because nothing is perfect.

"Are you interested in any kind of art, Max?" Fish asks.

"Yeah," I say. "I like drawing. Actually, I take a sketchbook with me wherever I go."

"Me too," says Fish. "Ever think of taking an art class?"

"Nah," I say. "Taking a class would ruin it."

"How long have you been drawing?"

"As long as I can remember," I say. "I started my first sketchbook when I was five."

"I remember that one," says Dad. "Seems to me it was filled with dragons."

"Mine had unicorns," says Fish.

We keep walking, slower now. We pass more Baldwin

students talking with each other in animated voices. A few kids wave to Fish and she waves back. One guy, this extremely tall dude with John Lennon glasses, grabs her waist, twirls her toward him, and kisses her cheek. Then he pushes her away and continues to his class.

"Sorry about that," says Fish, blushing. "He's in the drama club. Theater kids are pretty demonstrative around here. But don't worry. Even if you're shy, you'll get along fine. This is a good place for all kinds of people."

"Glad to know it," says Dad.

I don't say anything. I'm thinking about how it would feel to take Fish by the waist and kiss her too.

Fish walks us up a wide stone staircase to a building with stained glass windows and a carved wooden door.

I whip my sketchbook out of my jacket pocket and do a quick drawing of the doors. There are ghosts of a mother and child escaping from the cracks. The mother has a thin face and willowy arms reaching upward. Her hair rises from her head like smoke. The child is floating above her head, reaching down for her.

"Whoa," says Fish, watching over my shoulder as I sketch. "That's amazing."

"Thanks," I say. I draw the building rising up behind the doors, filled with spires and gables and ornate nooks and crannies.

47

"What's the name of this building?" I ask.

"Skinner Hall," says Fish, her eyes still fixed on my sketch. "It's my favorite."

I write the words *Skinner Hall* on the bottom of the page in twirling letters like ivy. "Now it's my favorite too," I say.

Fish smiles. "I love that," she says. "I really do." I tear out the picture and give it to her. She holds it against her heart for a moment, and then folds it neatly and puts it in her pocket. "In the seventies and eighties, Skinner used to be the administration building. Now it's where they store the records and the old black-and-white photographs of the first headmasters and the founding families. Sometimes I go down there and rummage around in the crates. I like to pull them out and look at the pale faces. They kind of freak me out. But between you and me, I sort of like being freaked out."

"Being freaked out is actually a permanent state of affairs for me," I say.

"This is true," says my dad.

"Well, I'm glad I'm not the only one," says Fish. "Most people think I'm a total lunatic. Maybe it's the hair. I don't know. So what else do you have in that sketchbook? Can I see?"

"Sure," I say. And then I surprise myself by handing it over without even wondering if it's such a good idea, and Fish starts skimming through the pages and looking at my bizarre imagination. Here is an emaciated woman lying in a bed with her hands folded over her chest. Here is a grinning tumor in a top hat with its tendrils reaching out in all directions. Here is a white face with one red eye bulging, all the veins detailed. Here is a boy cradling his own brain. His mouth is open and his eyes are closed. The brain is in a swaddling blanket. It nuzzles against the boy's chest. It wants milk, but he has none to give.

"Oh my gosh," says Fish. She gazes at that last one. "Oh my gosh, that is so twisted."

"Sorry about that," says Dad. He takes the sketchbook from Fish and hands it back to me, frowning. "Max is a bit dark."

"No," says Fish. "It's okay. I'm dark too, actually. Don't worry. Lots of kids are kind of intense here. I mean, this school is known for attracting complicated people. I guess that's why everyone is assigned a faculty advisor and a student fellow. That's one of the things that makes Baldwin so great. They really take care of you. Even if hard things are going on. Someone's gonna watch out for you here."

My dad doesn't say anything. He wipes his eye with the back of his jacket sleeve.

"You okay?" asks Fish.

"Oh yeah," says my dad, clearing his throat. "I'm fine. Just an eyelash in my eye."

But I know there wasn't an eyelash.

49

Fish leads us all around campus. From the dorms where the boarding students sleep to the playing field, which was once destroyed by locusts, and inside Trowbridge Hall to the dining room with its long tables where students carve amusing titles into their lunch trays with paper clips (*The Tray of Existential Angst, The Tray of Hideous Incurable Diseases*) to the possibly haunted library with its stained glass windows and, finally, to the place she calls her "sanctum sanctorum," the auditorium, with its polished stage and its long, black velvet curtains that smell like dust and sweat and standing ovations.

"Want to go up onstage?" Fish asks us.

"You guys go," says Dad.

"Okay," says Fish. "But don't get upset when we're having a ton of fun without you."

She grabs my hand and drags me up onstage.

That's when I notice the white scar that snakes below her thumb, across her wrist, and down the inside of her arm.

She sees me noticing it and smiles. "Long story," she says, as though she were reading my mind. "If you decide to come here, maybe I'll tell you one day."

Then she pulls me center stage, gets up on her toes, and spins.

Dad slumps into a chair in the front row and watches us.

"This place has amazing acoustics," Fish tells me. "The drama director just announced we're gonna do *Hamlet*. We always do a Shakespeare play right before spring break. I'm completely psyched. You want to hear something cool?"

"Yeah," I say.

Fish stands on her tiptoes, spreads her arms to either side, and screams, "TO BE, OR NOT TO BE: THAT IS THE QUESTION!" at the very top of her lungs. The whole auditorium fills with her voice and you can hear the words bouncing around on the ceiling, echoing faintly at the back of the room.

"Cool," I say.

"Now you try it," she says.

"Oh," I say. "No thanks. I'm not really into being loud."

"Come on," says Fish. "No one's here but me and your dad. Come on. It'll feel good. Just do it. Really. It'll make you happy. I promise. Come on, Max."

"Okay," I say. "But I'm not going to be as loud as you."

"That's okay," says Fish.

So I spread out my arms and I stand on my tiptoes and I scream, "TO BE, OR NOT TO BE: THAT IS THE QUESTION!" at the top of my lungs, only my voice cracks and I end up sounding like a drunk donkey reciting Shakespeare, which, I suppose, would have been appropriate if it had been a line from *A Midsummer Night's Dream*, but it's *Hamlet*, and as far as I know, there are no donkeys in *Hamlet*, so when the words reverberate in the auditorium it sounds ridiculous and silly and hilarious and really strange, and all at once I start laughing, without even knowing why. I feel like I might shatter because I haven't laughed in a million years, and soon Dad is chuckling from the front row and Fish closes her eyes and throws back her head and starts laughing this amazing, alarming, contagious, rollicking belly laugh that makes me and Dad stop short for a second to look at each other, because if we close our eyes, we could almost imagine that Mom is with us, but instead, it's this strange girl with pink hair, and we look at each other, startled and heartsick, but Fish is still laughing, and her laughter rises to the ceiling like sunlight.

ASSISTED LIVING FACILITIES HAVE GOOD ICE CREAM

WHEN THE TOUR IS OVER, FISH WHIRLS US BACK TO the bottom of the stairs that lead to Trowbridge Hall. "I hope you decide to come here," she tells me. "I think you would really like it." She shakes Dad's hand, she shakes my hand (is it my imagination, or does she hang on for just a few seconds longer than she needs to?), and then makes her way up the stone steps. Halfway up, she takes my drawing of Skinner out of her pocket, waves it to me, presses it against her heart, twirls, and then hurries up the remaining steps, where I lose her in the throng of students heading to class.

I am still thinking about how her hand felt when Dad announces that we're going right out to Green Meadows Assisted Living Facility to see Grandma.

When Grandpa Marty died, Grandma moved from their brownstone in Brooklyn to this incredibly tiny apartment at Green Meadows. It looks more like a hotel room than a home. The bedroom only has room for a bed. In the visiting room, there's a dresser in one corner, a lamp in the other, a ridiculously uncomfortable orange tweed couch for visitors, and a sad little corkboard on the wall where Grandma pins birthday cards and faded pictures of her dwindling family. Mom had asked Grandma to come live with us, but Grandma said no, she would just be in the way. No one wants an old lady farting around the house all day, she said. But I think the real reason she didn't move in is that it would hurt too much to see her only daughter wasting away. Of course there were visits. Mom would stop at Green Meadows when she still could, and Dad would bring Grandma to our house for dinner every Friday night. We would light Shabbat candles and say the prayers and try to smile across the table at one another, but inside, our hearts were breaking.

We pull into the parking lot and walk to the front entrance, where Darlene of the voluminous girth waves to us from the desk, buzzes us in, and gives us a polite smile.

"Oh my," she says. "Jean will be so happy to see you. How long's it been?"

"Too long," says Dad. "We try to get out here once a week. But things have been tough lately."

"Oh sweetie, I know," says Darlene. "I know all about it. Listen, why don't you go down and surprise her? She's in the TV room with the others. Wednesday's ice cream day."

The tumor is giddy. He is hoping for Toffee Bar Crunch.

If Green Meadows Assisted Living Facility was located in Disneyland, ice cream day would include a pastel room filled with happy, clean, talkative old people, all with full command of their bladders and cognitive abilities. They would be standing around a long table covered with cartons of various colorful ice cream flavors, whipped-cream canisters, squirt bottles of chocolate syrup, and bowls filled with gummy bears and rainbow sprinkles, telling one another stories in genteel English accents.

But in reality, the room is filled with sad plastic Thanksgiving decorations and old people sitting gaping in front of a television set no one's watching. Some are in wheelchairs, some are on faded couches. Some people are feeding themselves with white plastic spoons, which is a good sign because it means they know what spoons are for. Others are being fed by caregivers who open their own mouths wide to inspire their charges to do the same.

Grandma is sitting in an armchair by the window. The sun shines through the curtain and casts a triangle of light across her sleeping face. Her head is tilted back. For a moment, I think she might be dead. But she snores suddenly, a sharp, slurping breath, and I know she's still with us. Dad and I look at each other with relief and hurry over. I sit on a footstool and Dad pats her knee and rubs her shoulders until she wakes up.

She stares at us for a moment, blinking, disoriented.

"Hi Grandma," I say. "It's Max."

"And it's me, Joe," says Dad. "We came for a visit. We wanted to see how you're doing. How are you doing, Jean? Are you doing okay?"

"You came for a visit?" says Grandma, blinking.

We nod and hold her hands.

She looks over our shoulders toward the door.

"Did you bring Anna too?" she asks.

"No, Jean," says Dad. "Anna died."

"Anna died?"

"Yes," says my dad. "She had cancer."

Grandma shakes her head, as though shaking out cobwebs. Then she wipes her eyes and sits up straighter. "I forgot for a second," she says incredulously. "I was asleep and dreaming she was alive. And then when you woke me I had forgotten for just a second. People used to say she looked just like me."

"She did look like you," I say. "She had your eyes."

"So do you," says Grandma, reaching out to touch my face.

We look at each other.

"I want some ice cream," says Grandma.

"I'll get it," I tell her.

I bring three prefilled cups, each with a single scoop of vanilla ice cream, and three white plastic spoons to a table. We sit together and eat our ice cream, letting it drip down our throats. Grandma likes it. She closes her eyes every time she swallows.

The tumor is disappointed with vanilla. He doesn't realize that beggars can't be choosers. Presumptuous colonist. Most polyps and masses would be thrilled to have such delicacies. *Yes. I'll have one cerebral cortex with a tall glass of cerebrospinal fluid, please.*

"Jean," says Dad finally. "I want to talk to you about something."

"Okay," says Grandma. "What do you want to talk about?"

"It's Max."

He's dying of his mother's cancer.

"What's wrong with Max?"

The tumor has colonized his brain.

"Well, Max has been having a really hard time since Anna left us," Dad tells her, his face reddening. "At school, especially. He's stopped participating in classes and doing homework, and even though I've been trying to help him and the school has been trying to help him, he's failing all his classes."

"Failing his classes?" says Grandma. "Max Friedman. You should be ashamed of yourself."

"I am," I say.

"This is very bad news," she says.

"I'm sorry," says Dad. "And I wouldn't be telling you this—I wouldn't even be bothering you with it except we've found a private school, and we think it would be much better for Max. We visited today and he loves it. Smaller classes. Creative kids. Beautiful campus. It's called the Baldwin School. We think it would be a perfect place to help Max get back on track."

"Good," says Grandma. "This boy should not be failing classes. I'm disappointed in you, Max."

"I'm disappointed in me too," I whisper.

"So I had him apply and he wrote an essay and had an interview and took a test and he got in, Jean. Which is really wonderful news because they only take the top kids. And they're taking Max."

"He got in," says Grandma, looking at me and smiling. I nod.

"Even though he's been failing," she says.

"We're pretty happy about it," says Dad. "And we've applied for financial aid, which should help with some of the cost. But the thing is, and this is why I'm bothering you with it, if he goes, we need to pay tuition by next week and I don't have it, Jean. Things are slow in the frame shop right now. I haven't been doing very many photography jobs since Anna got sick, and I just don't have it. Normally I wouldn't ask. You know I wouldn't ask. Especially at a time like this when we've all been through so much. But I was just wondering if you could possibly help us out with this."

"Pay for the school?" says Grandma.

"Yeah," says Dad. "That's what I'm asking."

"How much is it?" says Grandma.

I swallow.

"Thirty," says Dad.

"Thirty dollars? You can't afford thirty dollars?"

"Thirty thousand," says Dad. "Thirty thousand dollars a year."

Grandma lets go of my hands.

"Oh my," she says. "That's a mint."

"Yeah," says Dad.

My heart sinks.

Grandma is quiet for a while. Her eyes are distant. Then she looks at us and smiles. "You know what?" she says.

"What?" says my dad.

"Thirty thousand is about how much I pay to stay here. Thirty thousand a year to be surrounded by sick people and strangers. I'd rather spend it on this boy, I can tell you that. But I can't live here and give it to you. I can't do both."

Dad and I look at each other.

I know he's thinking what I'm thinking.

"What if you come and live with us?" says Dad.

I'm grinning. I can't help it.

"Don't say things you don't mean," says Grandma, trying to stop herself from smiling. "I'm an old woman and I can't take more disappointments."

"I mean it," says Dad. His eyes are teary, and I have to look away to stop from getting teary myself.

"I don't want to be in the way," says Grandma.

"You won't be," says Dad.

"You think we can just walk out of this place?"

"I don't know," says Dad. "I can talk to Darlene at the front desk and find out how we go about it. I'm sure there's paperwork and things like that."

"Can I pack?" asks Grandma.

"Sure," says Dad. "Max, help your grandma pack."

I take her arm and we walk with slow steps down the hall to her apartment.

She drags a suitcase from under her bed and begins taking things out of her drawers. Nightgowns. Blouses. Slacks. Pullovers. Comfortable shoes. There aren't many things that belong to her in this tiny place.

In no time, the drawers are empty and the suitcase is full. The last thing to go is a framed black-and-white picture of Grandma and Mom on the dresser. Grandma is beautiful and young and Mom is a little girl in a white dress.

They have their arms around each other and they are laughing. You can tell, because Mom is throwing back her head the way she always used to do, and Grandma is smiling so wide it looks like her whole face is a sunrise. I show her the picture of the two of them, the woman and the girl. Forty years before tragedy. Grandma kisses the photograph and puts it in the suitcase facedown.

"Come on, Grandma," I say. "Let's get out of here."

DARK SIDE OF THE MOON

WE MOVE GRANDMA INTO THE GUEST BEDROOM, WHICH she has always loved because it's where she used to sleep when she came to take care of us. First when I was a newborn, then when Mom had her surgery, and then when Mom was so sick from chemo she couldn't be home by herself. The second time around, Mom was too far gone for chemo, Grandma was in Green Meadows, and the guest room remained empty. The walls are yellow, the way they've always been, with the same little white dresser that used to belong to Grandma when she was a kid, so she says it feels like home.

We love hearing her shuffling footsteps and seeing her hunched form sitting in the living room with the newspaper, or at the kitchen table with a cup of coffee. The house has been so empty lately, and there's something about Grandma that makes us think maybe a little bit of Mom is still around. So we treat her gently. When she talks, we strain our ears just in case a remnant of Mom's voice is still in there somewhere, a timbre, a note, a turn of phrase that will prove to us she is not entirely gone.

On Thanksgiving, no one's really up for the fuss, so Dad picks up three ready-made turkey dinners from Stop and Shop, each in its own cardboard tray with dividers for stuffing, mashed potatoes, gelatinous cranberry sauce, and corn. He lights a candle, and we sit at the kitchen table together while the light flickers across our faces. We try to smile at each other. We tell each other it's delicious. When the meal is over, Grandma excuses herself and goes upstairs. Most nights, she goes up to her room early, but I'm not sure she gets much sleep. I hear her slippered feet padding around the house in the middle of night, from the guest room to the bathroom and back.

Sunday night I'm lying awake in my bed with my sketchbook, trying not to think about second chances and trying even harder to ignore the tumor, who has decided that this is a good night to take up tap dancing. I hate tap dancing. There's a hesitant knock on my door, and before I have the chance to tell her I'm trying to sleep, Grandma shuffles in wearing her pink slippers and her long flannel night-gown. She stands in front of my bed and stares at me. "You're awake," she says. "It's almost midnight. You should be sleeping."

"I have a headache," I tell her.

Grandma kisses my forehead.

I lean my head back on my pillows. The tumor is Irish step dancing across my cerebral cortex. He has invited a hundred of his best friends to join him. Everyone is wearing spandex and those horrible clomping shoes. Good lord. I close my eyes and then open them again, hoping this will draw the curtain, but the show must go on. More tumors march out from the wings. They march down the center aisle. They fly in on ropes. It is a cast of thousands.

Grandma lowers herself down onto my bed. She's so small, it doesn't even shift with her weight. She is almost not there at all.

She closes my sketchbook, kisses me on the forehead, and runs a gnarled hand through my hair. "You look so much like Anna. Isn't that amazing? Oh, I could just tickle you until your mom jumps out."

Grandma tickles her fingers up and down my arm.

This excites the tumor and his dancing friends, who link arms and begin doing the cancan in unison across my frontal lobe.

Quiet down, crazy tumors. If I don't get some rest, I'm going to be a mess tomorrow.

I yawn tremendously.

Grandma kisses my forehead again. "Sleep," she says.

"Okay," I say. "You too."

Grandma winks at me. She rises from the bed and makes her way back to the door.

"I love you, sweetheart," she says.

It's my mother's voice.

"I love you too," I whisper.

The door closes. Her footsteps shuffle back to the guest room.

The tumors are shaking the stage with their clomping so I put in my earbuds and try to disappear into my favorite track on Pink Floyd's *Dark Side of the Moon*. I curl myself into a ball and pull the covers up over my head. I listen to that lady at the end of "The Great Gig in the Sky" singing her famous musical orgasm. She does these crazy, slow, soul riffs that swell and soar and get faster and louder and higher and louder and faster until they explode and shudder and purr and whisper and sigh and snuggle.

The tap dancing behind my eyes is driving me mad, so I turn the music up and roll onto my back with the lady whispering the end of her orgasm, and *resolving*, as they say in the world of music theory, pun intended, *resolving* into this gorgeous sustained chord, but the thought of her satisfaction makes me thoroughly depressed because of my own nonexistent love life and the relative unlikeliness that I will ever make a girl sound remotely as happy as the lady singing her glory into my ears, so I turn the music off and lie there, my pounding head on the pillow and the earbuds nestled in my ears like little turtles and the plastic-coated wire leading to nothing.

Most nights I can fall asleep with the music off and the earbuds in, because I like the feeling of something nestled in there. But tonight, the night before my first day at Baldwin, I am just too nervous to sleep, so I put the earbuds in my mouth and I suck on them while I google tumor statistics on my phone. By the time we learned that Mom's cancer had spread to her brain, we only had ten months left. She never said anything to me about the tumor tap dancing, but she did get headaches that brought her to her knees.

I find a list of different kinds of brain cancers listed in alphabetical order. Each one has a picture of a CT scan and a list of information. Diagnosis. Symptoms. Treatments. Prognosis. I suck on the earbuds and whisper the names of the tumors into the dark like an incantation: anaplastic astrocytoma, brain stem glioma, ependymoma, ganglioglioma, ganglioneuroma, glioblastoma, glioma, juvenile pilocytic astrocytoma, medulloblastoma, oligodendroglioma. I whisper their names and run my tongue back and forth

66

across the earbuds until I finally get sleepy. Pretty soon, the tumors stop dancing and begin to gather around my incantation as though it were a campfire. They put their tendrils around one another and lean their heads on one another's shoulders and they close their eyes while I name them over and over. No tumor has ever heard such a perfect lullaby. We fall asleep together, the tumors and me, our arms around each other, bathed in the milky blue glow of my phone in the dark.

MEASURE FOR MEASURE

WHEN I WAS LITTLE, MOM WOULD ALWAYS MAKE A
big deal about the first day of school. Getting ready was a
ritual I looked forward to every August, counting down the
days the way most kids count down to summer vacation.
First there was the annual back-to-school shopping trip to
Walmart for school supplies and new clothes. *I can't believe
you've outgrown everything in those drawers! Look how big
you're getting.* Then there was my last dinner of the summer, which always involved many burners and many pots
bubbling at once until the walls of our yellow kitchen would
sweat even with all the windows open and the fan going.

Mom hated using the stove when it was really hot, and
August dinners tended to be grilled outside on the barbe-
cue, or else they involved leftovers, cold cuts, and chilled

salads, but she was always willing to sweat on this one day so her little boy could start off his year right. I would sit at the table like a king, and Mom would smile at me while I ate my brisket or my baked chicken. I would wolf it down gratefully and she would laugh her amazing laugh and smile through her sweat even when it was ninety degrees and the kitchen fan didn't make a single bit of difference. That's how much she loved me.

After dinner there was the annual laying out of clothes and school supplies with the once-a-year prayer Mom said only on the night before the first day of school: *Tomorrow is going to be the very first day of your very best school year ever.* Words that sounded as sweet as a kiss on the forehead.

Each year I would wake before the alarm. I'd bounce out of bed and throw on my new clothes and brush my teeth because everyone likes a white smile. I would tumble down the stairs and Mom would already be there at the table with her coffee and newspaper. *Hey there, early bird!* she'd say, and there would be a whole plateful of matzo-meal latkes with grape jelly for breakfast because that's my favorite and they take so long to make you have to save them for special occasions.

Finally, just before the school bus rounded the corner onto our street, there was the once-a-year measuring of my height against the wall in the back hallway. *Don't cheat*, she'd say. *No tippy-toes. Feet flat on the floor, please.* And I would drop down an inch or two, and she would take a pencil and draw a line just like she had every first day of school since I was in kindergarten, and I could stand back and see how far I'd come from the year before and the year before and the year before.

Would you look at that? How can this be true?

But it is true. It is true.

———————————

Today my alarm goes off before sunrise. It's cold in my room. I peel the cell phone from my unshaven cheek. My desperate nocturnal Google search is still pulsing on the screen, laughing at me. The earbuds are still in my mouth, wires dangling down my chin. I know I should spit them out because they taste like morning breath, but the plastic against my tongue feels good and not much in this world feels good these days, so I suck on the earbuds while I drag a comb through my hair, and I suck on them all the way down the hall to the bathroom where I splash water on my face. Dark circles. Pale. Skinny. Look at you, dude. You look like a corpse already. How can that be true? But it is true. It is true.

I spit out the earbuds and brush my teeth.

"Max," calls Dad.

"Yeah," I call back.

"You dressed?"

I look down at the clothes I fell asleep in.

"Yeah."

"Come and eat something. We need to get going in a few minutes."

"Okay," I say.

Downstairs, Dad and Grandma are sitting at the kitchen table. Grandma's wearing her flannel nightgown and has her eyes closed.

Dad's hunched beside her, unshaven, bleary-eyed, wearing jeans, reading the newspaper, and drinking coffee.

I slide into a chair.

Dad looks up from the paper and says, "You look like you've been hit by a train."

"You don't look much better yourself, old man."

"Touché," says Dad.

He toasts me with his coffee mug and takes a long, noisy sip.

There isn't much left.

"Can I have some?" I ask him.

"Yeah," says Dad. "But go easy on it."

He hands over the mug. I like the feeling of the hot coffee moving down my throat. I can see why he does this every morning. Feels good. Not so many things in life feel good like this. Earbuds. Coffee. The list is dwindling.

I hand the empty mug back to him.

"Gee," says Dad. "Thanks."

"Got any more?" I ask.

"Nope," says Dad, putting down the mug and regarding me. "That was the last of it. Make your own coffee next time, you mooch."

"I'm your progeny," I remind him. "I'm supposed to be a mooch."

"Yeah?" says Dad. "Less than three years until college. Then I'm gonna kick you to the curb, you miscreant."

"Nah," I tell him. "I'm gonna live here forever, drinking your coffee and helping you lose what little hair you have left. Which, by the way, is not very much, in case you haven't noticed."

Dad runs a hand through his thinning hair. "Good plan," he says. "So you want a Pop-Tart or something before we leave?"

"Yeah," I say.

"Blueberry?" asks my dad.

"Okay," I say. "With frosting?"

"But of course," says Dad. He finds a package of Pop-Tarts from the pantry and throws it to me. I actually catch it. A minor miracle.

"Breakfast of champions," says Dad.

Then he goes over to Grandma. "Jean," he says close to her ear. "Jean. Wake up, honey. I'm taking Max to his first day at Baldwin." He rubs her shoulders.

Grandma opens her eyes.

"Where's Anna?" she says.

"She died, Jean," says Dad.

Her eyes widen and fill with tears.

"My Anna died?"

Dad sighs. "Yes she did," he says. "And you are living with us now. You said you wanted to say good luck to Max before I take him to his new school. Well, we're leaving in a few minutes."

Grandma wipes away her tears and shakes her head until she's fully awake. Then she pushes herself out of her chair, shuffles over to where I'm sitting, and puts her arms around my shoulders. She kisses me on the forehead. Her lips are soft and warm, like Mom's were. "Knock 'em dead," says Grandma. She smiles at me and I see Mom's eyes twinkling. "I love you," she says.

"Thanks," I say. "I love you too."

"We'll be back at three thirty," says Dad. "You gonna be okay?"

"I think so," says Grandma.

"You have my number at the shop?"

"I have your number. I'm fine. Don't you worry about me. I just need a little more rest. Didn't get much sleep last night. Good luck, Max. See you after school."

"Bye, Grandma," I say.

She makes her way up the stairs and back to her bedroom. I can hear her slippered footsteps and then the sound of her bedroom door pulled shut.

Our jackets are hanging on hooks in the back hallway.

We pass by the wall where Mom used to measure my height. Dad and I stop for a moment. We look at all the different years written in my mom's handwriting, letters and numbers that curl and twist, thin and slanted like tendrils.

The tumor is laughing at me.

I take a deep breath.

"You want me to measure you?" Dad asks.

He reaches in his back pocket for a pen.

"No," I say. My voice is harsher than I intend it to be.

He looks at me, taken aback.

"No thank you," I say, trying to sound gentler this time. "We better go."

Dad nods.

We put on our jackets and walk in silence to the truck. Dad gets in. I get in next to him. We slam our doors and pull onto the road, each of us thinking our own thoughts as we drive through quiet streets, down through the center of town toward Baldwin, where the sun winks through the bare trees like a tentative and uncertain promise.

MORNING HAS BROKEN

SOMEHOW, WHEN WE FIRST ARRIVE ON CAMPUS I expect a sign that my life is going to get better with my arrival and that this second chance will really be what I have needed all along. I want it to be true so badly it hurts almost as much as the tumor pounding behind my eyes. I imagine being serenaded by a chorus of angels singing Handel's "Hallelujah Chorus." I imagine the clouds parting and a shaft of light shining down. A rainbow. God's ancient promise that the flood is over. But that doesn't happen.

We see kids heading from their dorms, past the playing fields, and across the fallow gardens toward Trowbridge Hall. They walk in groups, beautiful, confident, sure of their paths.

"Well," says Dad, "you better get going."

"Okay," I say.

I stare out the window at the school. I'm worried that if I make eye contact with him I'll cry.

"See you later," I say.

I open the door to the truck. You can smell winter beneath the scent of the engine, the dirty seats, and Dad's old coffee cups.

"You got everything you need?"

"I think so," I mutter, still not looking at him.

"Hey," says Dad.

I pull my backpack onto my shoulders and get ready to leave.

"Hey." He puts his hand on my shoulder. "Look at me, would you?"

I do. I look at him.

His face is so full of concern, I think it's going to break me open.

"I want you to have a great day," he says.

"I will," I tell him, but my voice is uncertain.

"I'll be back at three to pick you up, okay?"

"All right," I say.

We sit side by side for a few more moments, watching the beautiful people.

We are enveloped in silence.

Finally, Dad reaches over and pulls my head closer to him.

He leans his cheek against the top of my head, kisses me, and then messes up my hair with both hands.

"Hey. I love you. You know that, right?"

"I know," I say.

"Mom would be so proud of you right now."

I don't say anything.

What is there to be proud of?

Calling her tumor into my brain like some kind of desperate landlord?

Failing my classes?

Taking Grandma's money to pay for my failure?

Worrying Dad so terribly that he looks ten years older than he did just a few months ago?

We were supposed to survive this. We promised her we would be okay.

"I better go," I say huskily.

"Okay," says Dad. "Break a leg."

"I'm not in a play, Dad," I say.

"Okay. How about good luck?"

"That's better," I say.

There's a pause.

"Well, good luck, then," says Dad.

We stare at each other.

"Thanks," I say.

I climb down from the truck and slam the door.

Dad waves.

I wave too.

You can go now.

But he stays in the parking lot and watches me as I start up the path toward the main office in Trowbridge Hall, hands deep in my pockets.

Students come from every direction with their backpacks and bags, and I fold into them, allowing myself to be carried by the current even though I know I cannot possibly fit in with all these faces, glowing about whatever things interest them, articulating their vowels and consonants like people who like the sound of their own voices.

Suddenly I feel very small, stupid, and unattractive.

I wish I had worn clean clothes. I wish I had shaved. I wish I had used mouthwash. I hope I don't smell. I hope the tumor isn't making my eye bug out of my head the way Mom's eye did. *The better to see you with, my dear*, and we laughed like it was the best joke in the world, even though no one thought it was funny. Not even her.

"Max!" A girl's voice behind me. "Hey! You're here!"

Running footsteps from the parking lot, and she is at my side. Fish. Breathless, with her pink hair cascading down her shoulders and her green eyes shining.

"Remember me?"

I feel myself smile. "Of course I remember you," I say.

"I didn't know you were coming."

"Well," I say. "Surprise."

"I am so happy you're here," says Fish. "Hey. Did you bring your sketchbook with you?"

"Yep," I say, patting my backpack.

"Me too," says Fish, patting her back pocket. Then she smiles mischievously and wiggles her hips. "I'll show you mine if you show me yours." But then, just when I think she is going to do something lewd, the alarm on her phone goes off. "Yikes," she says. "Almost time for first period. Mom woke up late as usual and we had to go, like, ninety through town to get me here. It was crazy. You commute too, right? I thought I saw your dad in the parking lot."

I look over my shoulder. The truck is still there, and he's still watching me, his hands resting on the steering wheel.

"Yeah," I say. "We live just across town."

"I think it would be better for me and my mom if I could board," says Fish. "But we could never afford it."

"Me neither," I say.

There's a pause. We watch Dad watching us.

A bell rings high up in the tower.

"We need to hustle," says Fish. "Want to wave goodbye?"

"Nah," I say. "He'll be okay."

"Aw, just wave to him. Come on. I'll wave too. It'll be cute. Like preschool."

We both wave, Fish on twinkle toes.

I see the scar on her wrist. I had forgotten about it.

Dad waves back.

"Come on," says Fish.

She grabs my arm.

We hurry up the path, up the stone steps of Trowbridge Hall, to the double doors.

Just before I enter the building, I turn around one more time to look at the parking lot. As if on cue, Dad's truck finally, *finally* pulls out of the spot and heads slowly back around the corner and down the road toward town. Even though I can't see him, I know he's turning up the radio so he can lose himself in something familiar. I know he's checking the rearview mirror to see if he can spot me one more time before I'm too far away and I fade behind him into the distance like a ghost.

WE'RE OFF TO SEE THE WIZARD

TROWBRIDGE HALL IS FILLED WITH EXCITED VOICES, the echo of quick footsteps on wooden floors, and the not-so-subtle bouquet of patchouli and sandalwood, the signature aroma of progressive youth. There's something overwhelming about being inside the school. Everywhere I look there's interest and intensity, clues that creativity is the rule rather than the exception.

One girl has doodled paisley Zentangles all up and down her arms, an intricate, interwoven pattern that alternates leaves and polka dots. A boy playing the ukulele is singing that completely sad Hawaiian version of "Over the Rainbow" that everyone loves. I stop for a moment and listen.

Fish pulls me into the front office, where Lydie greets me with a smile and hands me my schedule and an information page with the names of my student fellow and my faculty advisor. She explains that my student fellow will introduce himself during my first-period class and my faculty advisor, who also happens to be my creative writing teacher, will catch me afterward to schedule our first meeting.

"Think of this as your home base, Max. If you need anything, come find me."

"Thanks," I say. "I really appreciate that." And I mean it.

"I'm in creative writing too," says Fish at my elbow. "Dr. Cage takes a little getting used to, but he is really awesome. He's sort of a legend around here. What's your first class?"

I look at my schedule.

"World Literature with Dr. Austerlitz."

"Serendipity!" cries Fish. "I'm in that too! And so's my best friend, David. You'll like him. He's totally insane. He's also the tallest guy in the school. It's good to have tall friends."

"Are you talking about David Moniker?" Lydie asks.

"Yup," says Fish. "Everyone calls him The Monk. He's a junior. He was the Friar in *Romeo and Juliet* last spring, and everyone started calling him The Monk, which is ironic since he's one of the most un-monkish people on earth but still, the name kinda stuck."

"Well, it just so happens that David is Max's student

fellow. See? His name is on your sheet. What do you think of that?"

Fish pantomimes her head exploding.

"This is totally serendipitous. You know? Complete and utter weird-ass kismet."

"Fish," says Lydie sternly. "Watch your language, please."

"Sorry," says Fish. "I just really like it when things fall into place. *That's* the part that feels like kismet. You know what I mean?"

"I do know what you mean," says Lydie, half-smiling. "But nothing's going to feel like kismet today unless you two get to class quick. Dr. Austerlitz is strict about punctuality and I have a feeling he wouldn't make an exception even though Max is new. So you two better skedaddle."

"Skedaddling!" cries Fish.

She grabs my arm again and skips me down the hallway, Yellow Brick Road–style, all the way into class and into our seats, where she introduces me to her friend and my student fellow, The Monk, who kisses her hand and raises one skeptical eyebrow at me from behind his John Lennon glasses, and then Dr. Austerlitz appears, welcomes me to World Literature class, and tosses me a copy of *The Metamorphosis*.

"You're going to need this," he says. "It's the cornerstone

of our entire curriculum. No matter what we study, we will always circle back to Franz Kafka."

Then class begins.

I know he is speaking, but his voice is on mute and his face is faded and blurry.

The tumor unbuckles his belt and expands like an old man after Thanksgiving dinner. He sprawls out on my cerebral cortex and belches luxuriously, reaching for the remote. I can feel him unrolling his gelatinous folds, oozing into my cranium, bubbling between the coils of my brain.

I begin to unravel. Dr. Austerlitz says something about Gregor Samsa and how he has transformed, and I start thinking, Oh my God, he's talking about the tumor, he's talking about how my mother's favorite tumor is pushing against my left eye as though some heavy shoulder is leaning against it, and I wonder how my face will change after I die. Will my lips thin out and pull away from my teeth? Will my skin fall down against the bones in my face the way Mom's did, one eyelid sinking in, but the other, the one with the tumor, grotesque and monstrous? *The better to see you with, my dear.* I take my sketchbook out of my backpack and begin drawing eyeballs, hundreds of eyeballs, thousands of eyeballs. I draw eyeballs so quickly you can hear my pencil scratching across the page.

"Mr. Friedman," says Dr. Austerlitz. "Are you with us?"

I try to look at him, but the tumor is threatening to slice

my eyeballs open from the inside, so I put my elbows on the desk and bury my head in my hands.

"Mr. Friedman," Dr. Austerlitz says again, his voice touched with the slightest knife's edge.

The Monk nudges me with his copy of *The Metamorphosis*, but I don't budge. I breathe long and deep into my hands and try to come back into the classroom, where nothing strange is happening except a man turning into a cockroach. I clutch the edge of my desk.

"Hey," says Fish. She puts her hand on my elbow and leans over to me. "You feeling okay?"

"I think he's catatonic," says The Monk.

His theory is interesting but entirely devoid of possibility, because if I were catatonic I would not be able to do what I do next, which is drop my head on my desk where the wood is cool and smooth and rock my frontal lobe back and forth.

"Mr. Friedman," Dr. Austerlitz continues, "this is not a good way to begin. Please get your head off the desk and participate in this class. Or, if you are too ill, you may excuse yourself and take a walk down the hall to the infirmary. Which do you prefer?"

He is standing in front of my desk now, hands on hips.

I can't see him with my head down, but I can smell jock itch powder, and I am certain that if I raised my head and opened my eyes, I would be staring right at Dr. Austerlitz's crotch, a possibility that does not motivate me to come back to the equally disturbing world of Franz Kafka, no matter how much I love cockroaches or German literature. I choose to keep my frontal lobe on the desk instead.

"You may go, then," says Dr. Austerlitz's crotch. "Right now."

Look at this. Less than five minutes into my first class and already the teacher is telling me to leave. Mr. Mancini would be so proud. I press my head harder into the desk, at which point the tumor gets rowdy and begins knocking on the inside of my skull with his fists, pounding against nerve endings.

The doctors told us that at the time of my mother's death, her tumor was approximately the size and shape of a grapefruit. When did it start, this strange desire to make analogies between tumors and food? It is the size of a grape. A walnut. An apple. A grapefruit. A melon. A pumpkin. These days, I avoid spherical foods at all costs. I promised my dad I would be strong. Oh God.

"Someone help him out of here, please," says Dr. Austerlitz wearily.

"I'll do it," says a voice through the haze. "Hey. Dude. Let's go."

"Don't forget his backpack," says Dr. Austerlitz.

The hazy kid grabs my stuff, as though I were an enormous scuttling cockroach, and pushes me down the aisle and out the classroom door.

"Hey," he says, snapping his fingers in front of my eyes. "Come on, dude. Look at me. Come back to earth. Jesus Christ. What's the deal?"

It's my student fellow.

David Moniker. The Monk.

"Don't worry, dude," says The Monk. "I bet it's just nerves. First day in a new school? New kids? New teachers? *German literature*, for God's sake. Anyone would get stressed out. Maybe you should get a drink of water and come back in."

"I don't know," I say. "I think I may be coming down with something."

"You want me to walk you to the infirmary? See if they can give you a couple Tylenol? Maybe a shot of Jagermeister to wash it down?"

"Nah," I say. "Jagermeister's made with elk piss."

"Blood," says The Monk, clearly pleased with my knowledge of alternative trivia. "Elk *blood*, you sick bastard. And that's just a myth, by the way."

"That's what they all say."

The Monk starts giving my stuff back, ceremoniously, one item at a time. My pencil. My backpack. Then he hands over my sketchbook, still open to the page with all the eyeballs staring in different directions.

"Good God," he says. "That's completely disturbing."

"Thanks," I say.

"I collect oddities," says The Monk. "Those eyeballs would look perfect on the shelf next to my two-headed cow embryo. I just may need to procure it from you one of these days."

"It's not for sale," I say.

"Oh my dear boy," says The Monk dolefully. "Everything is for sale."

Then he smirks at me from behind his round glasses and hands me my copy of *The Metamorphosis*. "Kafka appeals to me," he says. "Think about it. Gregor Samsa starts out as a regular old middle-class slog like the rest of us. Sleepwalking through life. Then he turns into a *cockroach*, for God's sake. Six legs. Antennae. The whole nine yards. Now that is truly twisted shit. You agree?"

"Ja," I say, in my best German accent. *"Und* now I must go to the infirmary. Because I vell azleep. And as I vas vaking up from anxious dreamz, I discovered that in bed I had been changed into *ein* monstrous vermin."

"A monstrous vermin. Ha. Well, listen. If you need anything, I'm here for you, vermin-dude. Bratwurst. Blood sausage. Wiener schnitzel. You want it, you got it. Anytime. Okay?"

"Jawohl," I say.

The Monk points toward the infirmary and clicks his combat boots.

I salute him, flash him the peace sign, and hitch up my

backpack. I pretend I'm a cockroach saying goodbye with many legs. I raise one shoulder like a hunchback and start to scuttle down the hall toward the infirmary, with its yellow door wide open like the mouth of some huge yellow smiley-faced clown, revealing yellow walls, an orange vinyl sick-couch, rows of pink Dixie cups, and a glowing, toxic, neon-pink hand-sanitizer dispenser hanging on the wall. My head pounds and pulses with the tumor raging inside it, scratching against the backs of my eyes, a veritable cornucopia of irony and demise.

YELLOW SMILEY SICKROOM

I STAND AT THE DESK AND BREATHE ALL THE HAPPY colors into my lungs.

"Hi there," says the nurse. "How can I help you today?"

"I don't feel so good," I say.

Behind her desk, there's a window that looks out onto a courtyard. There are rows of gnarled trees shaking their fists at the sky.

"You must be our new student, Max Friedman. So not feeling good on the first day? That stinks. What's going on?"

"I don't know," I say. "I'm feeling really sick."

My words hang in the air.

Sick. Sick. Sick. Really, really sick.

"It's my head. It hurts right here in this area." I point to my frontal lobe.

"Is it a dull pain or a sharp pain?"

"Sharp," I say, wincing.

She raises her eyebrows.

"I mean dull. No. I think it's definitely sharp. Ouch." I close my eyes.

I lower myself down onto the orange vinyl couch and put my head in my hands.

"Wow," says the nurse. "It hurts that much?"

"Yeah," I say, making myself breathe slow and deep.

She brings me a Dixie cup filled with water.

I drink it and then crumple it in my hand.

"You want to lie down here for a bit and then go back to class?"

"No," I say into my hands. "I think I need to go home. It really hurts."

"Sounds like you have a little migraine. Have you ever had a migraine before?"

"No," I say. "I don't get migraines. This is something different."

The nurse takes out my medical file and starts riffling through my information.

"Hey," she says. "You have Ms. Grossman in the office listed as an emergency contact. Is she a family friend?"

"Yeah," I say. "I know her pretty well."

"Well, why don't we give her a call and see if she can come and keep you company for a while. Maybe you'll feel better after talking to someone you know."

I don't say anything. I am massaging my eyeballs.

I don't see how talking to someone is going to help shrink my tumor.

The nurse picks up the phone.

"Hi, Lydie. Karen here. I have Max Friedman in the infirmary. He says his head hurts. I looked at his file. Right. Exactly. So I was thinking maybe it would help if you came down to chat with him, and then we can get him back to class."

"I need to go home," I say.

"Ms. Grossman will be here soon," says the nurse.

She makes herself busy at her desk and I sit quietly until Lydie comes in.

"Hey, Max," says Lydie.

Her voice is soft.

"Hey," I say.

"Ms. Henderson says you have a headache."

"It really hurts," I say. "I want to go home."

Lydie sits down next to me. "Coming to this school is a change," she says. "You've had a lot of changes lately. But give this one a chance, Max. I think you'll like it here."

"This isn't about changes. It's about my head. My head hurts. Why won't anyone listen to me?"

"Where does it hurt?"

"Here," I say. I point to my left eye. "There's something pushing against my eyeball. See? Look at it. Look at my eye."

"You have lovely eyes," says Lydie.

"It's bulging."

Lydie frowns. "It's not bulging," she says. "It's fine. Ms. Henderson, can you come over here a second? Max is wondering if his eye looks like it's bulging. Does his eye look unusual to you?"

The nurse looks into my eye with a tiny flashlight. "Nope," she says, smiling. "His eye looks just fine. Gorgeous, in fact."

There's another wave of pain. I curl into it.

"I want to go home," I say. "Please call my dad."

Lydie and the nurse look at each other.

"I'm not making this up," I say. "Please."

"Okay," the nurse says finally. "I'll give him a call."

I look out the window. It has started to snow. Snow falls on the bare branches, the stone benches, the fallow gardens and the flagstone paths, and farther out, where I can't see, beyond the gates, where the concrete starts, it falls on the long stretches of nameless buildings and the busy people in their cars with the windows rolled up and the whole, wide, godforsaken world.

TRUTH AND TRUANCY

LYDIE WELCOMES DAD INTO THE NURSE'S OFFICE.

"Max," she says. "Your dad's here."

She and the nurse wander to the other side of the room so Dad and I can talk in private.

He looks completely out of place in this school. Too rough around the edges. Too unkempt in his work boots and his plaid jacket, his two days' growth of beard.

"So what's the deal?" says Dad.

"I don't feel good," I say.

"Do you have a fever?" He puts his hand out to feel my frontal lobe but I push it away.

"I don't have a fever," I tell him.

"Then why are you telling them you want to go home? You're fine."

"I'm not fine," I say. "I have a headache."

"You want to go home because of a headache? Max. It's your first day of school. You need to deal with this. Go back to class."

I push in my left eye and wince.

"What?" says Dad.

"Do you think one of my eyes looks strange?"

"Your eye is fine," he says again, more sternly this time. "What class did you leave?"

"World Literature," I say.

"When's it over?"

"Nine thirty."

Dad checks his watch. "Good. It's only nine twenty. If you go now, you might just get back in time to catch the homework."

"But Dad," I say.

"No," he says. "Stop it. I don't want to hear another word about this. You need to be strong."

"Aren't you worried about me?"

"Yeah," says Dad. "I am. I am very worried about you."

"Because you think there's something wrong with my eye?"

"No," says Dad. "Because this school can give us a second chance and I'm not going to let you ruin it. So I'm not taking you home. You need to deal with your headache, man up, get back to class, and do your best."

Dad calls Lydie and the nurse over from the corner of the room where they have been pretending not to listen to us.

"Ms. Grossman, Ms. Henderson, thank you so much for being so kind and helpful. But Max will go back to class now."

"Are you sure?" asks Ms. Henderson.

"Yeah," says Dad. "He's sure."

"I'll pick you up at three," says Dad. "Be strong. Make me proud."

"Okay," I say, expressionless. "Thank you for helping me."

"You're welcome," says Dad. "Now get going, please. And no more melodrama."

I have no choice. I have to do what he says. I make a silent promise to myself that no matter how bad it gets, I will never mention the tumor to him. I swing my pack onto my shoulders, put my hands into my pockets, and trudge back to Dr. Austerlitz's class, where I take my place at my desk.

The Monk reaches over and shakes my hand.

"Are you ready to join us now?" asks Dr. Austerlitz.

I nod and try to give him a look that means I'm sorry.

The tumor is shouting obscenities, but I try to ignore him.

I take my copy of *The Metamorphosis* from my backpack and pretend to read.

In a few minutes the bell will ring and it will be time

for second period. The school day stretches before me in even, never-ending rows. It's portioned into minutes and hours and grade books and calendars and megapixels and websites and text messages and doors opening and closing and arteries and veins and valves opening and closing and hearts, all those hearts, one in each kid, beating, because that is what they do when the person is still alive.

BOTTLE OF COW

ON TUESDAY, AFTER WE EAT LUNCH, THE MONK TAKES me to his dorm room to see his collection of oddities. He kicks off his combat boots and sprawls on his unmade bed, watching me examine the tiny bovine in a jar of formaldehyde with a satisfied smirk on his face. "That's Bertha," says The Monk. "She is my destiny." I shove a jumble of notebooks aside so I can perch on the edge of his desk and examine the strange specimen under the light. At closer inspection, it seems that Bertha is not actually one cow with two heads but two cows with one freakishly conjoined body and four translucent legs that wave vaguely if you turn the jar: the tiny, perfect hooves milky and delicate, rearing up, almost luminous, even under the harsh light of The Monk's green desk lamp.

"See what I mean?" he says. "She's amazing, right?" I nod but don't say anything. I have never been in a dorm room before, and I'm so struck by the utter profundity of his squalor that I'm finding it difficult to focus on the cow, which is probably a good thing because frankly I find it disturbing. The floor on The Monk's side of the room is covered in books and T-shirts, folders, towels, sheets, and blankets all rumpled together in a swirl. There are socks and boxers shoved hastily underneath the bed, along with empty tissue boxes, energy drinks, and packs of gum. It is immediately evident that The Monk, despite his apparent coolness, is also in desperate need of either an intervention or a garbage can or both.

There is a clear division across the middle of the floor, an invisible but completely recognizable line where The Monk's tornado of stuff ends and the ordered, organized world of his roommate begins—poor Thomas A. Trowbridge the Fourth, with his perfectly stacked books, his white duvet, and his plastic containers of black socks stored neatly under the bed, who must be forced to look with narrowed eyes into The Monk's swirling tornado every morning. Thomas A. Trowbridge's bed, I notice, perhaps in direct reaction to The Monk's aggressive disorganization, is so incredibly neat and tidy that it actually has hospital corners.

I know all about hospital corners. Mom's hospice nurse used to do them every morning when she made the bed. She would help Mom to the armchair while she changed the sheets, tucking in the edges and smoothing out the wrinkles before she put the blanket back on and found a fresh pillowcase from the linen closet. Then she would help Mom back into bed, walk to the windows, and say, *Let's get some light in here*, her voice always gentle, always pleasant, as though dying was the most natural thing in the world, which, I suppose, it is.

Mom would smile faintly as the nurse opened the curtains and the morning's first sunlight streamed in across the newly made bed, across Mom's pale hands, and across the ridges of her face, so that her eyes, (the bulging one and the normal one) gleamed so brightly for just a moment that, if you weren't careful, you might forget she was going to die. You might forget that this sudden shine, which was really a simple reflection, was not actually coming from inside her. You could almost forget, if you ignored the pill bottles, the dirty sheets in the hamper, and the yellow smell that issued from her parted lips, that soon she was going to turn her face away from us and leave this earth forever.

Bertha is white and veiny and covered in a viscous glaze.

"Shake her and see what happens," says The Monk, still smiling from his bed.

I shake the bottle. The embryo dances. The little legs wave. Both blind heads bob up and down in the tide, nodding acquiescence, their eyes milky blue and bulging behind membranous lids.

I wonder what my mother would be like in a jar of formaldehyde. I imagine her hunched form inside the bottle, her head and hands white and bobbing with the tide. The embryo looks strangely peaceful. Can you say that something is dead if it has never been born? Can you say it's gone if it never came into being in the first place? I study the tiny body and I am suddenly overwhelmed by the tragedy of the little thing.

"So?" says The Monk after a while. "What do you think?"

"I think it's cool," I say.

"Not *cool*," says The Monk, obviously disappointed by my choice of adjectives. "Not *cool*, dude. Cool is like a vintage cereal box or something. This cow is frigging *beautiful*. She's so completely and totally *bizarre* that she's transcended reality and she's become *breathtaking*. I mean *look* at her. She has *eyelashes*, for crying out loud. She has a *tail*."

"Actually," I say, turning the jar so I can get a better look, "I think she has *two* tails."

"Um *no*," says The Monk, rising from the bed to show me. "Not *two* tails. That other thing is an umbilical cord. Look closer. It's coming out of the belly, not the butt."

"Oh," I say, squinting. "Right."

"You think I don't know my own *cow*?"

"I didn't say that."

"Good," he mutters. "Because it sounded like you were saying I don't know my own *cow*. Which is *ridiculous*, dude. Because I look at this thing *a lot*. I mean I *study* her. She's one of my prized possessions. And I think after all this *time*, I would *know* the difference between a *tail* and an *umbilical* cord. *Okay?* I'm not an *idiot,* dude."

As he talks, The Monk comes closer and closer until his face is all up in my face and I have to give him a little push to maintain my body-space comfort zone.

"Jesus," I say. "I never said you were an idiot. Calm down."

He snatches the bottle from my hands, kisses it, breathes on it, polishes it on his sleeve, and places it on top of his bookshelf in between a jackalope and a framed photograph. In the photograph, The Monk is standing with Fish in front of an orange-and-white VW Microbus. He has his arm around her waist. Her head is buried in his T-shirt, and her pink hair cascades over half her face, just her nose and chin peeking out. She is wearing cutoff jeans and a tank top. One of The Monk's hands is touching her bare arm. Part of me wants to get a closer look at the photograph to see if I can figure out if The Monk and Fish look like they are in love, but another part of me doesn't want to know, so instead, I pretend to notice the jackalope and I say, "Oh *man*, I *love* that jackalope," which is a sentence I never expected to say in my lifetime.

"You like it?" asks The Monk. "Really?"

"I *love* it," I tell him. "It's so twisted. It's so awesomely, freakishly twisted."

I pick up the jackalope as though it were alive, this taxidermied rabbit corpse with fused reindeer antlers sticking out of its skull and I get all over-the-top weird, and pretend that it is sucking the blood out of my neck like a vampire. I make it snuffle and grumble and moan because it loves my pulsing, cancerous blood. Then I waggle it toward The Monk and make it burp.

"You *do* get it," says The Monk, relieved. He comes closer and punches me in the arm. "You *do* get why this stuff is so awesome. Don't you?"

"Oh," I say. "Totally. It's like mind-blowingly weird."

"*Yes*," says The Monk emphatically. "Yes. Mind-blowing. Thank you."

"And the cow. I mean, those tiny eyelashes. They're beautiful. And those hooves. I'll never forget those hooves."

"You better not," says The Monk. "Bertha doesn't like it when you forget her hooves. So listen. You got the eyeballs with you?"

"Yeah," I say, patting the front pocket of my backpack.

"Well, what are we waiting for? Bring it on, dude."

I take out my sketchbook and open it to the page with the eyeballs.

"Yes," says The Monk. *"Yes.* There they are. God. That's *gorgeous.* I can't believe you drew something so perfect."

"Believe it," I say.

"Are you going to let me procure it from you?"

"You really want to buy it?"

"I'll give you ten bucks."

"You want to give me ten bucks for something I sketched in two minutes?"

"Yes," says The Monk.

"That's crazy," I tell him. "I'll just give it to you." I tear the page out of my sketchbook and hand it over.

"No," says The Monk, pushing it away. "I have ethics. I can't let you do that. I have to give you something for them. Something valuable. Look around. You want a magazine? A little toy?"

I glance around his side of the room. It's filled with weird stuff. The bottle of cow. The jackalope. A row of fuzzy little windup chicks. A stack of freaky-looking children's books with questionable titles: *Dick and Jane and Vampires. Fluffy Pussy and Friends. The Uncle Wiggily Book.* And then, finally, that picture of him and Fish, her hair, even from here, a small pink beacon of light, gleaming in the distance.

"No man," I say. All at once I am remembering the sound

of Fish's laughter. I turn my face away. "It's a nice offer but you don't have anything I want. Listen. Think of it as a gift. For helping me out yesterday when I was being a moron."

I hand him the sketch.

He leans it against the photograph so that it covers the picture of him and Fish.

"I'll think of something," says The Monk. "One of these days I'll pay you back."

BILDUNGSROMAN AND OTHER FOUR-SYLLABLE WORDS

DR. CAGE IS ONE OF THE FEW TEACHERS AT BALDWIN who doesn't even pretend to like kids. Maybe that's why he never introduced himself as my faculty advisor after class on Monday like Lydie said he would. He didn't want me to get the wrong idea. Other teachers want their students to worship them. They quote the classics. They make easy reference to operas and political speeches. They know the derivations of words. They know which kings ruled in which century, and if it ever becomes necessary to quote Voltaire, their French accents are impeccable. They do not, however, know how to turn themselves off. Even Dr. Austerlitz, with his spit-shined shoes and his bow tie, is like a puppet dancing on a string. Hello, silly puppet. I will make you dance. Doop de doo.

Dr. Cage is different. He has gray hair and a beard. He smells like stale shirts. He wears sandals with wool socks, and faded jeans. He glowers at the class from beneath bushy eyebrows as he sits at a desk overflowing with papers and folders in the corner of the classroom.

Kids take their seats in the circle of desks. The Monk's roommate, Thomas A. Trowbridge the Fourth, sits across from me. His hair is combed and his pants are pressed. He looks at his watch. The late bell rings. Fish bursts into the room, a flurry of papers, pink hair tousled and uncombed. She flops, out of breath, into the desk next to mine, and tries to get herself organized, stacking notebooks, squaring the edges of things so the sides are symmetrical, putting loose papers into folders. But clearly the universe is against her today. A wrinkled Latin quiz falls on the floor. Then a math paper. Then her sketchbook, and her pencil box, and when she leans over and tries to pick up her mess, the entire stack of notebooks topples and her stuff goes everywhere, which is when Fish lets loose a stream of invectives, the magnitude of which I have never heard coming out of a human being. I leap from my seat and help her gather up her stuff. Pencil case, Latin quiz. Her sketchbook has fallen open revealing a drawing of a face. In colored pencil. Pink hair. But something's wrong. The eyes and the mouth are sewn shut with black thread. It is the face of a corpse.

I close the sketchbook and hand it back to her gingerly.

107

Our eyes lock. Something silent passes between us.

Then Cage pushes himself up from behind his desk and picks up a stack of papers covered in red ink. It must be an assignment from last week. When he walks by me and Fish, he knocks each of us on the top of our head with his fist, and then continues slowly around the circle until he comes to the ripped armchair that he calls his throne. He sits down, puts the papers in his lap, and reminds us that the assignment was to write about a childhood memory. He asks for volunteers.

Some of the kids take their assignments from him and read them out loud.

The class gives compliments.

Cage gives criticism.

When it's Fish's turn to read, she takes a deep breath and sits on the edge of her seat. She also takes a breath at the end of each sentence. She is lovely when she breathes. I wonder if The Monk has ever noticed this. If they're only friends, maybe he hasn't. If they're more than friends, if they're in love, I bet he has noticed how her T-shirt rises and falls when she breathes, or how she bends her head so her neck shows and her pink hair cascades over one of her eyes. Why is she drawing herself with her mouth and eyes sewn shut? What has she seen that she doesn't want to see? What is it she's afraid to say? Her voice trembles when she reads, but somehow even the trembling is beautiful.

*You hear them screaming at each other. They used
to close the door, to shield you from it, but these days
they don't even try. The arguments are too loud to be
kept inside small spaces. They seep like ink through
the cracks in the floor. And so you listen. You hear
them curse each other. And you hold yourself. Which
is why you are not surprised when, later, you find
his bags packed by the door. His two shabby
suitcases, leather, faded and frayed, filled with his
clothes. He lifts you up and holds you. You are still
small enough for him to do that. He swings you
around and calls you his little mongoose, and he
kisses your nose. But you are old enough to know
that goodbye means something different this time.
This time goodbye is forever.*

There are sounds of appreciation from around the circle.

"I liked the line about the ink."

"I liked the image of the suitcases."

"I liked the line about the mongoose."

Cage is disgusted. "Anyone have any criticism, or are we
simply going to appreciate each other today?"

No one says anything.

"Ah. So it will be another class of vapid affirmations.
Well, I have some criticism. Are you ready?" Cage leans
back in his chair and looks at Fish, who nods and grits her

teeth. "Get rid of the second person," he says. "It was a tremendous mistake. It makes me want to puke. And it gives new meaning to the word *sophomoric*."

"Sophomoric?" says Fish, crestfallen.

"Yes," says Cage. "It means you think you are being wise, but really you are being foolish. Get rid of the second person. *You do this and you do that*. It's distracting. Also it makes the reader feel as though the author is hitting them on the head. Read it out loud again. In first person this time."

"But I like it in second person," mutters Fish darkly. "It makes you feel like you're experiencing it in the moment."

Our classmates agree. They make supportive sounds in her direction.

"No," says Cage. "You're wrong. It's pretentious. And it gets extremely annoying after the first few sentences. The piece would be better if we could hear the narrator telling her own story. Read it again in first person. You'll hear what I mean. Oh please. Stop pouting at me like that. It's not becoming. Come on. Let's go."

Fish takes a deep breath and reads it again.

I hear them screaming at each other. They used to close the door, to shield me from it, but these days they don't even try. The arguments are too loud to be kept inside small spaces. They seep like ink through

the cracks in the floor. And so I listen. I hear them
curse each other. And I hold myself. Which is why
I am not surprised when, later, I find his bags packed
by the door. His two shabby suitcases, leather, faded
and frayed, filled with his clothes. He lifts me up
and holds me. I am still small enough for him to do
that. He swings me around and calls me his little
mongoose, and he kisses my nose. But I am old
enough to know that goodbye means something
different this time. This time goodbye is forever.

Everyone is impressed.

"Are you with me?" says Cage.

"Okay," says Fish, resigned. "I guess I see what you mean."

But her face is red and her eyes are filled with tears.

I wonder if The Monk has ever kissed those eyes.

"Simple language," says Cage. "Simple choices. Unpretentious. No one likes pretentious writing. Just tell it like it is." He makes his way around the circle, handing papers back to the rest of the students. "I want you to do this assignment over again for Friday with that advice in mind. First person. Present tense. Find the immediacy. And for God's sake, stop trying to be clever. It never works. You saw evidence today when our sophomoric friend read her terrible draft to us. Pretension always fails. See you tomorrow."

Class is over.

People start gathering their books.

Fish runs from the room.

I want to run after her. I want to tell her I thought her story was beautiful both ways. I want to ask her what happened afterward. And most of all, I want to find out if this story has anything to do with the scar on her wrist, but she is already gone, and I can't think of what words I would use if I caught up with her. In the photograph, The Monk had his arm around her. His fingers were touching her bare arm. My hands are clenched into fists.

I put my head on my desk and keep my head down until everyone has left.

Cage paces around, fixing chairs, picking up pieces of paper.

"So," says Cage, when he gets to my seat. "What's up with you, anyway?"

He smells like coffee.

I don't answer. The desk is cool beneath my forehead.

"Hey. Mopey. I'm talking to you. I'm supposed to be your advisor. This counts as our first meeting, by the way, so give me the decency of responding in some way. Stomp your hoof. Blink your eyes. Anything. What's the deal, Friedman? What's bothering you? Baldwin got you down? It's only been a few days. You already had your fill of all the bullshit?"

I shrug.

"Life can stink sometimes, can't it?" he says.

I shrug again.

"Two equally inarticulate gestures. But I get the message anyway. I'm good at making inferences. Trick of the trade. So I get it. You've lived through hard times. We all have. But listen. I have some advice for you. Stop wallowing in it. Start writing about it. Pain makes good prose, my dreary friend. Trust me. I speak from experience."

I sit up and glare at him.

He glares back at me harder.

I frown at him.

He smiles and then laughs. His teeth are yellow and crooked.

Then, in an unexpected gesture of familiarity, he reaches out and messes up my hair.

"Get out of here," he says. "Go home and write."

ERNIE'S JUNK SHOP

In the winter, when me and Daddy are stir-crazy from stay-ing inside too many days, when the kitchen feels too small, like the walls are holding their breath, Mommy picks up her purse and says, You know what? I think this would be a nice day for a drive. And even though it means we will have to bundle up in hats and scarves and tromp out into the snow, and even though the windows are covered with ice and we have to slap our arms and breathe steam into our hands to keep warm, we know it's a good idea. Once the windows defrost and the heat pumps into the truck, we begin to feel glad Mommy thought of this, even though neither of us tells her so.

Just forty-five minutes from our house is Ernie's Junk Shop, Mommy's favorite place on earth. Past empty cornfields covered in snow, past the boarded-up vegetable and fruit stands, and the cider mill and doughnut place that says Closed for the Season. *Ernie's Junk Shop with three floors of stuff no one wants. The shop stays open all year long, even in winter, and Ernie sits there watching the old television set with his gray face and his space heaters and his pellet stove going full blast. When we come in, the bell above the door tinkles and Ernie raises his heavy head. He never acts like he recognizes us even though one time Daddy talked with Ernie for almost twenty minutes about why antique cameras are better than digital. I was watching the grandfather clock, counting minutes, and after a while I lost track so I squinted my eyes and counted the pieces of dust that floated around the bare lightbulb hanging from the ceiling instead.*

Here is what Mommy says: We can each buy something small if it's not broken and it costs less than ten dollars. Yay, I say. And yay, says Daddy, even though he's a grown man and can spend money whenever he wants. I walk slowly up and down the aisles looking for treasures with my ten-dollar bill in my fist, letting my eyes slide across each piece of junk: orange-haired trolls, vintage lunch boxes, jars full of marbles, eggbeaters, ice cream scoopers, leather gloves, button jars. Daddy spends most of his time looking at the old cameras, opening the backs, squinting at us through the little square windows. I like the buckets of Matchbox cars the best. Not shiny new ones like they have in Sunday-morning TV commercials, but really old ones with paint chipping off and doors that open and close. Who played with this one? That kid is probably someone's father by now.

Daddy and I are looking at the treasures we want, me a bucket of Matchbox cars, and Daddy a tattered old Nikon camera, when Mommy bounds up to us, breathless, holding a blue plate to her chest and smiling like she has just found the gold at the end of a rainbow. This is when I realize she has red in her cheeks again, and her hair is already two or three inches long, and she looks like she is going to live forever.

She holds out the china plate. It has a pattern all along the rim. It's just like the one we had when I was a little girl, she says. I never thought I'd see this pattern again. Look at it. See the bridge? The pagoda? See the tiny blue woman walking with her walking stick? I used to love that little blue woman. When I was a little girl, I used to sit there and talk to her and talk to her. Can you see the woman, Max? See her on the bridge?

Yes, I lie, I see her. Do you like my cars?

That whole bucket? Mommy says. That's a lot of cars, Max. How about you choose three?

I start making myself cry. I am good at this.

Choose three. Or none at all, says Daddy.

His voice can be very final when he wants.

So I stick out my lip and flop on the dusty floor and plunge my hand into the bucket and rummage around until I find three black ones, because black is my favorite. They feel good in my hand and they sound good when they crash into each other. Clunk. The sound of one little metal car hitting another. Clunk. And then they spin away backward.

How much is the plate? asks Daddy.

Twenty, says Mommy. But it's special.

I want these three, I say.

Good choice, says Daddy.

In the end, Daddy doesn't get the camera.

"I haven't seen a plate like this since I was a little girl," Mommy says to Ernie.

"It sure is a beauty," says Ernie.

Except he's not looking at the plate. He's looking at Mommy.

See the little blue woman? she asks him in a voice filled with wonder, pointing at the plate, her eyes wide. Really, really tiny? Crossing the bridge? That's what makes it special. There are lots of Blue Willow china plates, but this is the only pattern I've ever seen with the tiny blue woman. Can you see her? Look close. Can you see her crossing the bridge?

Ernie takes off his glasses and peers at Mommy's plate. Then he puts his glasses back on and peers at her.

Sure, he says. Sure, I can see her. Pretty little thing. He is staring right at Mommy, who stares back at him.

Daddy moves to Mommy's side and puts his arm around her.

Ernie offers to wrap the plate in newspaper, but Mommy says no thank you.

Goodbye, goodbye, see you next time. The little bell above the door tinkles behind us. Maybe there won't be a next time, Daddy mutters, and Mommy throws back her head and laughs, but not too hard, because she doesn't want to drop her plate.

She cradles it against her heart all the way home, past the cider mill and doughnut place, past the boarded-up vegetable and fruit stands and past the cold, empty fields all covered in snow. Mommy and her special Blue Willow plate with the little blue woman on the bridge.

Are you glad we came, Mommy? I ask her. Oh yes, says Mommy. She reaches back for my hand behind the seat. Her hand is warm. We drive in silence, Daddy at the wheel with his arm around her shoulder, windshield wipers pushing back the snow, the Blue Willow plate with the blue woman against Mommy's heart, and me and Mommy holding hands, and holding hands and holding hands, all the way home.

BLUE WILLOW

IT IS THE FIRST NIGHT OF CHANUKAH, BUT INSTEAD OF celebrating, we are sitting at the kitchen table with Chinese takeout from Panda Wok. Mom loved Chanukah more than anything. We never had a lot of extra cash, so sometimes she would give us gifts she found or made. On her last Chanukah, Mom gave me fifteen turkey feathers that she had collected on her morning walks after she had been diagnosed the second time. *Because when I'm gone, I want you to spread your wings.*

Dad sticks his chopsticks into the lo mein and eats straight out of the take-out container. He slurps a few wayward noodles into his mouth.

"You can't just ignore it," says Grandma, frowning at Dad from across the table.

"Yes I can," he says.

I take a sparerib and gnaw on it.

"If I made latkes, would you eat them?" she asks.

"I might eat them," says Dad. "But I don't want to light candles this year. It just feels wrong."

"Anna loved Chanukah," says Grandma. "She was always my little candle monkey."

Dad and I exchange glances.

When I was little, Mom used to say *I* was her candle monkey. Something she passed down to me, I guess. That and a tumor who likes to call me a pussy.

It was always my job to chip the wax off the menorah with a toothpick and then choose what color candles for each night. Sometimes, when I said the blessing, Mom's eyes filled with tears of joy, which, in case you were wondering, have an entirely different chemical makeup than tears of sorrow.

"Have some Chinese food, Jean," says Dad. "It's good."

Grandma scowls at the paper containers filled with fried rice and lo mein. "I used to make latkes for Anna. I think I still remember the recipe. Potatoes. Onions. Matzo meal. Salt. Oil. Eggs. You got eggs?"

"Actually," says Dad, "I think we're out of eggs."

"How can we be out of eggs?" says Grandma.

"I don't know," says Dad. "We just are."

"Do you have a grater?"

120

"A what?"

"A grater. To grate the onion and the potatoes."

"Oh," says Dad. "That thing. Well, we probably do. But we haven't used it since Anna was well enough to cook." He shuffles into the pantry, rummages around, and then comes back out and plunks the grater on the table in front of Grandma. "There you go, madam. One grater."

"Thanks," says Grandma, "but the grater's no good if you don't have the rest of the stuff. Can you go to the store tomorrow?"

"Sure," says Dad. "If you want me to."

"I do," says Grandma.

"Well, then I will," says Dad.

"Good," says Grandma.

Everything around the table feels prickly and dismal all of a sudden.

Dad continues eating his Chinese food.

Grandma continues staring down at her empty plate.

I pull another sparerib out of the container and take a bite.

There's a knock on the front door. Then a quick pattering of smaller knocks.

"I'll get it," I say, grateful for the chance to leave the table.

I walk through the front hallway to the door.

A gust of winter.

A stomping of boots.

It's Lydie and Luna and Soleil.

Luna is carrying a menorah in one hand and candles in another. Soleil is carrying a wooden dreidel by its stem. And Lydie is carrying a plate of potato latkes.

"Happy Chanukah!" sings Luna.

Soleil smashes the dreidel into my palm, stem first. Then she licks my hand.

I wipe my hand on Soleil's dress.

"Hello!" Lydie calls into the kitchen. "We brought you some latkes!"

Dad hurries into the front hallway.

"Oh my goodness. This is so nice."

They hug.

Then Dad hugs the twins. He picks them up and twirls them.

"I hope it's okay we didn't call. We were very bummed out celebrating at home and we were thinking it would be nicer celebrating with you."

"Thank you so much," says Dad. "Max, would you take their coats?"

"Okay," I say.

They pile coats on me. They take off their boots and go into the kitchen where I hear Dad say, "Jean, this is our friend Lydie Grossman. The one I told you about who helped us get a spot for Max at Baldwin. And these pretty girls here are Luna and Soleil."

"Twins!" says Grandma.

Soleil meows and pretends to be cleaning her paws.

"Twins on Chanukah are good luck," says Luna.

"Good luck?" says Grandma, smiling. "I could use some good luck."

I come back into the kitchen.

"We won't stay long," Lydie is saying. "We just wanted to light candles and give you some latkes and spin the dreidel and then we'll be on our way."

"Joe doesn't want to light candles this year," Grandma says. "My Anna's favorite holiday is Chanukah."

"It was," says Dad. "She loved it."

"So did my husband, David," says Lydie.

Everyone is somber for a moment. Then Grandma says, "What are we waiting for? Let's have Chanukah." She starts to remove the Chinese food and plates from the table.

"Let's have Chanukah!" agrees Luna. Luna picks a pink candle from the box, and Soleil picks a yellow one. Then Soleil places them in the menorah with absolute care, as though this were the most important thing in the whole wide world.

I feel a pang of jealousy. I'm supposed to be the candle monkey.

Lydie takes two bags of chocolate gelt out of a big cloth shoulder bag and sets them on the table along with two little glass jars. She stands in front of the menorah and lights the match herself, setting Luna's pink *shamash* aglow before shaking out the match. Then she uses the pink candle to light Soleil's yellow one. She sings the prayer. Her voice spreads into the room like golden wings unfurling.

Baruch atah, Adonai
Eloheinu, Melech haolam,
Asher kid'shanu b'mitzvotav
V'tztivanu l'hadlik ner
Shel Chanukah. Amein.

Suddenly, I feel so thankful that it hurts.

Dad is looking away so no one except me sees him wiping his eyes with the back of his sleeve. Mom couldn't carry a tune. When she sang the Chanukah blessing, or "Happy Birthday," or "The Star-Spangled Banner," or anything really, we used to laugh like crazy because she had no shame. She would just shout it out like she was some kind of drunken opera singer. She could be like that. And the awesome thing was, she knew her singing was horrible. But she didn't care because singing made her happy.

My head hurts.

"Latke time!" shouts Luna.

Soleil jumps up and down and claps her hands and spins in crazy circles.

Grandma smiles. "Okay!" she says.

Lydie takes the tinfoil off the latkes and all at once the room smells glorious and golden.

"Voilà!" she says.

"Oh my!" says Grandma.

Lydie opens up the little glass jars filled with sour cream and applesauce.

Soleil claps her hands and licks her lips.

"Max," says Dad. "Would you get some plates and silverware for us?"

"Okay," I say, even though the tumor behind my eye has started shouting obscenities.

I bring out silverware and six plates and set them around the table.

I give myself Mom's Blue Willow plate. I follow the pattern with my eyes.

Lydie serves us latkes. We spoon sour cream and applesauce onto our plates.

Everyone eats. There's laughter and talking and people reaching over people to take more food. I use my spoon to spread sour cream across the landscape, the little mountain path that the tiny woman walks each day, her back curved from the exhaustion of trudging uphill for so long. I spread sour cream on the little bridge and on the jutting mountains and on the head of the bird flying over the mountain looking down. The woman is singing while she walks.

"So Max," says Lydie, noticing my silence. "Let's have an update. How are you liking Baldwin so far?"

"Pretty good, I guess."

She wants to have a conversation with me, but it's hard to have a conversation while I am trying to hear the woman singing. She is out of tune, but she doesn't care. Her voice is the tiny buzz of a mosquito. The bird flying overhead is laughing, and his laughter makes me furious. Stop laughing at her. She can't help it.

"Have you had an advisory meeting with Dr. Cage yet?" asks Lydie.

I look at her, but I don't answer.

"Answer her, Max," says Dad.

"We talked a little after class yesterday. He told me to stop moping. I guess that was our first meeting."

The tiny woman stops on the path and looks straight at me.

She's trying to tell me something. She cups her hands around her mouth and shouts, but all I hear is the tiniest buzz.

"Dr. Cage is Max's faculty advisor," Lydie tells Dad and Grandma. "He's a real legend in our school. He's a published author. A total nonconformist, political activist, ex-hippie."

"Sounds great," says Dad.

At the sound of Dad's voice, the tiny woman begins jumping up and down and waving her arms.

"Max has Creative Writing with Dr. Cage. Don't you, Max?"

I nod without looking up.

"I'm sorry," says Dad. "This holiday is hard for him."

"I know," says Lydie. "It's hard for all of us."

The tiny woman drops to her knees in the snow.

It's such a long walk up the mountain.

If I could, I would put you on my finger and carry you to the top.

Luna and Soleil are finished with their latkes.

"Can we be excused?" asks Luna.

"Yes, you may," says Lydie.

Luna takes a bag of gelt and sits herself down on the floor. She arranges the chocolate coins in rows from biggest to smallest.

Soleil bounds from her seat and begins galloping around the kitchen table. She neighs and tosses her head and stomps her feet.

"That's cute," says Grandma, smiling.

"She does a lot of this," says Lydie. "Everything is about animals right now. Sometimes she gets carried away. Be careful, Soleil!"

On her next pass around the table, Soleil stumbles into Grandma, who catches her and tickles her until she is a giggling mass of craziness. And now Grandma is part of the game and each time Soleil passes by, Grandma tickles her, and Soleil squeals and squirms out of her grip and gallops around the table again.

The tiny woman is pounding on the surface of the plate from the inside. Her whole body heaves with the power of her screaming, her curved back, her knees, her arms all rigid and clenched.

The tiny woman puts her head in her hands.

It's such a long way up the mountain.

All the paths are covered with snow.

I begin removing sour cream with my finger, careful not to crush her. I plow the paths, lifting the plate closer to my face to make sure I see all the places where the trail twists and turns.

My head hurts so badly that my hands start shaking.

Luna arranges her coins into the shape of a heart.

Soleil barrels into Grandma, who catches her again and tickles her until she squeals and wriggles out of her grip. Then she comes crashing into my dad, who tickles her, and then she crashes into me.

I drop the plate.

It shatters all over the floor. There are shards everywhere.

I fall to my knees, screaming.

"That was Anna's favorite plate," says Dad.

"Oh my goodness!" says Lydie. "Oh my goodness, I am so sorry. I am so, so sorry. Soleil! Stop it! Stop it!"

"Stop it, Soleil!" says Luna.

Lydie grabs Soleil's hand and pulls her close. Soleil puts her thumb in her mouth and starts to whimper.

I search desperately, sweeping my hands across the floor. I can't find the shard with the screaming woman. It has to be here. It has to be here. Somewhere. Oh my God. Oh my God, what am I going to do without her?

"Max," says Dad.

He is on the floor with me. Trying to calm me down.

The tiny woman is screaming but I can't find her anywhere.

She screeches my name, her voice frantic and broken. Finally I spot her under the kitchen table, trapped on a tiny triangular shard. I reach for her and fold her into my palm. I put the shard in my mouth and run my tongue over the smooth glaze. I drop my head into my hands and squeeze my eyes shut and I rock and rock until Lydie and the twins are gone, Grandma has gone up to bed, and only Dad is left, kneeling next to me on the kitchen floor, broken pieces of plate scattered all around us, the shard under my tongue like a bitter pill, the snow falling softly outside the window like ashes.

AFTER

THE NEXT MORNING, I PUT THE SHARD IN MY BACK pocket. My brain hurts and everything feels surreal, the way the world always seems different after a storm. Grandma is waiting for me at the kitchen table as always. There is no trace of the broken plate. After I eat breakfast, she says, "Sweetheart, come over here." I go stand next to her and she reaches out to hold my hands.

"I love you," she says.

"I love you too," I tell her.

"We'd better go," says Dad.

Grandma nods. She's not smiling.

I swing my backpack onto my shoulder and follow Dad out the door and into the cold morning. We both climb into the truck, he puts his key in the ignition, and we head down the road. Dad doesn't know what to say. Every once in a while he looks over to make sure I'm okay. He puts his arm around my shoulder, but I'm rigid so he doesn't keep it there for long.

I can feel the corner of the shard poking into me. I shift in my seat just a little so the sharp end presses harder. There's something about that discomfort, that tiny spot where the edge pushes into me, that feels right somehow.

We drive through town and make the slow turn up the snowy hill toward Baldwin campus. Dad pulls into the parking lot and stops the truck. We sit for a while looking out at the icy world, the frosted paths, the buildings hooded in snow, the beautiful students with their hands plunged deep into their winter jackets on their way to Trowbridge Hall.

Fish's mom pulls into the parking lot in their battered old car. Fish slams the door, screams in pink fury, and runs to catch up with The Monk, who's walking with his buddies. She bounds up to him and he twirls her ceremoniously. They continue up the path together, talking to each other with dramatic and animated gestures, Fish still skipping because that's the way she is. We watch them as they talk and laugh and climb the stairs of Trowbridge Hall and then disappear through the huge double doors.

"I should go," I say finally.

"Try to have a good day," says Dad.

"You too," I say.

But I know neither one of us is going to have a good day today, because my screaming from last night is still echoing in our ears and Mom's plate is broken and everything feels raw. I head up the path. Fish and The Monk are nowhere to be seen. When I walk past the front office, Lydie comes out to meet me. She has dark circles under her eyes and she looks like maybe she didn't get any sleep last night either.

"You okay?" she asks quietly.

"I don't know," I say.

"I'm really sorry about what happened, Max."

"You don't have to be sorry," I say. "You didn't do anything wrong."

"I should have seen things escalating," says Lydie. "Soleil was having such a good time with your grandma. She just kinda went nuts with all that running around. I should have been more careful watching her."

"Don't worry about it," I say.

But I can see she's going to worry because my reaction to the broken plate was so huge and so overwhelming that it beat everybody up and now we all are bruised.

"Just let me know if there's anything I can do," says Lydie.

"Okay," I tell her. "I will." And I turn around and start to head off to class.

"Hey Max," Lydie calls.

I turn back around. "Yeah?" I say.

"I hope you don't mind, but I sent an e-mail to Dr. Cage last night. I wanted him to know what's been happening with you. He's supposed to schedule regular meetings with you, not just a few words after class. Do you mind?"

"I don't mind," I say.

"I don't know where that guy gets off making up his own rules. He knows what an advisor is supposed to do. He has the handbook." Then she composes herself. "Anyway," she says, "don't be surprised if he makes some kind of contact with you today."

"Okay," I say. "Thanks."

She reaches out and gives me a hug.

Her hair smells like peppermint. At first I am rigid and then, despite myself, I relax into the hug. I close my eyes and breathe.

When I get to Creative Writing class, it's hard to believe that Cage could ever do anything that would make me feel better. He is in rare form today. He hates everything that anyone has written. He sits in his throne with his arms crossed over his belly and looks disgusted, rolling his eyes at every cliché. He shakes his head at every run-on sentence and moans whenever a metaphor falls flat. By the time half an hour has gone by, he has completely trashed two different papers and both writers are on the verge of tears. Thomas A. Trowbridge the Fourth excuses himself and stalks off to the bathroom to cry in private. Forty minutes into class, kids are so intimidated and demoralized that no one wants to read or give feedback. We all just look around at one another, check our watches, and try very hard to disappear.

"Really," says Cage. "I don't know how many times I need to tell you people the same thing. It's December, for crying out loud. You've gotten it into your heads that to be good, you have to twist your sentences into pretentious pretzels. Your grammar is bizarre. Can't you hear that? Haven't you ever heard of subjects and verbs? English is your first language, people. There's no excuse for this kind of garbage. Just say what you want to say and be done with it. If the guy is walking across the street, say *He walks across the street*. Period. End of sentence. You think your reader wants to sit there listening to you ramble on and on? Jesus Christ, I want to shoot myself sometimes." Then he checks his watch. "Who wants to be next?"

No one volunteers.

Cue crickets.

"Mr. Friedman," says Cage, "what about you?"

I look down at my desk.

More crickets.

134

Cage comes to my desk and puts his face up close. "Hello!" he says. "Hello, anyone in there? What, you think you're auditing this class or something? You just here for the cruise? The free food? The shampoo samples, what?"

I smile, but I still don't say anything.

"Blink once for yes and twice for no."

I close my eyes and keep them closed.

"Ah," says Cage. "Rebellion."

"Cage?" says Fish in a quiet voice. "I'll read."

"And then, just like that, the mopey boy is saved by the masochistic girl with pink hair who's willing to risk her soul despite the fact that I lambasted her on Wednesday. Who says reverse chivalry is dead? The end. Four stars. Rave reviews. Pulitzer. Go ahead, Miss Santacroce. Read. We'll listen."

"Okay," says Fish. "Here goes nothing."

I keep my eyes closed while she reads.

Her voice is so lovely, listening to her is like being coated with honey.

If I had known what she would become when he left
us, I swear I would have gone with him. I would
have packed myself into his suitcase or traveled in
his back pocket along with his cell phone and his
cigarettes. But how could someone as young as I was
ever guess that the woman who called herself Mother,

135

*who gave birth to me and braided my hair, would
crash and burn the way she did. Hot mess. Broken
woman. Dirty dishes in the sink. Dirty clothes on the
floor. A half-empty bottle on the counter. Her words
slurred at night when she should have been singing
me lullabies.*

I open my eyes.

Fish is staring down at her story, smiling faintly.

I open my mouth. I am about to tell her how amazing
she is. But suddenly Cage is giving her a standing ovation.
Fish is so shocked and relieved that she stands up, bows,
twirls, and then falls into her chair, exhausted.

"There it is, folks," says Cage, grinning at us with his
crooked yellow teeth. "There. It. Is. The first real writing
of the year. Hallelujah. Better late than never. Thought it
wasn't gonna happen. But it did. Yesss." He walks over to
Fish and knocks on her head with a soft fist. "Someone is
home," he says. "Thank the lord."

The bell rings.

Cage tells us to leave our papers on his desk and get the
hell out of his room.

Kids start filing out.

Fish is surrounded by kids who want to congratulate
her, high-five her, pat her on the back. She looks at me.

I swing my backpack onto my shoulder, put my paper on his desk, and start to go over to her, but Cage's hand comes down on my shoulder like a bear's claw.

"Hey, Mopey," he says.

Before I can call out for Fish to wait up, she's out the door, still surrounded.

"You really aren't much of a talker, are you?" says Cage.

I shrug.

"Are you like this with everyone or just with me?"

"Most people," I say.

"Oh!" says Cage. "He speaks! I was beginning to wonder if you had problems with your vocal cords. I've started referring to you in my notes as Mr. Muteness."

"My vocal cords are fine," I say.

"But other parts of you not so much?"

I shrug.

"Again with the inarticulate gestures. I thought we had made a breakthrough, you and I. Ah well. Two steps forward, one step back. Life is a cha-cha. What can you do. So listen, Mr. Muteness, remember when I told you that I'm supposed to be your *advisor*?"

He says the word *advisor* with a Kermit the Frog accent.

"Yeah," I say. "I remember."

"Good," says Cage to an invisible audience. "He's speaking again. That makes things easier." Then back to me. "Well, did you know that you and I are, apparently, supposed to meet a whole bunch of times this year so that I can, as they say, *advise* you?"

"Yeah," I say. "I knew that."

"Good," says Cage. "We're two for two. So what are you doing for lunch Monday?"

"Nothing," I say.

"Fabulous. I'm taking you out for Chinese food. As your advisor. Because you obviously need advice. Also egg rolls. Ever hear of Panda Wok?"

"Yeah," I say. "We get takeout from there all the time."

"You like it?"

"Sure," I say. "They have good lo mein."

"That they do," says Cage. Then he leans down and whispers in my ear. "And their piña coladas ain't so bad either. If you're a good boy, I'll let you have a sip."

BEEF LO MEIN

PANDA WOK IS ONE OF THOSE ICONIC CHINESE restaurants that were once popular in the seventies and eighties but have mostly become hangouts for lonely old men who like to sit at the bar, order neon-colored drinks and watch ESPN, passing gas from time to time, far away from their wives. Don't get me wrong, normal people still go there to eat every once in a while, families who are drawn to the enormous combination plates (number 6 comes with pork fried rice *and* an egg roll), but it's obvious that Panda Wok is in decline because there are two empty rooms, an empty function hall upstairs, and a huge, mostly untouched lunch buffet filled with stale scallion pancakes and vats of congealed moo goo gai pan.

There are three times as many waiters as the place

really needs to service the handful of customers who come out for lunch to feel ethnic, eat with chopsticks, and add *in bed* to their fortune cookies, so that *You will be respected and admired*, becomes *You will be respected and admired in bed*. This makes the cholesterol and triglycerides entirely worth it, in my opinion.

A waitress in a Santa hat comes to our table. She smiles at Cage like she knows him.

"Hey," she says. "Long time no see."

"I know it," says Cage. "My doctor says I need to lay off fried foods. Do you believe it? What a killjoy."

"He's right," says the waitress. "Fried foods are bad for your heart. So what will it be? Lunch buffet as usual?"

"But of course," says Cage, in a very bad French accent. "And a piña colada?"

"Yes. Thank you kindly. And a Coke for the kid."

"Coming right up," says the waitress.

Cage watches her go.

We proceed to the buffet, where we pile appetizers onto our plates. Egg rolls, spring rolls, dumplings, pork strips, chicken wings. Scallion pancakes, crab Rangoons. When we run out of room on our plates, we head back to our table for two by the window. Cage pulls out my chair and then seats himself. He struggles out of his too-small cable-knit sweater. He is wearing a faded undershirt and suspenders. He pats his belly. The waitress returns with our drinks.

Cage mutters something appreciative and then dives into his heaping mound of fried food.

"Do you keep kosher?" asks Cage, grabbing a sparerib in one hand and a crab Rangoon in the other and dipping them both into sweet-and-sour sauce.

"Nah," I say. "My grandma used to. But not anymore."

"Good," says Cage. "Because this stuff breaks those laws in like a hundred different ways. Cloven hooves and bottom-feeders galore. You gotta love it. You know what? I don't care what my doctors tell me. I just want to smear it on my face. I want to swim in it."

He does, in fact, have small pieces of food in his beard and his eyebrows. It looks like he has recently gone for a swim in a vat of Chinese food.

I take a bite of a chicken wing. It's greasy, but it's good.

"So," says Cage, "Ms. Grossman tells me you've been through some hard times lately."

"Yeah," I say.

"Your mom died over the summer. Cancer, right?"

"Yeah."

"How you holding up?"

"I don't know," I say. "I'm kind of a mess, I guess."

"You know what might help?" says Cage.

"What?"

"Egg rolls."

"Egg rolls?"

"Yup. Egg rolls make everything better. Also spareribs."

"Thanks for the advice," I say.

"No problem. Believe me, there's a lot more where that came from. I'm a veritable storehouse of good advice. That's why they pay me the big bucks for being your advisor."

"They pay you to do this?"

Cage takes an enormous sip from his piña colada. "Are you kidding?" he says. "You think I would hang out with someone like you for free? You must think I actually like you or something." He winks and grins at me with his yellow teeth.

I bite into a steamed dumpling and the juice squirts onto his undershirt.

"Thar she blows!" cries Cage, throwing up his hands.

I laugh.

He dips a cloth napkin into his ice water and starts dabbing at the stain, which strikes me as odd because he has all kinds of other stains on his undershirt and dirt under his nails and his crazy gray hair is long and unbrushed. I watch Cage scrub at his undershirt and wonder if he ever catches flak from other teachers for being so rough around the edges. I can imagine Dr. Austerlitz raising his eyebrows, straightening his bow tie, and shining his shoes in response.

"So," says Cage. "How come you don't talk in class?"

"I guess I'm just not much of a talker," I say.

"You've always been like this?"

"I don't know," I say.

"You don't know? Okay, new rule. From this moment on, you are no longer allowed to answer questions with *I guess*, *yeah*, *yup*, or *I don't know*. You owe me a dollar any time I catch you using any of them. You up for that?"

"Okay," I say.

"No *okay* either. *Okay* is just as bad as *I guess*. So tell me. In a full sentence, please. How long have you been like this?"

"I guess it's been worse since my mom died," I say. "I just never know what I'm supposed to say to people anymore."

"You could start with what's been on your mind."

It turns out the tumor is an even worse tenant than I thought he would be. He throws these crazy keg parties every night. He ruins stuff. Pees in corners. Scratches off the wallpaper.

"Go ahead, Friedman. Tell me what you're thinking about."

"No thank you," I say. "I don't think that would be such a good idea."

"And why would it not be such a good idea?"

"If I tell you what's on my mind, you're gonna think I'm completely crazy and then you're going to tell me I need to see a shrink."

"First of all," says Cage, "there is nothing wrong with needing to see a shrink. I happen to see a shrink. Second of all, I *like* crazy." He leans forward and wiggles his shaggy eyebrows.

"You sure?"

"Are you kidding? Look at me," says Cage. "I'm a weird-looking dude. I'm a writer. I teach teenagers I don't even like. Nothing you could say would surprise me. Here. Let me guess. You hear voices? You believe in unicorns? You see things that aren't there?"

"Kind of," I say.

Cage pounds the table with the meaty palm of his hand.

"No *kind of* either. *Kind of* is just as bad as *I guess*. I'm putting *kind of* on the verboten list. *Kind of* is dead. Good-bye, *kind of*."

"You're not leaving me much to say."

"Au contraire," says Cage. "I'm leaving you the entire world. Everything except the repertoire of uncommunicative monosyllabic caveman grunts you've been using. Listen, Friedman." He leans forward and speaks into my ear very softly as though he were sharing a secret. "Some kids don't have much upstairs. They're dull. I know. I know. It's Baldwin. Everyone is supposed to be brilliant. But I'll tell you a secret. Even brilliant people can bore you to tears after a while. The thing is, Friedman, I've been watching you. Yes. I read your short story. And I happen to believe there is some good stuff going on in that funky little noggin of yours. I like your brain. It is a good one. I wish you would share it more often. Why not start now?"

I take a deep breath.

"You can tell me," says Cage. "Why don't you give me a chance?"

It started out as a way to keep part of her close to me. It was imaginary. But it changed fast. I know it's crazy to believe what I believe, but somehow it became real. And now I'm pretty sure I'm dying of my mother's brain tumor. You, my good man, are looking at a kid who is about to kick the proverbial bucket.

Cage leans forward and looks into my eyes. "You gonna tell me or not?" he asks.

"I don't think so," I say.

"You sure?"

"I'm sure," I say.

"Suit yourself," says Cage. "But if you change your mind, or if you want more egg rolls and bad advice from a hairy, fat mammal, come find me in my office. Or if it's after hours, call me. Here's my number." He hands me his business card.

I put it in my back pocket next to the shard.

"Mission accomplished," says Cage.

He sighs and polishes off the appetizers on his plate.

I watch him.

145

After a while, he signals the waitress, who comes over with the check.

"How are those arteries?" she asks.

"Let me put it this way," says Cage. "If I die tonight, I'm going to die happy. Thanks to Panda Wok."

"Don't go into advertising," she says.

"You don't think my statement would win you customers?"

"*Come to Panda Wok. Have a coronary*? I don't think so."

Cage pokes me. "This is what you want one day," he says. "A girl who is beautiful and brilliant. These are the benefits of being as articulate and witty as yours truly. Girls are always nice to men who like to talk."

"So where's *your* girl been?" asks the waitress. "You always leave her at home?"

"And observant too," says Cage. He winks at the waitress and puts two twenties on the table. "Keep the change."

"Don't be a stranger," says the waitress.

Cage pats his belly and puts his sweater back on. "Couldn't even if I tried," he says.

The waitress picks up the check and walks away.

We put our jackets on in silence. Cage opens the door for me. It's snowing and cold outside. We walk back to campus in silence, our hoods and collars flipped up to protect us from the wind. Every once in a while, Cage tries to say something funny, and I know I should respond, because

146

that's what people do, but the tumor is shouting at me and I'm tired from almost but not quite telling my secret.

We climb the steps to Trowbridge Hall, which, as always, is filled with the confident voices of people who love the sound of their own words that buzz into the air like insects, filling the space with a deafening cacophony that mocks me as I walk through the halls with my fingers curled around the shard in my pocket, and my lips clamped shut.

THOMAS A. TROWBRIDGE
THE FOURTH

IN THE LATE AFTERNOON, THE SUN SLANTS THROUGH
the frosted windows of The Monk's dorm room casting a triangle of light across the floor. Now that I've been at Baldwin
almost two weeks, and there haven't been any visible catas-
trophes, Dad's decided I can take the bus home any time I
want to stay late, so I'm hanging out, reading *The Metamorphosis* on The Monk's rumpled bed amid a swirl of blankets
and notebooks. We are guzzling energy drinks, eating corn
chips, and listening to Led Zeppelin on his vintage record
player. Thomas A. Trowbridge the Fourth is sitting ramrod
straight at his perfectly organized desk, trying to write.
Led Zeppelin shakes the walls of the room, a wonderful
pounding bouquet of angst.

Thomas puts his hands over his ears and groans.

The Monk turns up the volume. He leaps onto his bed and jams out on air guitar, biting his lower lip, narrowing his eyes, and pretending to slide into the high notes. Then he scissor-kicks from the bed, struts across the floor, and begins leaping around and playing vigorous make-believe chords in Thomas's direction.

"Do you *mind*?" says Thomas.

"Do I mind what?"

"Do you mind stopping, please? I'm trying to *write*."

"Oh. *Dude*. You're trying to *write*. I'm so sorry."

"That's okay, *dude*. Just try not to distract me while I'm working."

The word *dude* sounds bizarre coming from the small, tight lips of Thomas A. Trowbridge the Fourth. It rings unnaturally in the room the way it does when my dad tries to win me over by using teen lingo. No matter what words he uses, in the end he just winds up sounding kind of desperate.

Thomas is too worried about his reputation with adults to ever use slang comfortably, even in his own room. It's the downside of his legacy. He crosses to The Monk's side, and in a fit of pique, yanks the arm of the vintage record player off the record with a hideously loud scratch.

"Hey!" screams The Monk, snatching the scratched record off the turntable. "I can't believe you *did* that, *dude*. This record is part of my *collection*."

"*Everything* is part of your stupid collection," says Thomas, red-faced. "All your precious little oddities. Your weird friends. You're obsessed with everything."

"I'm not obsessed with *you*," says The Monk. He flops next to me, places the record gently on his pillow, and puts his arm around my shoulders. I try to squirm away, but he holds tight. "In fact, I couldn't care less about you anymore. I tried to help you be cool. I staged a whole intervention. I introduced you to my people, took you under my wing. But you're a lost cause, man. I'm into *this* guy now."

"Oh, of course," says Thomas, narrowing his eyes. "I'm too boring for your collection, right? I'm not interesting enough for you?"

"That's right," says The Monk. "I tried my best, but you give me no choice. I'm dropping you, man. I have decided you aren't worth the effort. You are status quo. You are The Man. You are corporate greed, dude. You are the top one percent of the top one percent. You are everything that is wrong with the world."

"That's a little harsh," I tell The Monk.

"Yes," says Thomas. "Thank you."

The Monk tightens his grip on my shoulders.

I continue to squirm.

"See this guy?" The Monk asks, jabbing one finger into my chest. "Now *this* guy is worth collecting. He's a nonconformist. And unlike *you*, he doesn't give a shit about

150

what people think of him. *You*, on the other hand, have *sold out*."

"I haven't sold out," says Thomas. "You keep saying that, and I want you to know it's really starting to get to me."

"I just tell it like I see it," says The Monk. "I gave you a chance. Now I'm done."

He finally lets me go. I move from his bed to his desk.

The Monk picks up his record and wanders to the window to get a better look at the scratch. He rubs at it with his sleeve. "Jesus Christ," he says. "Look at this thing. It's totally ruined."

"I wish you wouldn't swear in front of me," says Thomas.

"Jesus. Fucking. Christ."

Thomas puts his head in his hands.

"Maybe you should give the guy a break," I suggest.

"I can't," says The Monk. "Picking on Thomas is part of my religion."

"You don't know what religion is," says Thomas into his hands.

"Oh, so pious," says The Monk.

Thomas looks up.

"He doesn't let me come out with him and his buddies anymore," Thomas tells me. "He invited me along at the beginning of the year, and we had some good times, but now he says I'm not welcome." Thomas glares at The Monk.

"That's because you snitch on us," says The Monk.

"I only snitch when you break rules."

"Oh, so you're admitting it now?"

"Maybe," says Thomas. "Maybe I'm admitting it. Maybe I'm not."

"You know what?" says The Monk. "I think I'm done with this conversation."

He puts the record back on the record player and turns it on. The psychedelic music pours into the room. You can hear the scratch below the bass line, a loud, frightening *rip* every time the record turns. *Rip. Rip. Rip.* The Monk frowns in Thomas's direction, but he doesn't jam and he doesn't crank the volume. Thomas turns his face away. He goes back to his writing. But I can see the hurt in his shoulders, in his neck, and in the way he is trying to slow his breathing down. The Monk grabs my copy of *The Metamorphosis* and pretends to read. He turns pages furiously.

We sit in silence for a few moments, but the air is almost too heavy to breathe. Finally, Thomas rises, red-faced, from his desk. He crosses the room and opens the door. He looks back at The Monk, maybe hoping an apology is coming his way, but The Monk does not look up. He turns so he is facing the wall instead. Thomas turns away too. His shoulders slump and he sighs, lingering for a moment in the doorway. Then he walks out of the room and slams the door behind him.

"You weren't very nice," I tell The Monk.

"You think?" The Monk mutters, still leafing through *The Metamorphosis*.

"Yeah," I say.

The Monk looks up at me.

"What if I told you he reported me to the dean of students a couple weeks ago."

"What? Why?"

"For breaking curfew. Good old school rule number A-4. *All licensed juniors and seniors in good academic standing have permission to operate registered motor vehicles off campus as outlined in transportation bylaws*, blah blah blah, *but all drivers and passengers must be signed back into dormitories no later than ten o'clock Sunday through Thursday and eleven o'clock on Friday and Saturday nights.* Trowbridge has the whole frigging handbook memorized. You think I was too harsh? What if I told you they gave me a demerit because of him?"

"What does that mean?"

"It means if they catch me breaking curfew again I'm screwed."

SOPHOMORES ARE SOPHOMORIC
AND OTHER TAUTOLOGIES

I'M SITTING ON A BENCH IN THE BOYS' FIELD HOUSE
lacing up my Converse All Star sneakers after gym. Boys
are doing what they always do in locker rooms, even in progressive places like Baldwin. They are flexing their muscles, whipping each other in the butt with towels, and
checking out their acne and their facial hair in tiny square
mirrors over the sinks. They are boasting about their girl-
friends, their field goals, and the cars they want to buy one
day. Interestingly, because this is the Baldwin School and
not my public high school, they are also making jokes
about existential philosophers, discussing string theory,
and practicing their Latin declensions. But this doesn't
do anything to mitigate the fight-or-flight feeling I always
get as soon as I set foot in a locker room. Maybe it has to do

with my concave chest and my enthusiastically detailed rib cage.

The Monk is hanging out with a strange assortment of guys over by the lockers. There's a heavyset kid with a shaved head, various piercings, and a Rage Against the Machine T-shirt, there's a shifty-eyed kid with a Mohawk who speaks in a whisper and can't stop snickering at everything anyone says, and then there's this kid with a curly red fro who has shaved off his eyebrows and penciled them back in with black eyeliner. The Monk pounds the bald kid on the back. Then he fist bumps the kid with the eyeliner, who tries to grab his fist and push him backward, but The Monk yanks his fist away, and because he's so tall the kid can't even reach him. They scuffle and tackle each other and crash against the lockers. Other kids stare warily at them and then move silently away.

The Monk spots me and motions for me to come over. I think about doing it, because these guys just might be weird enough not to ignore me the way so many kids at the public school did, but the tumor is drinking beer and making snide remarks about why I suck, so I stay put and pretend I don't notice the invitation. I concentrate on my shoelaces.

The Monk strides over to where I'm sitting and slides in beside me.

"Dude!" he says.

"Hey," I say.

"You don't look so good."

"I don't?"

"No," says The Monk. "You're kind of pale."

"Yes, well," I say. "Winter and being Caucasian and all that."

"Come meet my buddies," says the Monk.

The tumor kicks the back of my eye with his boot.

"Nah," I say. "I have to study for a quiz."

"You should meet these guys," says The Monk. "They're quality."

I look over. The curly-red-haired one is waving at me. I raise a hand to them, and then look back at my sneakers.

"Holy crap," says The Monk. "We need to do something about your antisocial behavior. Look at you. I threw you a lifeline and you totally ignored it, dude. What's with that? You want to drown? You want to get eaten by sharks? I have to tell you, as your student fellow and your friend who sees your potential coolness, that is extremely pathetic behavior."

"So now I'm pale and pathetic?"

"Yes," says The Monk. "You are."

"Great," I say. "Thank you."

"I just tell it how I see it."

"Shut up," I say.

"Now you are just being rude," says The Monk.

"Oh," I say. "Pale, pathetic, and rude. Anything else?"

The Monk puts his face in my face. "You are also

infuriating. Has anyone ever told you that? You are in a pit. You need to dig yourself out right now. You *need* to frigging *do* something, dude. Snap out of it. Snap *out* of it, dude!"

The Monk grabs me by my ears.

"Please stop," I say.

"No," he says. "I'm *not* going to stop. Not until you promise to change your *attitude*. Otherwise I'm going to shake you until your scrambled brain comes out of your *asshole*. You think I'm *joking*? You think I won't *do it*?"

The Monk grins at me insanely and shakes my ears to prove his point.

I have never had someone shake me by my ears before. Ears are not meant to be used as handles. The skin on the earlobes is sensitive. It does not appreciate fingernails. The harder he shakes, the harder the tumor crashes into the walls of my brain. The tumor is getting pissed off. He doesn't like crashing into walls unless he is doing it on purpose in a mosh pit with a crowd of gorgeous women. My brain, despite all the pounding noise, is most definitely not a mosh pit.

The Monk gets up from the bench to get a better grip on my ears.

"Stop," I say. "You're hurting me."

"*That* is the *point!*" says The Monk.

"Okay," I say.

"Okay, *what*?" says The Monk.

157

"Okay, I'll try to be less pathetic."

"And less rude?"

"Yes," I say. "Yes. Less rude. And less pale."

The Monk lets go of my ears.

"Good man," he says, sitting back down.

"Good God," I say.

I slump forward.

"You shouldn't get me aggravated like that," says The Monk.

"I'll keep that in mind."

"So will you meet my buddies?"

"Sure," I mutter, rubbing my ears. "Anything you say."

"Guys!" shouts The Monk, turning around toward the lockers where the misfits were standing not moments before, but they are already hustling out the door, one after another. First the bald one, then the shifty-eyed one with the Mohawk, then the curly-red-haired one with the eyebrows. We watch the door to the locker room close behind them.

"Damn," says The Monk. "You scared them away."

"You think?"

"Yeah. They're definitely frightened. 'Cause of all that ruckus you made while I was shaking the snot out of you. But don't worry, dude. There will be other chances. In fact I have an idea. I have an awesomely wonderful idea. This is gonna be great. I can't believe how perfect this is. I am a genius."

"What," I say.

"A week from Friday we're auditioning for *Hamlet*. All of us. You need to be part of this, dude. I can see it."

"No thank you," I say. "Theater's not my thing."

"You think I didn't know that?" says The Monk. "You keep underestimating my brilliance. Which pisses me off. I know theater isn't your thing. You can barely talk to me. You think I don't know you wouldn't be comfortable talking to an auditorium full of people? I get it. But listen, dude. I think you are in great need of getting out of your comfort zone, okay? You need to get out of this *rut*. Plus you promised to be less lame. So no more conversation is necessary. You're *doing* this."

"You're wrong about something," I tell him.

"No," he says. "I'm not. I have you figured out, dude."

"You don't. I'm never in my comfort zone. So cut me some slack."

"No slack," says The Monk. "Auditions. After school. A week from Friday. My buddies will be trying out. Fish'll be there too. You know Fish, right? From our World Lit class? With the hair?"

I feel my face flush.

"Yeah," I mutter. "I know her."

"Good," says The Monk. "She's part of my collection. It's always good to have a girl in your collection. Just in case." He winks at me.

He checks his phone. "Shit," he says. "I gotta go." And then, without waiting to hear what I have to say about his proposition, he swings his backpack onto his shoulder, starts texting furiously, and strides away.

I watch him head past the lockers and toward the door, which swings back and shuts so that I am left alone to think about what he said.

If I was in the play, I would have a chance to spend more time with Fish and that would be worth it. But would someone as amazing and beautiful as Fish ever really notice someone as pathetic as me?

I sit alone on the bench with my concave chest and my shard and my tumor and my pathetic, pathetic sadness leaning against my eyelids, breathing in the ghosts of a thousand generations of boys so filled with sweat and acne and hormones and optimism, so filled with expectations of health and years on this earth, it makes me want to fall to my knees and pray, even though I haven't prayed since I was five years old. *Dear God, if you are up there, please help me find the courage to try out for this play so I can hang out with this gorgeous pink-haired girl named Fish who you have placed on this earth in your infinite, twisted wisdom, and may I one day have the chance and the guts to kiss her. Amen.*

The tumor only laughs.

TRUST FALL

THE AUDITORIUM SMELLS LIKE OLD PAINT, FRAYED ropes, moth-eaten velvet curtains, and about a hundred generations of dusty costumes. It's not an unpleasant odor. If you've ever been onstage, you know exactly what I mean. It smells like folding chairs, like the insides of violin cases, like cast-iron music stands, yellowed scripts, clipboards, sandbags, and the sweat of hopeful understudies.

We sit in a circle of chairs on the stage and wait for the director to arrive. The Monk introduces me to the misfits, who clearly remember me from the locker room incident, because they crack up when they see me, and the bald kid grabs the curly-red-haired kid's ears and starts shaking them, which I don't find very funny. The bald one's name is Smitty. He is wearing a Green Day T-shirt and black combat boots and black skinny jeans that are way too tight on him and he has disks in his ears and he speaks in this crazy booming voice that carries over the stage as though he were God. The shifty-eyed one with the Mohawk is Griswald. Griswald doesn't seem to talk, but he snickers at everything anyone says as though every utterance contains a sexual innuendo. Finally, there is Ravi, the kid with the red fro and the shaved eyebrows who gesticulates madly with both hands and pokes at people's chests for emphasis but no one seems to mind because he is amusing. Dude, says The Monk. Tell Max why your parents named you Ravi. Because they are hippie wannabees, that's why, says Ravi, flashing double peace signs. Plus they worship Ravi Shankar, who happens to be the sexiest sitar player who has ever existed. Peace and love, dude, man. Don't trust anyone over the age of thirty.

And then of course, there's Fish.

Fish is wearing black combat boots and black leggings and a ripped black Dead Kennedys T-shirt held closed at various places by safety pins. The scar on her arm looks even whiter against all the black clothing.

Smitty and The Monk have been watching Second City do improv comedy on YouTube. They start to imitate the act they liked the best, newscasters reporting a national disaster. What's funny is Smitty pretends to be narcoleptic and he keeps falling asleep in the middle of sentences and toppling out of his chair just in time to wake himself up and start all over again. The Monk is obsessed with opera and can only sing his sentences. The two of them are amazing. Between the snoring and the singing, they have the rest of us in stitches, especially Fish, who is laughing so hard she has tears streaming down her face.

The director strides onto the stage in the midst of all this hilarity. She's a tall white-haired woman, much older than Dr. Austerlitz. She smiles at us with her entire face and suddenly the whole space seems to light up. She wears black pants and a black tank top and a long purple jacket that flows behind her, so when she strides onto the stage, it looks as though she's riding the wind.

She grabs an empty chair, turns it backward, and straddles it.

"Good afternoon, everyone," she says. "Welcome to auditions for Shakespeare's wonderful tragedy *Hamlet*. For those of you who don't know me, my name is Donna Pruitt, and I'll be your director. Today I want to see who you are. I want to watch you use your wits, your imagination, and your instincts. I want to find out how well you think on your feet. Here's our first exercise. For every action there must be a reaction. Please stand in a circle so I can demonstrate . . ."

We rise and form a circle. She reaches into the pocket of her jacket and takes out an apple. She gazes at it for a moment and all our eyes are drawn to the apple through the force of her gaze and her breath.

Oh apple. Oh lovely apple.

The redness of it. The perfect shape.

Suddenly, Donna Pruitt hauls back and throws the apple to The Monk.

He catches it without blinking and throws it back.

Action.

Reaction.

"Not bad," says Donna Pruitt.

She shines the apple on her jacket. Then she takes an enormous bite and shows with her entire face that this is the best apple she has ever eaten in her life.

She passes the apple to Fish, who kisses it and takes a bite. Fish passes it to Ravi, who passes it to The Monk, who passes it to Griswald, each of them taking a bite. When it gets to Smitty, he takes a gigantic bite, chews with his mouth open, and then belches, widemouthed, much to everyone's pleasure, before passing it on to the next person.

I am the last one to receive the apple.

I don't take a bite.

I hold it by the stem and hand it, gingerly, back to Donna Pruitt, who raises an eyebrow at me and pitches it over-hand toward a wastepaper basket on the other side of the stage.

It goes in.

"That was amazing," says Fish.

"Yes it was," says Donna Pruitt. "It's good to be able to take a risk every now and then. Accept what another person gives you. Say yes to the moment."

"Yes . . . ," says Fish emotionally, like she has just received a marriage proposal.

"That's right," says Donna Pruitt. "*Yes*. A three-letter word. A simple word. But it's the most important word in the world. You know why? Because without *yes*, none of us would exist. *Yes* is creation and procreation."

She rises from her chair and starts striding around. She has very long legs for an old woman.

"Ever say yes to a stranger before? Ever say it to someone you love? Good acting can only happen when everyone onstage says yes with their body and their voice. Risk is what makes theater delicious. Someone throws you an apple. You catch it. You take a bite. Are you ready to do it?"

"Yes!" Fish shouts. She leaps from her seat and pumps her fist.

"Oh yes," intones Ravi. He is looking sideways at The Monk.

Everyone else goes around the circle and says their golden line.

When Griswald says it he hunches up his shoulders like a spy and holds on to the *sssss* so it sounds like hissing. When Smitty says it, he shouts *Yayes* and waves his arms like a Holy Roller. When The Monk says yes, he strikes a pose like a constipated guy sitting on a toilet, and he squats and flexes and curls so the word comes out like a grunting bark that resonates across the stage, and everyone applauds because it is so funny and inspired.

When it is my turn, I do not say yes.

Instead, I say *hamburger*.

Donna Pruitt winks at me.

Next, she hands out slips of paper. Each one has a line from Hamlet's famous soliloquy. We are going to stand in a circle and take turns jumping into the middle and reciting our line with some kind of grand gesture. Everyone else will watch and listen and then imitate what they see in the center.

The Monk, of course, goes first. He runs into the center of the circle, goes down on his knees, raises his face and his arms to the ceiling, and shouts, *"To be or not to be: that is the question!"* Then he pretends to stab himself in the heart and falls to the floor. Everyone laughs, especially Ravi, who laughs the loudest.

The Monk is so easy to watch. His motions are so fluid. He'll get the part hands down. David Moniker as Hamlet. I can already see it.

But there's no time to think because now it's our turn to fall to our knees and shout the line and die.

Then Smitty staggers in like he's a drunk in an alley.

166

He hiccups, takes a swig of something in a bottle, and slurs his words: *"Whether 'tis nobler in the mind to suffer the slings and arrows of outrageous fortune, or to take arms against a sea of troubles."* He doubles over and pretends to vomit. Then he pulls his Green Day T-shirt over his belly, wipes his mouth, takes another swig of his bottle, and exits.

We do it too.

Fish twirls to the center. She skips around, flashing us the peace sign and handing each of us invisible flowers. Then she stops as though she has been struck by an arrow.

She clutches her heart and kneels on the stage. *"To die,"* she moans, *"to sleep; No more; and by a sleep to say we end the heartache."*

Then she falls.

She is beautiful lying on the stage crumpled like that. A broken dove.

Instead of imitating her, I stand back, shaken, while the others come forward and die together, as though around a mass grave, a terrifying action. They think it's funny. I know this because they make faces while they die. They stick out their tongues and twitch and make strangled noises. I envy them. They have not yet learned that there is nothing funny about death.

Now it's my turn.

I walk into the center of the circle with my slip of paper.

I take a shaky breath.

I don't do anything momentous. I just stand there and think about my mother.

I tell them, without telling, how it was.

I tell them, without telling, how hard it is to be on this earth without her.

"To die," I whisper, *"to sleep; To sleep: perchance to dream: ay, there's the rub; for in that sleep of death what dreams may come."*

None. I tell them with my silence. No dreams. Nothing.

When my line is over, people are staring at me.

Fish wipes her eyes.

Donna Pruitt is smiling.

Then the rest of them do what I did.

Donna Pruitt puts her hand on my shoulder when I come back to the circle.

After the last one in the circle says their line, Donna Pruitt brings us down into the pit and arranges us in two parallel lines facing each other, perpendicular to the stage. She puts me and Fish across from each other closest to the stage and she puts Smitty and The Monk on the ends. She tells us to extend our arms and clasp the wrists of the person across from us. Fish grabs my wrists and smiles.

I see the scar, but pretend I don't. There is something beautiful about it. The way it snakes across her wrist like a white bracelet.

I hold her wrists.

Suddenly I want to hold more of her.

I look into her eyes.

"Hi," she says, smiling.

"Hi," I say. "Nice day."

And now I'm blushing like a moron.

Donna Pruitt climbs back onto the stage and faces us.

"I am going to fall into your arms," she says. "I weigh a hundred sixty pounds. Do you think you can catch me and keep me safe? I'm a tall woman. If you drop me, I'll break my neck. But I trust you. I know you can do this. I'm going to turn my back to you. Then I'll compose myself, get myself ready to take the risk. When I'm ready, my line is *Ready to fall*. You all check your grasp. Make sure you have each other's wrists and you're spread out just enough so that my weight will be evenly distributed. My head and shoulders weigh the most, so those of you on the far end need to be most careful. When you are ready, make eye contact with each other. Nod your head to each other and your line is *Fall away*. Then I'll say *Falling*. I'll cross my hands over my chest like this. I'll keep my body as rigid as possible and I'll fall into your arms. Sound good?"

Everyone nods.

She's completely crazy. We're going to drop her and she's going to die.

She turns her back to us.

She breathes in and out. I watch her breathe. We all watch her breathe.

"Ready to fall," she says.

We tighten our grip and position our bodies so we're strong on our feet.

We make eye contact all up and down the line.

"Fall away," we say.

She takes another deep breath and squares her shoulders.

"Falling," says Donna Pruitt.

She crosses her arms against her chest like a corpse and makes herself rigid like a corpse and just as I begin to be distracted by a bad thought about my mother in the open casket, Donna Pruitt falls backward.

We catch her.

Smitty and The Monk get her shoulders and the rest of us lower her down, real easy, until she's standing in front of us grinning, and the rest of us are hooting and cheering, and everyone's heart is going quicker.

People take turns going onstage and falling backward. Each time, we catch them, and it is triumphant. Each time I almost get swallowed up by the image of my mom in the coffin, but the person falls before I drown completely and it's like my brain snaps, like a lasso, into the moment and out of the image.

It's Fish's turn to fall. She climbs onstage and faces us.

"This is scary," she says.

"I know it's scary," says Donna Pruitt. "Everything important is scary."

Fish breathes in and out. She is smiling at us, but her eyes are filling with tears. "I'm not the kind of person who trusts other people very easily. There are reasons . . ."

"There are always reasons," says Donna Pruitt. "Everyone has scars."

"I've never done anything like this before."

"That's good," says Donna Pruitt. "You'll feel strong when it's over."

"You guys seem like pretty nice people," she says, still smiling and teary.

"We are nice people," says Ravi, wiggling his eyebrows.

The Monk elbows Ravi in the ribs.

"Fish," says The Monk, "I'll catch you."

"Okay," she says. "Okay. I'm gonna do it."

Fish turns her back.

She has narrow shoulders and a narrow back and her pink hair goes down almost to her waist. It's such pretty hair.

"Ready to fall," she says.

We tighten our grasp and move closer together because she is small and we know this will be easy. When Smitty and The Monk fell, they were so heavy they left red marks on our wrists, but catching Fish won't be like that. "Fall away," we say.

She breathes in and out a few times. Then she puts her arms across her chest.

I don't know why they arrange some bodies that way in the coffin.

It's not as though people sleep with their arms that way.

It must be the desire of the living to gaze on those hands one last time.

"Falling," says Fish in a voice that is really a whisper.

She falls backward.

We catch her. I lower her feet down.

She is crying and smiling and triumphant.

She hugs every single one of us.

When she comes to me, she puts her face up to my ear and whispers, "You should try it, Max."

I reach out and pet her hair. I don't think about it, I just do it.

Fish smiles.

The Monk glares at me.

"Max is going next," says The Monk menacingly.

"He needs to make that choice," says Donna Pruitt. "Max, are you ready?"

"I don't know," I say.

"Max! Max! Max!" says Fish. She is clapping her hands

and soon they are all clapping their hands and chanting my name.

"Okay," I say. "Okay, I'm going to do it."

Fish is jumping up and down.

I climb the stairs onto the stage.

I stand at the edge and look down at them. It seems like a long way down.

They arrange themselves, clasping each other's wrists.

"I don't know about this," I say.

"You can do it," says Fish. "I was scared too."

"I don't know if I can."

"Stop talking about it and do it already," says The Monk. *"Ready to fall. Say it."*

I turn my back on them and close my eyes.

I feel them get quiet. I feel them watching me and waiting.

"Ready to fall," I whisper.

I feel them getting ready for me.

"Fall away," they say.

I put my hands across my chest.

I close my eyes.

This is how I will look in my coffin.

Dad will stand beside me. He will look down at my face.

I will not look like a human being.

I will look like a wax sculpture.

With a bulge behind my left eye.

What does it feel like to be lowered into a grave?

"Fall away," says Donna Pruitt.

Fall away, says the tumor. *Six feet is not such a long way down.*

"I'm sorry," I say. "I can't."

"Are you sure?" asks Donna Pruitt.

"I'm sure," I say.

"Next time," says Donna Pruitt. "Next time we'll try again."

"Okay," I say.

But it's not okay.

I am silent when Donna Pruitt brings us back together onstage and tells how proud of us she is and how she will post the cast list after winter break, and how no matter what part we get, we are about to become part of something wonderful. I stay still when everyone bursts into applause. At the end, when everyone is hugging each other and congratulating each other, and telling each other about their plans for winter break, and theorizing about who will get what role, I find my backpack and leave the auditorium without saying goodbye. I walk down the aisle and out the door and I rush as fast as I can into the boys' bathroom where I lock myself into an empty stall.

I sit down on a closed toilet.

I pull the Blue Willow shard out of my back pocket and

hold it in my hand. Then I put it in my mouth and run my tongue across the smooth surface.

People come in and people leave.

Someone flushes a toilet in another stall.

Someone washes his hands.

I sit on the toilet and close my eyes until I can breathe again.

When I finally leave the boys' bathroom, the hallways are strangely quiet. I spit the shard into my palm and tuck it back into my pocket. If I move fast, I can catch the six o'clock bus. I zip my jacket and shoulder my backpack.

I pass a janitor with thinning white hair and a baseball cap who is whistling "Silent Night." He's walking down the hall with a broom, pushing papers and milk cartons as he goes. He smiles at me and I try to smile back but I just can't do it. He shrugs and continues down the corridor, "Silent Night" and the sound of the broom and his footsteps getting fainter and fainter, and makes his way toward the classrooms on the other side of the building, pushing our garbage and whistling to himself, the strange, empty echo of wind and a failed attempt at goodwill. The most lonesome sound in the world.

TO BE OR NOT

WINTER BREAK PASSES UNEVENTFULLY. IT'S COLD BUT it never quite snows. Lydie stops by with homemade gluten-free gingerbread cookies. We thank her profusely and take polite bites, but once she leaves, I throw mine in the garbage. It tastes like cardboard. Outside, the sky is full of heavy clouds and we can see our breath rising from our lips like ghosts so I spend the break in my room, on the Internet, googling cancer statistics and reading the PDF of *Hamlet* on my computer. I dream about Fish. I obsess over the possibility that she and The Monk are seeing each other over the break, doing whatever they do without me. His family lives an hour out of town, so it's not out of the realm of possibility. I imagine them laughing together, their arms around each other. I count down the days.

Finally Monday comes. First thing in the morning, the stage manager hangs the cast list on the auditorium door. We all rush over to see who we are. I look for my name at the bottom, expecting to find myself among the throng of Lords, Soldiers, Attendants, or Guards. I find Griswald, but my name is not there. I move my eye up the page, part by part. I am also, as it turns out, not Fortinbras or Lucianus or the First Ambassador, or the Priest or First Sailor or Captain. My stomach sinks. I wasn't cast. It's because I said *hamburger* instead of *yes*. It's because Donna Pruitt looked in my soul and could see that I am dying.

Masochist that I am, I keep looking up the cast list to see who got the good parts. I try not to allow myself to feel the sting of defeat, but for some reason I care a lot more than I expected to. It's not as though this disappointment will kill me. I am already dying, for God's sake. I was dying before I knew about the auditions. I'll be dying after it's over. My path is set one way or another.

The Monk, of course, is Hamlet.

Ravi is Laertes.

Smitty is Polonius.

Fish is Ophelia.

A couple kids I don't know are Gertrude and Claudius.

And then I see it. My name.

177

Ghost of Hamlet's Father—Max Friedman.

What do you know?

I was cast. As a ghost. Which I basically am already. So it's perfect.

But also kind of insulting.

The first thing I think is: *How did she know?*

The second thing I think is: *This is ironic.*

The third thing I think is: *Perhaps this is the opposite of irony. Perhaps this is precisely what they mean when they use the word* apropos.

I am pondering the derivation and spelling of the word *apropos* when The Monk suddenly crashes into me.

He screams, *"Heck Yeah!"* and uses me as a pogo stick to vault himself into the air. "You are gonna *haunt* me, dude. This is *good*. This is going to be *awesome*. Are you *psyched*?"

"Sure," I say.

"Don't be pathetic, Friedman," says The Monk.

"I'm not being pathetic."

"You are," he says. "Change. Now."

"Okay," I say. "I guess I'm excited."

The Monk looks down his nose at me, unimpressed. Then he gives me a tremendous dope slap that nearly topples me over. "Careful," he says. "There's more where that came from."

There's a whirlwind of activity and suddenly the rest of

the kids are all around the door of the Baldwin Theater high-fiving each other and giving each other hugs and kissing each other's cheeks and rubbing each other's backs and wiping each other's tears. Fish was right. Theater people really like touching.

After school we meet in the auditorium for our first rehearsal. The sea of actors parts for Donna Pruitt, who walks through the middle of the crowd. She's wearing brightly colored silk scarves that flow behind her while she walks and she carries a box of scripts, which she hands over to The Monk ceremoniously. There's an air of expectancy. You can hear it in people's voices as we climb onto the stage from the wings. People spread out. They stretch like dancers. They lean on each other, and they put their arms around each other and they listen.

"*Hamlet* is a play about grief," says Donna Pruitt. "It's also a play about secrets. It's a play about betrayal and revenge and about madness and about being haunted."

The Monk elbows me.

"Our sets and costumes are going to be gothic, steampunk. Iron bars, alleyways, ripped tights, studded collars, and corsets. Think dry ice and steel pipes and graffiti. In addition to playing Laertes, Ravi has volunteered to be our designer. We are so lucky to have his artistic genius in our production once again. We have a host of talented volunteers who will begin work on sets and costumes as soon as Ravi gives the thumbs-up."

"Prepare to be dazzled," he says.

Fish squeals with delight and throws her arms around Ravi, who pats her gently.

"You are so adorable I almost can't stand it," he says. He touches her nose and she pretends to bite him.

Donna Pruitt smiles at them. "Ophelia, in act 4, scene 5, you go mad. You walk around singing nonsense, holding a bouquet of herbs and flowers. That bouquet will be in direct contrast to the starkness onstage. Ophelia and her flowers will be the only delicate things on a stage filled with metal and sharp edges. Can you imagine it?"

We nod, already transported.

Fish rises as though pulled by an invisible string. She gazes at the ceiling and begins tiptoeing, tripping, whirling, wandering across the stage, her eyes already wide and glistening, her breath already coming in uneven gasps, the way Mom's breath came before the end. We watch her, amazed at how completely she is able to enter Ophelia's character. She begins to sing Ophelia's songs, snatches and riddles, her voice a whisper, her face drawn and filled with pain. When she sits back down, The Monk puts his arm around her and she buries her head in his shoulder. My stomach curls into a fist.

"Hamlet," continues Donna Pruitt, gazing at The Monk, "the big question of this play is whether or not you are mad. In this production, I want you to consider that a human can, in fact, be both mad and sane at the same time. We each experience a range of emotions at once. Love. Sadness. Anger. Can you imagine that?"

The Monk nods, smiling, then frowning, then scowling, then sneering.

"Nice," says Donna Pruitt. "We have a strong cast this year, that's for certain. I think we are all going to learn a lot from one another. And now we will begin."

I don't have any lines in act 1, scene 1, but I'm there as an apparition, the ghost of the dead king, Hamlet's father. When the Guards see me for the first time, I'm dressed in armor, floating through the hallways of Elsinore Castle as a wraith. I sneak around the stage, tapping on their shoulders. I blow on the backs of their necks. They whirl around, terrified. I whisper in their ears and they shudder and hold each other. They try to swing at me, but their swords cut through me. I am nothing. I am air. I am dread. I am regret.

When the sun rises in the morning, I am nowhere to be found. I am the ghost of a king. A dead man walking. But

I wonder who I am when I am not haunting this castle. Do I exist? Do I lie in my grave? I look at my hands again. I want to reach into my back pocket, find the shard, and put it in my mouth. I want to run my tongue over the edges, the smooth, cool glaze, but I can't do it in front of these people. I hug myself. I curl my fingers into fists.

When rehearsal is over, I head to the boys' bathroom to make sure I am alive. A few guys from the cast come into the bathroom to look at themselves in the mirror and use the urinals. I climb onto the toilet so they can't see my red Converse All Stars at the bottom of the stall. I wait for them to leave.

They are laughing together, making plans to go out after rehearsal. I stay standing on the toilet until I'm sure no one is in the building except the janitor, who comes in with his keys jangling, whistling. I hear him empty the garbage and push his broom across the floor. I put the shard in my mouth and run my tongue over its surface.

"Hey," says the janitor, when he gets to my stall. "You okay in there?"

"Yeah," I say.

"I'm locking up in a half hour, so you're gonna have to get moving soon."

"Okay," I say.

"You sure everything is all right?"

"Yeah," I say. "Everything's good."

I let the shard click against my teeth. I feel the corners against my gums. I taste something warm and salty and I know my tongue is bleeding, but I don't stop. There is something about the pain that feels right.

The janitor lingers in front of the stall. I hear him breathing, getting ready to ask me if I need any help. But then, after the seconds tick by, I guess he thinks better of it and he moves on with his broom.

He whistles a lonesome tune into the empty bathroom and nothing moves except the broken sound of his song and the broom pushing dust, and finally, once he closes the door to the bathroom and I know I am alone, I spit the shard and a stain of blood into my palm. Then I wipe my palm and push the shard back into my pocket like a secret, safe and sound in the perfect and inscrutable darkness.

LADY J. AND THE AGE
OF AQUARIUS

AT HOME THAT NIGHT WE EAT FROZEN PIZZA ON PAPER plates. We try to make conversation, but as usual we are too numb to be amusing. The tumor loves frozen pizza. He has enough enthusiasm for all of us. Whenever I take a bite he yodels like a cowboy, kicks his spurs against my eyelids, and shoots bullets into my brain with silver pistols. *Yippee ti yi yay*, screeches the tumor in a voice so shrill it breaks several windows in my hippocampus. I rub my left eyeball. I can feel him in there flexing his muscles.

There is a knock on the front door.

Dad and Grandma and I look at one another.

"Are you expecting someone?" says Dad.

"Who would I be expecting?" I say.

"Why don't you get the door," says Dad.

"Because it's probably Lydie with another batch of cardboard cookies."

"Ha," says Dad. "I don't think so."

Someone knocks again. This time louder.

"What should I say if it's for you?" says Dad.

"Say I'm not home."

"Okay," says Dad. "It's a plan."

Dad walks into the front hallway. He opens the door wide. It's Fish and The Monk and Ravi.

They're all wearing strange winter hats. The Monk has a red-and-white-striped top hat. Ravi is wearing a squid, his red fro spilling out the sides. Fish has a furry white hood with ears. She spots me in the kitchen and waves to me.

"Hi Max," calls Fish. "Want to come out with us?"

"He can't," says Dad, smiling. "He's actually not here. That guy at the table over there is an apparition. A hologram. Weird, I know. But true."

"I'm here," I moan. I get up from the table and head into the front hall.

"I stand corrected," says Dad. "He *is* here, it turns out."

Dad invites them in and they tumble into the house with their hats and scarves. The Monk shakes Dad's hand. "I'm David Moniker," he says. "This pretty polar bear here is Felicia Santacroce."

"We've met," says Dad, smiling at Fish.

The Monk continues on blithely. "Well, you haven't met

185

this funky guy over here with the squid hat. He is the one and only Ravi Gunderman. We're all in *Hamlet* with Max. We're headed out for some pizza and we wanted to know if he was up for joining us."

"Pizza?" says Dad. "What a fabulous idea. It just so happens that Max loves pizza. Ms. Santacroce, it's so nice to see you again. Mr. Gunderman, nice to meet you. Go get your jacket, Max. These fine people want to feed you."

"I've already had pizza tonight," I say.

"It had freezer burn," says Dad, "so it doesn't count."

"But it's a school night," I say.

"Live a little," says Dad. "And bring back a house salad and some spaghetti and meatballs for Grandma."

"Ooh," says Grandma, rubbing her hands, "good idea."

Fish peers into the kitchen and waves. "Hi Grandma," she says.

Grandma smiles and waves back.

"Go ahead, Max," says Dad. "Go have fun with your friends."

"Are you sure?"

Dad hands me a twenty-dollar bill and his red plaid lumberjack jacket. "I'm sure," he says. "Just call if you're going to be late."

"Okay. Thanks."

He walks us toward the door, shakes everyone's hand, and then ushers us out. The door closes behind me.

186

The Monk and Ravi and Fish receive me by jumping on me, messing up my hair, and pounding me on the back. The Monk helps me with my coat and then gets me in a headlock. Ravi tosses me a leather pilot's hat with flaps that go down over my ears. It's lined with fake rabbit fur.

"You can't be with us unless you have the proper attire," he says.

I put on the hat.

"Very good," says Ravi. "You look better now."

"Your grandma has a nice smile," says Fish.

She grabs one of my arms and Ravi grabs the other and they skip me down the sidewalk toward The Monk's rusty orange-and-white VW Microbus that waits for us like a big, smiley time machine. There is a dent in the passenger door and the front fender is held together by duct tape.

"What is this?" I ask.

"This," says The Monk, gesturing grandly, "is my BUS." He says the word *bus* two octaves lower than he says the rest of the sentence so it sounds as though this one word comes from the mouth of a three-hundred-pound man or a movie voice-over artist.

"Her name is Lady J.," says Fish. "She is a very wise and venerable old woman. As you can see." Fish runs over to the bus and throws herself over the bumper for a hug and kiss.

"She's a hippie like my parents," says Ravi. "Lady J., that

is. Not this silly young woman who makes love with inanimate objects. You know what a hippie is, Max?"

"Yes, Ravi," I say. "I know what a hippie is."

"Excellent," says Ravi. "Then you'll also understand when I say, power to the people, stick it to The Man, feeling extremely groovy, and so forth."

"It turns out Ravi is a bit peculiar," says Fish.

"Yes, you are," says The Monk. He pinches Ravi's cheek. Ravi pretends to swoon. Then The Monk opens the door to the bus and gestures for us to climb in. Smitty and Griswald are already in there waiting for us. Smitty is wearing a wool army hat and Griswald is wearing orange earmuffs, because let's face it, there is no way in hell that guy is going to get a hat to fit over his Mohawk.

Smitty turns around from the seat in front of me. "Greetings, human," he says. "Welcome to your kidnapping!"

"I thought we were going out for pizza," I say.

"Poor deluded soul," says Smitty.

"Today is the first day of the rest of your life," says Fish. Smitty gives Fish a high five.

"Max," says Ravi, with an evil grin. "There will be no pizza tonight."

"Say goodbye to the universe as you know it," says Fish. Griswald laughs maniacally.

The Monk shoves the key into the ignition and Lady J. lurches down the street, boogying in her treads like a coked-up disco queen, just in case we forgot she was born in the same decade as most of our parents. The world speeds by outside the tinted windows. Houses and streetlights and mailboxes. The ceiling and the walls of Lady J. are covered in carpeting the color of rice pilaf. There are three rows of seats. Ravi and The Monk sit up front. Then Smitty and Griswald. Then Fish and me. Ravi hands out five pairs of John Lennon glasses, which we don with extreme seriousness. We get on the highway heading north.

"Can I tell Max where we're going?" begs Fish.

"No," says The Monk. "It's secret."

Griswald puts one finger to his lips.

"If we told the human where we were taking him it would not be a kidnapping, it would be a date," says Smitty.

"I like dates," says Fish.

"I can vouch for that," says The Monk.

The thought of The Monk on a date with Fish makes my heart implode.

"If this were a date," says Ravi, "it would be one girl and five dudes. And while you are quite lovely in the round glasses, Miss Fish, you are not nearly enough woman for all five of our appetites. You're just a very small person. A tiny little female."

"A minnow," says The Monk.

"A smelt," says Smitty.

"Oh yes. I think I'll call her Smelt from now on," says Ravi. "Smelt's a good name. Hello, little Smelt. Swim into my net."

"That's enough, Ravi," says Fish.

"I'll take out your bones and then I'll dip you in egg and bread crumbs and I'll fry you in a pan and eat you."

"It stopped being funny like a hundred years ago," says Fish.

"Okay," says Ravi. "I apologize."

Everyone is quiet for a while. We get off the highway and drive in silence behind our round glasses. It starts to snow lightly. The Monk turns on the windshield wipers. Soon there is a thin white powder of snow across the world. Snow makes everything hush.

"Where exactly are you taking me?" I ask again.

"To Nirvana," says Ravi.

"Hey," I say, remembering something. "What happened to A-4, breaking curfew, the demerit, being screwed, and all that?"

"I like to live on the edge," says The Monk. "And besides. It's only seven thirty. We have plenty of time to get back before curfew."

Suddenly, The Monk swerves left onto a dirt road and we head into the forest.

"Welcome to the Age of Aquarius," intones Ravi.

Fish throws back her head and laughs, a deep, rollicking belly laugh.

It's a glorious sound.

NIRVANA

IN THE OLD PHILLIPS ROCK QUARRY, THERE'S A footpath that goes right down to the water, just wide enough to follow single file if you're intrepid and don't mind heights. It goes down in an even slant from the dizzying rim into the quarry and all the way down to the frozen water where it's a good fifteen feet over your head at the deepest point.

During the summer, when you are too hot to exist, if you make it the whole way without chickening out, you can reward yourself with a swim, maybe climb one of the jutting rocks, grab on to the ancient rope swing someone's great-grandfather tied up in a pine tree a hundred years ago, pull yourself onto the knot, and swing forward so your feet splay out over the water. If you time it just right, you can let go into the deepest part of the swimming hole, in the shade of the trees and stones, so all around you is green water singing over your head and the wonderful thrill of being alive.

I've never been here during the winter. Mom and Dad used to take me in the summers when I was little. Dad would walk behind me keeping his hands on my shoulders so he could grab me if I lost my balance, which I did, frequently. When we got to the bottom, Dad would take out his camera and Mom would sit herself down on one of the flat rocks and look out over the water with her lovely feet out in front, her summer feet, white as doves, with dark red toenails. She never wore a bathing suit after her surgery, but in the summer she would wear sleeveless dresses and flowing smocks. I would sit down next to her and touch each of her gleaming toenails as if they were jewels.

Now we walk single file down the ice-covered footpath, which is barely visible in the dark with the new snow coming down. We are a strange clan of clowns with our hats and glasses, the whole mismatched lot of us. There is something incongruous about our seriousness, how closely we watch our feet, the depth of our silence as we make our way from the rim of the quarry, between the jutting rocks, and down toward the water, which they tell me is thick with ice.

The Monk goes first. He has a flashlight on his phone, and his tiny LED light shines a halo before him. The snowflakes dance in the glow, and I catch a glimpse of our treacherous path.

On our right the chiseled rocks jut up like shark's teeth. On the left is the pit. Every once in a while, one of us slides forward, mutters an obscenity. We steady each other and laugh to keep ourselves from crying. Or maybe that's just me. We grab on to elbows and shoulders. We keep our hands on each other.

I'm lucky.

Fish walks behind me.

Whenever I lose my balance she touches my back, my shoulder, my elbow, my waist. I start stumbling a lot more than I need to, because it feels good having her touch me. I want to reach back and grab her hand, but I'm worried I'll lose my footing completely and we'll both catapult into the pit. That would be bad. Plus it would greatly reduce the chance of more touching in the future. So instead of holding her hand, I call out, "Whoa!" and then when she puts her hands on me to help steady me I say, "Wow, thanks, Fish. Jeez."

"Everyone okay?" The Monk calls back.

"Just dandy," screams Ravi behind us. "It's Monday night. A great night to die."

"Not funny, Ravi," says Fish.

"Who was being funny, Miss Bossypants?" says Ravi.

"I've never been funny in my life. I don't even know how to be funny, thank you very much, you small pink-haired caterpillar. Now let me concentrate on not plummeting to my death."

"Ravi can be kind of bitchy," says Fish.

"Um. By the way," says Ravi, "I heard you. And it turns out that this statement is the third time you have assassinated my character and also, by the way, I don't appreciate the constant patronizing back-chatter, and finally by the way, I can see you petting Max as though he were a pussy cat and it makes me want to puke."

"He's just joking," says Fish.

"No," says Ravi, "not joking. Not joking at all."

I stop walking and turn around to glare at Ravi.

"What," says Ravi. "You think that look is intimidating? You think you're upsetting me?"

"Just cut it out, Ravi," says Fish. "You're being melodramatic."

"Again, the character assassination."

"Now, children," says The Monk. "Don't make me come back there."

"She started it," says Ravi.

"We're almost there," says The Monk from his place in the lead. "Look, just a few more yards. There's the swimming hole right down there. Oh man, look at it."

The swimming hole is frozen, circled by the rock wall on

all sides. It's the color, or the lack of it, that catches me off guard and makes me almost gasp, the way the faded sky and the rock and the ice all take each other's shadows, so it becomes a muted watercolor, as though someone had brushed a gray painting with their thumb, smearing the lines so all the parts of the picture blend together and it becomes impossible to distinguish where one natural body begins and the other one ends. I want to be part of that. I want my body to be part of that faded landscape.

We stand on the edge, just staring at it. I raise my face to the sky and watch the snowflakes dance. I open my mouth and stick out my tongue and allow snowflakes to twirl in, cold as tin. Inside my pocket, the woman on the shard shivers deliciously. She lets the snow fall on her cheeks.

If I die tonight, I will die having swallowed glorious snowflakes. I breathe the snow. I want to take winter into my lungs. I close my eyes and metastasize.

The Monk checks the time on his phone. "Okay, guys," he says. "It's eight o'clock. Me and Ravi and Smitty and Griswald need to be back in the dorm at ten. Are we going to waste our precious time standing here staring at this thing, or are we going boot skating?"

"Boot skating!" screams Smitty at the tops of his lungs as though it were a battle cry.

"Boot skating!" screams Fish.

Griswald grins and gives a silent thumbs-up.

"Okay, then," says The Monk. "Let's go."

The Monk lets out a barbaric battle cry and runs the rest of the way. We follow, propelled by the momentum of his sudden dash.

The frozen swimming hole stretches in front of us.

The Monk leaps onto the ice and slides out to the middle. He twirls around and around, whooping and gliding, a dark form moving in the snow.

One by one, we join him. First Smitty and then Griswald, then me and Fish and Ravi, each of us finding our own way onto the ice.

At first, we circle in our own orbits, arms outstretched, twirling, testing our balance, running and then sliding, falling down on our knees and crawling on all fours. There is nothing in the world besides the ice and the quarry and the snowy sky and the six of us. And the tumor expanding like a beer belly in my brain, but I won't think about that sadness now, I will just twirl and at least I'll know that I had one good night before I died. Besides my dad and Grandma and Lydie and the twins, there will be at least five other people at my funeral, which is not bad, considering my track record. Maybe we could get Donna Pruitt to give my eulogy. That would be eleven of us. Good enough for a party. Too bad I'd miss it on account of being dead.

It doesn't take long for people to begin orbiting closer to each other, except Griswald, who just stands there looking up into the sky like he's waiting for the mother ship to come back and take him home. Ravi skates over to The Monk and tries to waltz with him. The Monk grabs Ravi, puts him in a headlock, and flings him across the ice. Smitty falls on his knees and slides, screaming *Stellllaaaa!* Fish just spins, her hair a wild pink blur. I spin too. The world whips around me like a merry-go-round. A blur of gray. Again and again and again. At a certain point I become aware that Fish is spinning near me, and then, suddenly, she has grabbed my wrists and we are spinning together and the whole world spins around us. We are the vortex, smiling at each other, our faces a crazy blur, and for just a moment, for just a single blessed moment, I am happy.

ALL THINGS FRAGILE
AND DESPERATE

ON TUESDAY, THERE'S AN INCH OF NEW SNOW ON THE
ground. Not enough for a snow day or a delayed school opening, but enough to make the world look new, with the sun
coming through bare trees, making things sparkle. There is
something so hopeful about snow in the morning before it
gets covered in footprints and tire tracks, the way it covers
the gray in the sidewalks and the streets, brushing its smooth
white palms over everything.

Grandma's in her flannel nightgown, sleeping at the
breakfast table. One hand is curled around a coffee mug,
the other is open in her lap.

"Jean," says Dad at her shoulder. "We're heading out
now."

Grandma doesn't move for a moment, but then she stirs, inhaling sharply.

It's strange how much smaller a person looks when they're not moving. They seem so fragile, impermanent as paper. Movement gives the illusion of immortality. Stillness catches in your throat and makes your heart ache. It promises more stillness one day, just like Hamlet says, *To die, to sleep—no more*. Grandma's fingers are crooked, her white hair rising from her head like smoke.

I uncurl her fingers from the mug, hold her hand, and put my face down to her. "Grandma," I say near her ear. "I'm heading to school."

She opens her eyes and looks at me, blinking.

"We'll be heading off now," Dad says gently.

Grandma takes my other hand and pulls herself up until she's steady and planted on two feet. She looks into my eyes.

"I wanted to ask you something. Did you have fun with your friends last night?"

"Yeah," I say. "Actually I did. I'm sorry I didn't bring home dinner for you."

"That's okay," says Grandma. "I'm just glad you had a good time. Why did that girl have pink hair?"

"I don't know. I guess she likes it that way."

Grandma laughs. "You crazy kids," she says. "You beautiful, beautiful crazy kids." And then she swings my hands back and forth the way she always does, kisses each fist, and shuffles out of the kitchen. We hear her footsteps up the stairs and then above our heads to her bedroom.

Dad and I never talk much on our way to school, but today our silence is as comfortable as new white socks as we drive past the frosted houses, most cars still parked on the side of the road, each still dusted in a layer of snow. Dad turns on the radio and we listen to the country-and-western station, all the way through the center of town, the shops and office buildings still sleeping. Normally, I'm not a fan of country music. The way it pulls at you. But today, for some reason, I don't mind it. I lean my head back and listen to the promises it makes. Music. The new sun leading us down the road, rising through the trees in the school parking lot, where we stop for a while and sit in the car, the heat still going. The tumor is sleeping. When I cover my mouth to yawn, I slip the shard into my mouth and let it rattle against my teeth like a lozenge, sliding my tongue against the surface, and it's all kind of peaceful because we're early, and there's no point in rushing. Because somehow, sitting here together, just the two of us, surviving like this feels almost okay.

Then, suddenly, a battered car peels into the parking lot and the world is filled with dissonance again. A woman, elbow out the window, cigarette between her lips, sucks in and blows smoke out fast so she can scream at the kid slumped down beside her as she jerks into the parking space. We can hear them arguing above the music, their voices shrill and frightening.

"Slut!"

Dad turns off the truck.

I put the shard back in my pocket.

We listen to them shouting at each other.

"Stupid, selfish slut!"

"You think I should do something?" says Dad.

"I don't know," I say.

The voices rise even higher.

"I wish I lived with Dad! I hate you! I've always hated you!"

Movement inside the car and the sound of the girl sobbing.

We rush out of the truck.

That's when I see who it is. Fish.

She flings open the door.

"You're not leaving until you apologize!"

"I'm not apologizing to you!"

The mother grabs her backpack.

Fish yanks and pulls until the strap breaks from her mother's grasp.

She falls forward with the backpack out the open door of the car and onto the pavement.

I run over to help her up.

Her lip is bleeding.

Her mother slams the passenger door, cranks her music, and starts backing up, cigarette butt sailing out the open window. She tears out of the parking lot at full speed, the pounding music fading as she roars down the road toward town.

"I'm going to call the police," says Dad.

He reaches into his pocket for his cell phone.

"No!" says Fish. Then she puts her hand on his arm. "No need to call the police, Mr. Friedman. I'm fine. We were just having an argument and it got a little heated. Please. I'm okay."

"Has she ever been rough like that before?" Dad asks.

"Never," says Fish. "I swear."

"Your lip is bleeding," says Dad.

"Please, Mr. Friedman. We just get on each other's nerves. But most of the time things are fine. I fell out of the car, that's why my lip is bleeding. It's my own fault. I've always been kind of a klutz. Please don't call the police. She didn't lay a hand on me."

"I'm calling the school then," says Dad. "Somebody should know what happened."

"What should they know?" says Fish, her eyes blazing. "That we got in an argument? Why do they need to know that?"

Dad strides back to our truck and starts dialing numbers on his phone.

We watch him turn away from us to talk.

I reach into my pocket to find a folded Dunkin' Donuts napkin. I take it out and press it against her lip very, very gently. Her eyes are red from crying.

"Ow," she says.

I press it even more gently, barely touching her.

"What happened?" I ask, looking into her eyes.

"Mom doesn't like The Monk," says Fish. "She knows I was out with him last night. And then this morning she saw this drawing I did of us in my sketchbook and she just lost it. I didn't mean for her to see it. I was so stupid."

"What drawing?"

Fish doesn't say anything. She just looks at me.

"What drawing?" I say again.

"You don't want to see it," she says.

"I do," I tell her. "I want to see what you drew."

"Okay," says Fish. "I guess, if you really want to."

Fish reaches into her backpack for her sketchbook.

She opens it.

There is a drawing of Fish and The Monk in the nude, handcuffed together.

My heart stops. Fish is looking at me, waiting for me to say something, but I don't know what to say. The tumor wakes up and sets off a flare. He starts waving red flags behind my eyes. Fish reaches out and touches my arm. I can't look at her.

Dad walks toward us.

Fish shoves her sketchbook into her backpack. I help her zip it closed.

"Hey," says Dad. "I just called the nurse's office and told them what happened. She wants you to stop by right now so she can take a look at you, okay?"

"Okay," mutters Fish. "But you're making a big deal out of nothing. I'm completely fine." She starts walking away.

"Go with her, Max," says Dad. "Make sure she gets there."

"Yeah," I say. "I'm going."

Dad watches as I catch up to her. Fish is crying again. At first I can't tell, but then her shoulders start shaking. I take her backpack and put my arm around her hesitantly. She stiffens, but then she looks at me, and gently, slowly, we walk together up the path to Trowbridge Hall, Fish leaning against me, until all of a sudden The Monk comes hurtling toward us from nowhere.

"What's going on?" he says.

She looks down so at first he doesn't see her lip, but then he takes her chin and moves her face toward him.

"Jesus Christ!" he screams.

He pushes me, as though I am the one who did this to her.

"What the hell *happened*?"

"My mom," says Fish, crying harder. "She knew we were together."

"Did she hit you?"

"No," says Fish. "It wasn't like that."

"What did you see?" The Monk asks me.

"They were fighting," I tell him. "We heard it. And then they were pulling on the backpack and Fish kind of fell out of the car. She's supposed to go to the nurse's office so they can check her out. My dad called."

"Oh," says The Monk. "Your *dad* called. Well, aren't you a *hero. Daddy* made a flipping *phone call.*"

The Monk puts his arm around Fish's shoulders and takes over like he belongs there, walking fast, owning her all the way up the staircase, guiding her like a person who knows how to take charge. Fish holds on to the railing and The Monk holds on to her. I trail behind with her backpack, watching how easily their bodies fit together, his arm around her all the way to the nurse's office, where he opens the door for her and sits her down on the orange vinyl couch and pretty soon the school counselor is there with a clipboard, and she is asking all kinds of questions and Fish is saying *No, no, it's not like that*, and The Monk is rubbing her back, with me holding her backpack like a dog.

I clear my throat so they can hear about what I saw, so they can know that I was the one who helped her up, I was the one who wiped her lip. I was the one who comforted her and walked with her gently, in the beginning, before The Monk came and took over. I was the one who was there. But there is no space for me. Now the nurse is putting ice on her lip and the counselor is still asking questions, and Fish is saying *No, no, I swear*, and The Monk keeps kissing her head.

I know I should wait, but I take a step backward instead because I can't deal with the jealousy. I should be the one at her side.

Selfish bastard, says the tumor. *This isn't about you.*

Gently, slowly, I lower Fish's backpack onto the nurse's desk, making sure it's upright so she'll see it and remember it when she and The Monk leave here together. The counselor sees me standing at the desk and frowns because this is none of my business, and she says, "Time for class," and ushers me out of the room with a single stern glance.

UNGEZIEFER VERWANDELT

FISH AND THE MONK ARRIVE LATE TO WORLD Literature together. He leads her to her chair by the elbow and helps her get settled. Dr. Austerlitz glances at Fish for a moment and frowns. Then he goes back to making grammatical connections between Rilke and Kafka. He is explaining the syntactical structure of their sentences, and the differences between the English translations and the original German. *Als Gregor Samsa eines Morgens aus unruhigen Träumen erwachte, fand er sich in seinem Bett zu einem ungeheuren Ungeziefer verwandelt.* I try to make eye contact with Fish, but she is looking down. All around us, kids are taking notes, scribbling furiously like little drones. Dr. Austerlitz lectures about subordinate clauses and the various and layered meanings of words like *Ungeziefer*, which could mean cockroach or dung beetle or vermin, but could also mean the symbolic separation between a human being and the order of his natural world.

According to Dr. Austerlitz, Kafka uses *The Metamorphosis* to struggle with the theme of the natural versus the unnatural. *He looks in the mirror and sees something unrecognizable.* This makes sense to me. My mother's face, for instance, was always moving and shifting in life, emotions flickering around her eyes and mouth and cheeks as thoughts occurred to her, like clouds across a sky, but in the coffin, her face was still and the blood had drained from her cheeks and her lips had already grown thin and grim. As a result, her face in death was almost but not entirely devoid of human characteristics, it looked instead like a mask, a terrible experiment in de-animation.

"You see," says Dr. Austerlitz, prowling between the rows and wiggling his bony fingers as though he were a tremendous insect, "Gregor Samsa is transformed both physically and metaphysically. But this is not the kind of metamorphosis that happens in nature—the pupa into an insect, the caterpillar into a butterfly. What happens to Gregor Samsa is hideous and unnatural. He has forgotten what it means to be human. Do you agree with this?" He is standing beside my desk, obviously expecting me to say something.

Even though they were the same cheekbones, the same bridge of the nose, the same skin, the same hair, the woman in the coffin looked nothing like my mother at all. The effect of these anomalies was both terrifying and profoundly disappointing, because instead of seeing my mother's face, I saw this monstrous caricature with colorless lips and waxy skin.

"Mr. Friedman, do you see Gregor Samsa's tragedy as natural or unnatural?"

I don't answer.

"Natural or unnatural?" Dr. Austerlitz says, louder this time.

I still don't answer. I look over at Fish.

"Mr. Friedman. I am asking you a question. Listen to me. And answer, please. Is Gregor Samsa's tragedy natural or is it unnatural?" He practically screams these words into my face.

"Natural," I whisper, surprising myself.

"Excuse me? I didn't hear you," says Dr. Austerlitz.

"Natural," I say again, louder this time.

"Why natural?" says Dr. Austerlitz. "He has changed into a cockroach. How can this be natural? Explain."

I stand up at my seat.

"Because sometimes you look at yourself in the mirror and you just don't believe what you're seeing. Sometimes you think you have become so horrible and cowardly and pathetic, you think there isn't anything human about yourself."

My heart is beating and I am breathing hard.

209

"You think that it's unnatural, like turning into a cock-roach. But it's not. We all feel reprehensible sometimes. We can't believe what we've become. But that disgust is part of being human. You know what I mean?"

"Yes," says Dr. Austerlitz, almost smiling. "Yes, I do. Very good, Mr. Friedman."

I sit down.

The Monk is staring at me.

"Does anyone want to respond to this?"

More hands go up. We discuss this point for the rest of the class.

I do not put my head down on the desk even though the tumor is shouting.

At the end of class, The Monk helps Fish from her seat and leads her out the door. He walks her past me, his arm around her shoulders. I gather my books and make my way to the door.

I hug the books to my chest.

"Mr. Friedman," says Mr. Austerlitz. He puts his hand on my shoulder.

"Yeah?"

"Nice job," he says.

"Thanks," I say.

The Monk whispers something to Fish and heads off down the hall alone. Fish is leaning against the wall by the water fountain arranging her folders in her backpack.

"Hey," I say.

She watches The Monk disappear.

My heart is pounding.

"Are you okay?" I ask her.

She shrugs.

"I'm glad they checked you out," I say. "I was worried."

"I think they wanted to call someone about my mom, but I convinced them I was fine. I don't want any trouble. All I need is another reason for her to be mad at me. So what happened to you? I was looking for you when I got out of the nurse's office. Where did you go?"

"I didn't want to get in the way," I tell her.

"What's that supposed to mean?" says Fish.

"I figured you didn't need me waiting around for you. It just seemed like The Monk had everything under control."

Fish frowns. "You really don't know me at all, do you?" she says.

"I don't know anyone," I say. "I don't even know myself."

"Well, whose fault is that?" says Fish.

I have no answers.

She sighs and heads off down the hall toward Cage's class without me.

I watch her go, ashamed of the monstrous vermin I have become.

MISERY MAKES GOOD FICTION

DR. CAGE SMELLS LIKE OLD YOGURT. AS SOON AS I open the door and step inside, it hits me right in the face, his odor, yeasty and pungent, like something that should be wiped up and put out with the cat. I take my seat next to Fish and pull my notebooks from my backpack. We look in opposite directions until class begins. One by one, the other students enter the room. They take their seats uneasily, breathing through their mouths. It's not clear which part of Cage's body is emitting this foul odor. It could be his feet or his armpits. It could be his breath or his hair or his beard. It could be dirty underwear or socks. It could be all of the above. Stinky man, we love you anyway.

The class begins the way it always does. Students read their drafts. We go around the circle, giving feedback, appreciating every flimsy simile no matter how clichéd. And then Cage tears each piece apart. His cruelty is strangely amusing, the way it is always entertaining to watch the meanest judge in a television talent search. Even though you cringe when he does it, there is an element of delicious tension in waiting for him to lambast a contestant, ruin someone's dreams in precisely the way you hope your own will not be ruined. And then when he rips them to shreds, you smile because deep down inside you are a selfish son of a bitch. The Germans have a word for this kind of joy: *schadenfreude*. It means taking pleasure in another person's suffering. The Germans are nothing if not articulate.

Thomas A. Trowbridge the Fourth stands at his chair and reads his story in a tremulous voice.

The city at night. Blood. Sweat. Tears.

A rat scurries down the train track like a tiny buffalo, charging, charging headlong into the yellowed, piss-stained concrete. The whores gather their skirts, raising their blouses like nursemaids to show the toothless old men how round they still are despite the years and the diseases and all the dead or dying babies who rang their breasts like bells.

Saunders only has five bucks in his pocket. He prefers credit cards.

But he wouldn't be caught dead giving one of

these hags his platinum. Oh no. Not just because
of the frequent-flier miles, but because you just can't
trust a whore these days. Let's face it. No one can.
Even though it is the oldest profession. Saunders
thinks about this as he offers one wrinkled dairymaid
his crumpled fiver, Benjamin Franklin be damned,
and walks with her, groping her, behind the train
station, where there is a mattress on the ground that
smells like piss and beer.

"Stop reading," says Cage. "I can't hear any more. Please. Don't go on."

"Why not?" asks Thomas.

"Because it's completely offensive. And there's no real value in anything you have written here. Please. Put me out of my misery. Stop. It's horrible torture."

"That's your opinion," mutters Thomas peevishly.

"Yes," says Cage. "It is. I don't even want to go around the circle to hear your classmates try to make you feel better by complimenting your similes. This story is garbage. Pure and simple. I refuse to allow you to continue."

"It's not that bad," says Thomas.

"It is," says Cage. "It's worse. It could kill a person."

"I think my grammar and sentence structure are pretty good."

"My dear boy," says Cage. "Saying that your story isn't

214

bad because it has pretty good grammar and sentence structure is like saying that Auschwitz wasn't bad because it had pretty good plumbing."

"That's not fair," says Thomas. "You're comparing my short story to a concentration camp."

"It has the same effect. Listen. If you grew up in the city surrounded by whores, or if your mother were a whore, or if you had recently taken a trip to the city in search of a whore, well, now then maybe you would have something worth writing about. But this is just titillating chauvinistic garbage. It's not even worth revision."

"You're saying I should go into the city and find a whore?"

"Are you really this concrete? Listen carefully. I am not saying you should go into the city to find a whore. No. I am not saying that. I am saying that you have written something that does not come from your own experience, so there's no sense of reality. The whores. The city. The piss. It's completely beyond you, Thomas. You see what I mean?"

"He might have had experiences with credit cards," says one of our classmates either in an attempt to be helpful or to break the tension. "Or five-dollar bills. I bet he has handled plenty of five-dollar bills."

"That's true," says Thomas desperately. "I have a credit card. I have also handled five-dollar bills."

"Well, congratulations," says Cage. "There are two details in your story that come from somewhere real. The rest of it is complete bullshit. Listen. I get it. You're sixteen years old. Right? You haven't lived for very long. You are looking for something to write about that will feel exciting and edgy. Borrowing someone else's misery, because you don't think you've lived through anything important. But I promise you, if you look hard, you'll find that your own small miseries are more than enough."

Cage takes a battered red bandanna from his back pocket and mops his face. He is sweating profusely. He takes off his blue cable-knit sweater and airs himself, fanning his damp undershirt with the folders on his desk.

"I don't have any small miseries," says Thomas miserably.

"Bullshit," says Cage. "You've never heard your parents fight?"

Thomas shakes his head.

"You've never wanted to kiss someone so bad it hurts? You've never had some crazy old creative writing teacher pull apart your story in front of all your friends? Nothing?"

"Nothing," says Thomas.

"I just handed you one," says Cage. "The creative writing teacher. It's happening. Right now."

"Oh," says Thomas. "That's not so bad. That doesn't even bother me that much."

Cage looks like he is getting ready to slap Thomas, who is completely unaware that he is experiencing existential angst for the first time in his life.

"Okay," says Cage. "I give up. Get into pairs. Talk to each other. Brainstorm as many miserable moments as you can. Some of you are going to have to dig. You didn't get what you wanted for Christmas. Your dog peed on the rug. Your teacher made you cry because he said your story was bullshit. Something. I guarantee you, even our boy Thomas has some misery in there somewhere. Go on, find a partner. Share your misery. Get busy. I need to take a break."

Thomas A. Trowbridge the Fourth heads off to the bathroom. Cage reaches one hand into his pocket and pulls out a small bottle of aspirin. He shakes two into the palm of his hand, pops them into his mouth, and puts his head down on his desk.

"I think we killed him," I say to Fish.

"Thomas killed him," says Fish.

Fish is looking out the window.

The tumor kicks the back of my eyelid with his cleats.

What are you waiting for? Talk to her.

I put my hand in my pocket and wrap my fingers around the shard.

"You said I didn't know you very well."

Fish keeps looking out the window.

"Well, I was wondering if we can be partners so we can tell each other some things that happened, and maybe it will help me know you better."

"Maybe," says Fish. "But only if you don't run away like you did this morning."

She turns toward me. I can't stand the pain on her face.

"I promise I won't run away," I tell her.

"Even if what I have to say bothers you?"

"Especially then," I say, looking into her green eyes. "I promise."

Fish exhales. "Okay," she says. "Okay. Let's do it."

All around us, kids are breaking into pairs and telling each other about their angst: we moved when I was nine, my dog died, they all made fun of me, I didn't win the competition, I studied my brains out and only got a B, he broke up with me, she broke up with me, they got divorced, I broke my leg, my tooth fell out, I never saw her again, he died before I was born, there was a fire in the kitchen, we got into an accident, I never had the chance to apologize. A strange litany of sadnesses from all sides of the room. Whispered voices, confessing their scars. Even the kids who look happy. Even the kids who look normal. Even the kids who look healthy. Even the kids who speak easily and make friends easily and walk without any visible burden in their step. All of them laying out their disappointments like paper boats in a river, hoping the current will be strong enough to carry them away.

Fish and I move to an empty corner of the room. We sit

facing each other, our knees touching. "Are you ready?" I ask her.

She nods. Then she takes a deep breath and begins.

"My dad had an affair," she says.

I say, "My mom got cancer the first time when I was five."

"My mom had an affair."

"Then she had surgery."

"They fought all the time. Screaming. Broken dishes."

"She had chemotherapy."

"Then one night he left."

"All of her hair fell out."

"She totally fell apart. She started drinking. Stopped taking care of things. The house is a mess. Sometimes I do things just to piss her off. Like taking ten bucks from her purse or going out with The Monk or dying my hair pink. She used to love my hair."

I reach out and touch her hair. "She became so fragile."

She touches my fingers. "She became so broken. I used to worry she would get worse if I did the wrong thing. But I still did a lot of bad things. Things are so bad I don't even know how to talk about them. Are you going to run away now?"

I turn her hand over and touch her scar. I trace it with the tip of my finger, across her wrist and down the inside of her arm. I want to kiss her scar so badly my whole body is flushed with it.

"No," I say. "I'm not going to run away."

"Your turn," she whispers. "What happened after the chemo?" She reaches out and holds my other hand.

"She was in remission for ten years," I say. "We thought we had it licked. And then it came back."

"She died?" whispers Fish.

"Yeah," I say, looking into Fish's wide green eyes. "She died."

"I'm sorry."

"Me too," I mutter.

"You miss her," says Fish. It isn't a question.

"Yes," I whisper.

"I miss my mom too."

We look at each other for a long time. I think I can see my reflection in her eyes. The faintest gleam. All around us, students are still whispering their sadness, the long, feathered flock of disappointments rising into the air like prayers. Slowly, carefully, as though we might break if we touch each other too quickly or with too much force, Fish and I put our arms around each other. We begin to rock. We rock each other back and forth so gently it almost tears me open. I have never rocked another person before. Her body is fragile and tentative, but it is warm. I can feel her heart beating. She looks at me with her sore lip and before I can say anything, she puts her head on my shoulder and I put my head on her shoulder and we breathe and breathe.

GET THEE TO A NUNNERY

THE WINTER WEEKS PASS. FISH AND I EXCHANGE phone numbers, but I never have the guts to call her. We rehearse every day after school, even on Fridays when we are tired from the week and eager for the weekend, we get up onstage and do our best. In act 3, scene 1, Hamlet delivers the famous "To Be or Not to Be" speech. The Monk wanders to the very edge of the stage and stares at us with shining, wild eyes. He is suffering. You can see it in the way he holds himself, the way he paces back and forth like a caged animal. He is trying to decide whether it's better to be alive or not, whether it's more noble to suffer all the horrors and mishaps of living or to take matters into his own hands and end it all. What is death, he wonders, but a long sleep? But then he suggests that death is really not at all like sleep, because once our spirit has left our body, there can be no dreaming, there can be no more thinking. The end is simply the end, a face in the coffin, a stone. And so we trudge through life and we keep on living. We try as hard as we can to avoid the nothingness that waits for us in the grave.

I am sitting next to Ravi in the audience. His eyes are glued on The Monk. He leans forward with his chin in his hands and studies him. When The Monk is finished with his monologue, Ravi sighs and nods and looks around at all of us dramatically to make sure we are appreciating the brilliance onstage. No one meets his eyes but me.

Enter Fish stage left as Ophelia, Hamlet's onetime girl-friend, barefoot, lovely, luminous with her pink hair against the black stage, a stack of Hamlet's love letters tied in a red velvet ribbon. She tells him he can have the letters back. Here they are. Back in your hands, where they belong. Hamlet stares at her with wild, furious eyes. He says he has no idea what she's talking about, and he begins raging about her beauty and her honesty and then he lunges at her like he is going to hit her, but instead he pulls her to him and kisses her neck and when she throws back her head in ecstasy he screams, *Get thee to a nunnery* so she will never have to set eyes on a sinner like him ever again. He berates her. He teases her. He confuses her. He flirts with her.

I am amazed at how comfortable they are with each other's bodies. Both the tenderness and the violence. How easily they move from one to the other. I put my hand in my pocket and curl my fingers around the shard. I let the sharp edge cut into my palm. This pain feels better than watching them onstage together. I rub my fingers over the shard. I press it into my thumb.

The Monk grabs Fish by the waist, touches her hair, kisses her eyes, and pushes her away so hard she falls to the floor.

I stand up.

Ravi pulls me down.

"Hamlet," says Donna Pruitt. "Why are you being so cruel to Ophelia?"

"I'm angry," says The Monk, staring at Fish with eyes that have seen her in so many more ways than I have seen her.

"Why?" Donna Pruitt asks.

Fish and The Monk continue making eye contact.

"She hasn't been paying attention to me lately," says The Monk. "And I am addicted to her attention. So I'm furious. I am also really mad at my mom for moving on to someone new so soon after my father died. So I guess you could say I'm down on women right now. I hate the sight of them."

"Ha!" says Ravi, standing at his seat. "I think it's the opposite, Oedipus. It's unfortunate, believe me, but actually

223

you love women. You especially love your mommy and you're jealous that another man has finally won her heart. Poor Hammy. You thought maybe now that Daddy's gone it would be Junior's turn. So transparent. Baby wants booby again. Well, I have news for you. Mommy's boobies belong to someone new."

"That's gross," says the girl behind us, who plays Gertrude.

"Hey," says Ravi, turning around. "Don't talk to me about it. Talk to my man Sigmund Freud. Oh yeah. Hamlet loves his mommy. He's destroyed by guilt. Sexual frustration drives us all mad. Mad, I tell you. Mad."

Ravi sits down and throws his arms around me.

"Please don't hug me," I say.

"Sorry," says Ravi.

"Well, I want to say something Hamlet should know," says Fish, still staring across the stage at The Monk. "Even though he acts crazy sometimes. And even though we can't be together anymore, I'll always have feelings for him."

"You will?" says The Monk.

"Yes," says Fish. "Because I will always care about this brooding boy. And I will hug him and pet him and call him Hammy."

"Awww," says The Monk. "You called me Hammy. Now you don't have to go to a nunnery. Come here, Ophelia. Hamlet misses your big fishy kisses."

224

"Yay," says Fish, who skips into his arms. He dips her backward and kisses her cheek noisily and dramatically.

This bothers me. I stand up again.

Ravi pulls me down again. "Easy there, lover boy," he says.

Donna Pruitt claps her hands to stop the nonsense. "Enough," she says. "We need to get back to work. Quiet in the house." Then she stands between Hamlet and Ophelia. She takes their hands.

"Hamlet," she says. "Are you crazy in this scene or are you sane?"

"I don't know," says The Monk. "I think a little of both."

"Okay," she says. "Tell me about what you are trying to accomplish."

"I want Ophelia to think I'm crazy so she won't suspect that I'm planning on exposing my uncle Claudius for the murder of my father."

"Why don't you want her to know what's on your mind?"

"Well, I'm confused. I don't know if I'm ready to be brave and take action, so I figure it's better to keep her at arm's-length while I'm trying to make up my mind."

"Okay, now tell me about the madness."

"Well," says The Monk, "I'm grieving over the death of my father. I'm furious with my mother for marrying my uncle, Claudius. And then there's all the stuff the Ghost of my father told me."

"What did the Ghost tell you?"

"He told me he was murdered by my uncle and that he wants me to seek revenge."

"So the Ghost's words propel you forward in this scene," says Donna Pruitt.

"Yeah," says The Monk. "They're driving me. Pushing me to do things."

"Then the Ghost's words need to be the heartbeat behind everything. You need to feel them in everything you do. Like a rope, pulling you. Did you feel the Ghost just now when we ran the scene?"

"No," says The Monk. "I wasn't really thinking about him. I was thinking about Ophelia."

"Try again," says Donna Pruitt. "Make it real."

"Hey," calls The Monk, squinting into the audience. "Max. Get the hell up here. Help me feel the Ghost."

"I'm not in this scene," I say.

"It's okay," says Donna Pruitt. "Come on up. Let's see what happens."

I walk up the stairs and stand onstage with The Monk and Fish.

"Hi Max," says Fish.

"Hi," I say.

"What do you want him to do?" asks Fish.

"I don't know yet," says Donna Pruitt. "Let's play the

scene again. But this time I want the Ghost in there somehow. You all figure it out. And the rest of us will watch."

"Boo," I mutter to The Monk.

"Action," says Donna Pruitt. She peers at us with shining eyes.

We start the scene again. Now when Hamlet recites the "To Be or Not to Be" speech I am standing near the curtain watching him. My eyes are on him every moment. When he begins talking about whether death is different from sleep, I take a step forward, I reach toward him. He doesn't turn around, but I know he can feel me, especially as I move closer to him as he kneels on the stage to say his lines, and then pretty soon I am kneeling behind him. I wrap my arms around him. I rock him. He turns and speaks his lines to me, gazing up at my face, and then I kiss him on the forehead and I let him go.

Applause.

"Amazing," says Donna Pruitt. "But stop the applause. I want them to stay in this space. Keep the scene going."

Ophelia enters.

"Stay with Hamlet, Ghost. Now. Do it."

Fish comes onstage barefoot with the love letters. Her eyes are wild.

Hamlet moves from my embrace and goes to her, but we are still attached as though there is an umbilical cord

227

between us. When I pull, he leans back. When I push, he stumbles forward. He falls into her arms. He teases her. He rants about her beauty and her honesty, he pulls her toward him, but then I push my arms into thin air and he pushes his arms against Ophelia and she is suddenly thrown across the stage. And now she is lying crumpled, looking back at him, her eyes filled with hurt. *"O, help him, you sweet heavens . . . O heavenly powers, restore him!"*

I will, dear girl. I will.

He chastises her, creeping over to her, petting her hair for a moment, then kissing her neck, hard, as though he wants to hurt her. She tenses up and draws away. Then, feeling my fury behind him, he turns from Ophelia to gaze at me, terrified to see the ghost of his father, who has been with him this whole time.

We are a triangle, me and The Monk and Fish. I back up and Hamlet comes toward me. I walk backward off stage right, pulling my hands as though I have a rope that is tied to his neck. Hamlet stumbles forward and then trips as though shackled and then, finally, gives up and follows me, stumbling, his eyes blazing. Ophelia is left alone onstage, weeping.

"Brilliant," says Donna Pruitt. "From now on this is how I want it to be."

TRIANGLES AND OTHER
THREE-SIDED POLYGONS

AFTER REHEARSAL, WE ALL HEAD TO THE MONK'S dorm room to play truth or dare. February has cast its shroud over the frozen campus and we slap our arms and legs to keep our blood moving. The crows jeer at us from bare trees. We hurry down the path to the dorm and push our way into the building, windows fogged from the heat inside. We climb the stairs, throw open his door, and pile into his room like clowns in a clown car. Then we dump our coats in the corner and thaw ourselves. The Monk sits on his desk with Ravi at his feet. Me and Smitty and Griswald push off a swirl of towels and books so we can fit on the bed, and Fish curls up on the floor with a pillow. Thomas A. Trowbridge the Fourth watches us from his desk on the other side of the room. Everyone ignores him except Griswald, who nods to him and then looks away.

"I have a surprise for all of you," says Smitty.

"Ooh," says The Monk. "I love surprises. What did you bring?"

Smitty unzips his backpack. "Contraband," he says. He takes out a wrinkled paper bag.

"Did you bring drugs into this room?" says Thomas.

"Not drugs," says Smitty, winking. "Tea."

"What's so good about tea?" I ask.

"We're gonna *smoke* it," drawls Smitty.

"What does it do to you?" I ask.

"Absolutely nothing," says Smitty. "But it tastes yummy."

"Smoking is bad for you," says Thomas.

"Not when it's herbal," says Smitty. "This is Lemon Zinger."

"Putting any smoke into your lungs is bad for you, no matter what it is," says Thomas.

"I don't think anyone asked for your opinion," says The Monk.

"It's not my opinion. It's a fact."

"Well, no one asked for your facts then."

"Children," says Smitty. "Stop fighting." Smitty shakes a plastic Baggie out of the paper bag. Then he takes a pack of rolling papers from his pocket and tries to make cigarettes, but he's all thumbs. Lemon Zinger goes everywhere and nothing stays rolled up.

"You have no idea what you're doing, do you?" says The Monk.

"Shut up," says Smitty. "I'm doing my best."

Griswald is laughing so hard at Smitty that his Mohawk vibrates. He reaches across me, slaps Smitty's hand, swipes the plastic bag and the rolling papers, and begins making joints like a pro, folding the paper in half, sprinkling in the tea, licking the edge, and rolling it up. He is fast. He works with deft and nimble fingers. It takes him a while, but in the end he has seven of them. Griswald kisses his fingertips like a chef and smiles at us.

Smitty swipes the cigarettes back from Griswald. "Show-off," he says, and then he hands out cigarettes to each of us like they are dollar bills and he is our uncle. Smitty reaches in his pocket and takes out a lighter.

"Don't you dare light up in this room," says Thomas.

"Careful or you'll exhaust yourself with all this self-righteousness," snaps The Monk.

"You'll set off the fire alarm," continues Thomas. "And then we'll all get in trouble. This school happens to mean something to me. Okay? If you're going to smoke, do it somewhere else."

The Monk gets up from the desk and opens a window.

"Problem solved," he says.

Smitty lights our cigarettes.

"What am I supposed to do with it?" I ask him when he comes to me.

"Just suck in," says Smitty.

I do. It is revolting. The smoke burns my throat and my lungs. But Smitty loves his. "Mmm," says Smitty. "Lemony."

"You're a lunatic," says Fish.

"I'm a daredevil," says Smitty.

"That's why I love you," says The Monk.

Ravi and Thomas roll their eyes.

"Smitty," says Fish. "Truth or dare."

"Dare," says Smitty, taking another drag on his tea.

"I dare you to kiss Thomas's foot."

Smitty looks over at Thomas's bare feet and wriggles his eyebrows.

"I don't want him to kiss my foot," says Thomas. "That's totally unsanitary. This is a really bad game. Please don't involve me."

Smitty walks across the room to Thomas. Then he kneels down in front of Thomas like he is going to propose.

"Please don't," says Thomas, but before Thomas can jerk away, Smitty grabs Thomas's foot with two hands and gives it an enormous sloppy kiss.

Thomas screams and kicks Smitty in the face. "Don't

ever do that again," he says. "That was horrible. I'll probably never recover."

Smitty wipes his mouth and returns to the bed, grinning.

"My turn to ask," says Smitty. "Thomas. Truth or dare."

"I'm not playing," says Thomas.

"Oh, you're playing. Come on. It won't be as much fun without you."

"Well, okay," says Thomas.

"Truth or dare," repeats Smitty.

"Truth," says Thomas.

Smitty narrows his eyes. "Okay. Here's one. Did you snitch on The Monk?"

Thomas doesn't say anything.

"Did you tell Administration that he was driving after curfew?"

"Maybe I did. Maybe I didn't," says Thomas.

"No," says Smitty. "You have to tell the truth. You chose truth."

"Well, dare then," says Thomas.

"Kiss Ravi," says Smitty.

"I'm not going to do that," says Thomas.

"Okay, then truth."

"Tell the truth, Thomas," says The Monk. "For Christ's sake stop being such a pussy and tell the frigging truth."

Lemony smoke rises into the room.

Thomas looks from one of us to another, trapped.

"I don't have to do this," he says finally. "I'm leaving. Have fun burning out your lungs. I hope you all get cancer and die."

He is not aware of the irony.

Thomas puts on his socks and shoes, gathers up his books, and marches out of the room. He slams the door behind him.

We all stub out our tea except The Monk, who keeps on smoking.

"Exit stage left," says The Monk.

"I think you guys were mean to him," I say.

"Give me a break, Friedman," snaps The Monk. "He's lucky I don't make his life a living hell."

"Maybe you do," I say.

The Monk takes a long drag of his tea and blows smoke into the room. Ravi, still sitting on the floor in front of the desk, leans his head against The Monk's leg and The Monk lets him do it, patting him absently like a dog, but then he realizes what he is doing and he stiffens and shifts so that they are no longer touching. Ravi reaches for his leg again but The Monk shoves him with his foot.

"Dude," he says. "You're freaking me out."

"Sorry," says Ravi.

"Ravi," says Fish. "Truth or dare."

"I don't think so, small Fish," says Ravi, frowning. "Not today."

"Please?" says Fish.

"No," says Ravi. "I'm not in the mood."

He leans his head back against the desk.

The game becomes more twisted over the next several turns. The Monk makes Griswald take off his pants and stick his bare butt out the window. Fish makes Smitty give her a huge, red hickey on her neck. Smitty makes Fish go into the closet, take off all her clothes, and cluck like a chicken. Fish makes The Monk grab his balls. The Monk makes me rub Smitty's belly as though he were a Buddha. Then it's my turn.

"Fish," I say. "Truth or dare."

"Truth," says Fish.

I take a deep breath. "Are you and The Monk a couple?"

Everyone freezes. Even the tumor.

Ravi closes his eyes.

"Are we a couple?" Fish asks The Monk.

The Monk doesn't answer.

Fish turns back to me. "It's complicated," she says.

"Yes or no," I say.

"It's not really a yes-or-no answer."

"Yes or no," I say.

Fish takes a deep breath. "Yes," she says. "I guess the quick answer is yes."

"Okay." I nod and I keep on nodding like some kind of deranged bobblehead. Inside, my body feels cold and I have to hold myself still so that I won't shatter right there in front of all of them. Fish watches me, wide-eyed. Then she puts her shoulders back and holds herself taller.

"David," says Fish, "truth or dare."

"Dare," says The Monk, taking one last drag of his tea before throwing it out the window. "And make it good. I'm in the mood for a big one."

"You want a big one?" asks Fish.

"Yeah," says The Monk. "Challenge me."

"And you'll do it? You promise?"

"Anything for you," says The Monk.

Fish stands up. "Come over here," she says.

The Monk grins and saunters over to her. Ravi puts his head in his hands. Fish gets up on her tiptoes and The Monk bends down and they kiss, tenderly at first, and then more roughly. I want to leave the room. I want to get out of here and wipe the image from my mind, but I promised I wouldn't ever run away again. When the kiss is over, Fish looks up into his eyes.

"Are you ready for the dare?"

The Monk pushes a stray lock of her hair back behind her ear.

"Yes," says The Monk.

Fish takes a deep breath.

"Okay," she says. "Here's your dare. I want you to end things with me."

"What?" says The Monk.

"I want you to look into my eyes and say, *Felicia, I think we should start seeing other people.* And then I want you to kiss me on the forehead and set me free."

"I don't want to do that," says The Monk.

"You said you would do anything I wanted."

"You want this?" asks The Monk incredulously.

"Yes," says Fish.

The Monk takes a breath and then lets it out. He looks down into her face. "Felicia," he says, "I think we should start seeing other people."

He kisses her on the forehead for a very long time.

He closes his eyes and stoops down to rest his cheek on the top of her head.

And then he lets her go.

BIRDS TO THE SLAUGHTER

OUTSIDE THE KITCHEN WINDOW, THE SNOW SWIRLS, illuminated beneath the streetlights. It scatters from the snowdrifts like mist rising through the night. I sit at the window and watch the slow cars. Their headlights shine beams of snow. No matter how old I am, I always feel excited about a snowstorm. There's something in the air that changes, something you can taste in the back of your throat, an orange glow in the sky, and even though I'm snug and warm inside the kitchen, I can still feel the pillowed hush of snow outdoors each time I breathe.

When I was in elementary school, I used to pray for a snow day. All night long I would wake every few hours and run to the window to check the streetlight to see if its beam still illuminated falling snow. Then I'd check the roof outside my window to guess how many inches had fallen. If, by midnight, the snow had already made a white hood, like the back of a large white turtle, chances were pretty good that there would be no school and I could spend the next day doing all the things I loved: sledding, making snow dragons, snow forts, and best of all, eating Mom's gourmet maple-drizzled snow cones.

Grandma rises from the kitchen table and stands behind me. She puts both of her hands on my shoulders and watches out the window with me. Then, absently, she begins petting my hair with her warm, smooth hands the way she used to do when I was little. I lean my head back into her hands and close my eyes.

There is a click.

"I got it!" says Dad putting his camera back on the table. "That was a good one. The light was perfect. Oh, you two are going to just love that."

"You took a picture of me loving him," says Grandma, smiling.

"I never like myself in pictures," I say, looking back out the window. "I'm so skinny. I look diseased."

"You don't look diseased," says Dad. "You just aren't used to seeing yourself. At that angle, with Grandma's face so close to yours, you both looked like Mom. Can you see your reflections in the window? Look at that. With the snow coming down. It's amazing."

He's right. Both Grandma and I look like Mom. It is something in our eyes and foreheads, something in the set of our jaws. We are her future and her past without the present. Our reflections are missing the middle. Mom's ghost looking back at us, through our own eyes.

Grandma puts her cheek next to my cheek. "Baby boy," she says.

"I should take more pictures of the two of you," Dad says. "I used to photograph Anna all the time. Do you remember? She never posed for pictures. Not like people these days with their selfies. She was always completely natural."

"She was beautiful," says Grandma still looking at our reflections.

"I wish I had taken more photos of her," says Dad.

As if on cue, all three of us turn to look at Dad's family photographs on the kitchen walls. Framed memories taken through the years. Dad and Mom standing on the top of a mountain, kissing. Mom in a bathing suit, nine months pregnant with me, her hands on her round, planetary belly, eyes closed, smiling. Me at age five, back to the camera, holding Mom's hand, looking out at the old Phillip's rock quarry. It must have been shortly after her first diagnosis, because there is a sadness in the shadows, a heaviness in her shoulders, the darkening sunset in the distance, resonant even in black-and-white.

Someone is knocking on the front door.

We all come back to the world. Pulled out of our various sadnesses.

Another knock.

"You want to get that?" asks Dad.

"Okay," I say.

Maybe it's Fish.

I go into the front hallway and open the door.

Lydie stands outside our door with a big copper soup pot. The twins are at her side, shivering.

"Hey, Max," says Lydie. "I made some organic chicken soup. Can we come in?"

"Of course," I say. "Come on in. You guys look like you're freezing."

"It's Gloria," says Luna.

"You cooked Gloria?"

"Yes," says Luna. "She's in the soup."

"Well, okay then," I say.

"She tastes like chicken because she *is* chicken," says Luna.

"Hey, Dad," I call. "Lydie and Luna and Soleil and Gloria are here!"

"Gloria?" calls my dad.

"In the pot!" I call back. "Chicken soup."

Dad and Grandma come into the hallway to greet them. Dad hugs Lydie and helps the twins with their wet things, unwrapping scarves, peeling off hats and gloves, placing boots by the side of the door. Grandma takes the soup from Lydie and walks it with one hand on each handle back into the kitchen.

"There goes Gloria," says Lydie.

"Bye-bye, Gloria," says Luna.

Soleil clucks and pecks and scratches. Then she runs around in circles like someone has cut off her head.

"This is such a surprise," says Dad. He tickles Soleil at her next pass, drapes Lydie's coat chivalrously over his arm, and brings it to the closet.

"We just made the soup and there's way too much for the three of us," says Lydie. "The storm's not supposed to get really bad until later, so we thought we'd drop by and bring you dinner while the roads are still okay. I hope you don't mind the visit."

"I don't mind at all," says Dad. "We love your company anytime. Don't we, Max?"

"Yup," I say. "Did you kill the chicken yourself?"

"You want me to lie or do you want to know the bloody truth?" Lydie asks, rubbing her hands together.

She is a calm-looking woman. It's hard to imagine her with a meat cleaver chopping off a chicken's head. But her hands are hard and calloused and her fingernails are short and ragged. She has muscles in her arms from all that yoga. And there is something hard about her, something about how she always walks on the balls of her feet with her shoulders back that makes me think there is more to her than meets the eye. Soleil is bumping into walls and flapping.

"You did it yourself, didn't you?"

Lydie nods. "I did all three of them, actually," she says. "It's hard keeping chickens in the winter. I made pot pies out of Gertrude and Camille. But Gloria was always my favorite so she needed to be soup. Don't look so shocked, Max. I grew up on a farm. Chickens are easy if you know how."

"Hey," I say. "No complaints here."

"Or here," says Dad, backing away. "But let's not get on her bad side just in case."

Lydie laughs and pushes my dad just a little. He pretends to fall over. "Ow," he says, rubbing his arm.

"Oh stop it," she says. "Let's have soup."

In the kitchen, Grandma has already put out bowls and spoons. She has the soup pot on the stove and the room smells wonderful: salty, yellow, and warm, the scent of onions and pepper rising to the ceiling. Grandma is sitting at her place at the table.

"How are you doing, Jean?" asks Lydie. "I haven't seen you in a while."

"It's snowing," says Grandma. "And it's nighttime."

"Yes," says Lydie. "Isn't it beautiful? There's nothing in this world that's better on a cold, snowy night than chicken soup."

Grandma doesn't say anything.

Dad spoons soup into everyone's bowls. We sit together around the table. Me and Grandma. Dad and Lydie. Luna and Soleil. Gloria in our bowls. The tumor is quiet and I am strangely at peace. We drink soup. The snow falls outside the windows. Dad pours wine for himself and Lydie and they clink glasses and take sips and everyone watches the snow come down.

After dinner, Dad turns on some music and pours more wine. He picks up his camera and starts taking pictures of everyone. He gets Lydie gazing out the window at the snow, and Grandma drinking tea and Luna twirling like a ballerina and Soleil jumping up and down and shrieking, and then he gets me with both girls in my lap and all of us laughing like crazy. Then he starts taking pictures of Lydie and the girls. He gets Lydie standing against the wall with her face in profile. She takes her long gray hair out of its braid. She twirls in circles. Click. Click. Click.

"Beautiful," says Dad. "Just beautiful. You are going to love these."

"I'm going to bed," says Grandma.

Everyone says good night to her, but she either doesn't hear us or doesn't want to respond because she keeps her eyes forward and just walks out of the room and then up the stairs. We can hear her footsteps over our heads crossing the hallway and then the door of her room closing.

"This is pretty special," says Lydie, holding her wineglass in one hand, "getting photographed by a real, professional photographer."

"Well," says Dad. "I wish I had more work these days."

The music swirls through the kitchen.

Lydie grabs the girls' hands and dances with them.

Dad is gazing at them and taking pictures from one angle and another, and Lydie and the twins are having so much fun that the kitchen is alive with the sound of their laughter. Soleil screeches and whirls around. Lydie is about to scold her but I am so happy tonight, I tell her it's okay, and I laugh when Soleil grabs Luna's hands and twirls her around the room. The two girls are beautiful, dancing together, like two yellow butterflies. They twirl and float right out the kitchen door and through the hallway into the living room where they lean back and spin in faster and faster circles. I follow, smiling at the way their hair cascades behind them like sunbeams and I stand in the doorway, watching them and wondering how two human beings can be so free.

They are so wonderful and so beautiful to watch, I want to show Dad and Lydie. I want them to see how the snow comes down outside the tall windows behind them, and

245

Luna and Soleil are dancing around the living room like sugarplum fairies, and even though I'm not the kind of guy who usually goes in for things like sugarplum fairies, I run back through the hallway and into the kitchen to get them the way a little boy might if he wanted his parents to see something wonderful. I don't think about it. I just do it. My mouth is already open, about to say, *Dad. Lydie. Come into the living room, Luna and Soleil are dancing like sugarplum fairies and I've never seen anything so beautiful in my life.*

But the words never make it out of my mouth because when I get back into the kitchen Dad and Lydie are kissing, their hands in each other's hair.

Oh baby, says the tumor.

The blue woman screeches her fury into my pocket.

I stumble out of the room, away from the kitchen, away from my father and this woman who is not my mother, kissing, breathing into each other.

On my way out I trip over a chair.

They jump apart.

"Max," says Dad.

"Oh my God," says Lydie.

I stumble backward into the hallway.

Luna and Soleil are still dancing in the living room.

"Max!" Dad follows me, his face red, his eyes filled with shame.

I grab his plaid jacket, which is hanging on the hook, while the tumor pounds his fists against my eyelids, while he rattles the bars and kicks the walls and the tiny blue woman on the blue shard in my pocket shrieks in her fury. I get the hell out of there.

I slam the door and disappear into the night like a drunk man, blind with fury, blind with the snow that swirls in chaotic, unbelievable circles until everything I can see before me and behind me is swallowed in the audacious irony of pure and untouched white.

PERCHANCE TO DREAM

IF I WERE DR. WHO, I WOULD STAGGER INTO THE NIGHT, eyes wild, hair outrageously unkempt (devilishly handsome, of course), and there, waiting outside my front door would be my trusty TARDIS in the form of a British telephone box, waiting to zoom me into some other dimension.

All my attractive friends would be inside, waiting for me.

They would put their arms around me and pat me ceremoniously on the back. Someone would say something glib and clever (we are British after all), then we would grin at one another, and off we would go into the post-BBC universe made of Styrofoam and cheap computer graphics, the Weeping Angels close on our heels.

Cue Moog synthesizer.

But this is not *Dr. Who*. This is my life.

So when I stagger outside into the snowy winter night and lurch down the street like a madman, there is no TAR-DIS.

I slip and slide down the street, using my flailing arms to balance myself, farther and farther away from that house that suddenly seems unfamiliar: where Dad has kissed a woman who is not my mother.

We have enjoyed soup made from the corpse of a feminist yoga hen named Gloria, who was beheaded on a chopping block and then drained into a metal bowl.

Lydie killed the chicken with her own hands. It's easy to do a chicken.

I imagine my footsteps in the white new snow filling with blood.

I run behind the houses and through the aqueduct where the snow cloaks the branches of trees, weighing them down so they look like beggars on some ancient road.

I'm suddenly thinking about Hamlet's question: *to be, or not to be.* I'm not so sure *whether 'tis nobler in the mind to suffer the slings and arrows of outrageous fortune* or *to die, to sleep . . . perchance to dream.*

For the first time in my life, I'm thinking that maybe it is *not* nobler.

Not nobler at *all.*

To suffer.

Because slings and arrows hurt like hell.

And so does cancer.

And so do lonely fathers and organic widows who smile at you and then go make you chicken soup out of corpses.

And so do four-year-old girls who could almost be your sisters if you let yourself love them.

And so does Gregor Samsa, looking into the mirror one morning and realizing his life has been meaningless the whole time.

So maybe Hamlet *is* right.

Maybe it would be nobler to just end it all.

To die, to sleep—no more.

The snow comes down like ash falling in the spaces between the trees. I wonder how long it would take to freeze to death out here. If I just sat here all night and didn't move, if I took off my shoes and my socks and my coat and lay down in the snow, how long would it take for my heart to stop?

I wonder if the tumor would die before me.

Would there be a moment when I would be finally free of him?

All I would need is a second or two, where I could take a deep breath without him. Or maybe he would linger after I was gone, waiting on tenterhooks, as he must have done when Mom took her last breath, for the next rube to come along and take pity on him, some unsuspecting dog walker, maybe, or a jogger out in the morning, passing by my frozen face, eyes wide open. The tumor will leap from my brain into the jogger's ear and burrow his way into a new pink host.

Not to be.

That is the answer.

One hundred percent. Not. To. Be.

I take off my coat.

I take off my shoes and socks.

I lie down on the icy ground and let the snow fall on my face.

I will myself to die.

This is not an easy thing to do.

There is no coffin above me.

Snow is cold.

It hurts my skin.

I squint my eyes and move my face to the side and curl my toes and clench my fists and try to stop my heart, but it is too cold to concentrate, even in a fetal position, even with my hands over my face, even breathing into my cupped palms.

I realize, with a kind of grim disappointment, that I am not capable of suicide.

Cursing, I bolt upright, pull on my socks and my shoes and my coat and scramble to my feet and blow on my fingers and rub my arms and stomp around from one foot to the other. I plunge my hands deep into my pants pockets. In my left pocket, I can feel my cell phone. I text Fish and she doesn't answer. Then I put my hand back in my pants pocket and I feel the shard and my wallet and remember the business card Cage gave me at the Panda Wok. The one with his number. I pull it out of my wallet and start to dial.

I am so cold my fingers almost do not work.

"Max!" screams Cage. "Max! Oh Max. Oh, you wonderful foolish person. I didn't think you would do it. Bravery abounds. What's going on?"

"Not much," I say looking up at the sky.

"Hey. You don't sound so good. Are you okay?"

"Not really. I was kind of wondering. You said I could call you anytime and we could meet. Is this a good time?"

"Is this a good time?" Cage shouts into the telephone as though he were ninety years old or drunk or both. "Are you kidding? This is a *perfect* time! Where are you? What's wrong?"

"Well," I say, "I'm in the aqueduct and it's snowing, and I'm kinda thinking about *whether 'tis nobler in the mind to suffer the slings and arrows of outrageous fortune* or if it is better to just *sleep: perchance to dream. There's the rub* at the current moment. As long as you were asking."

"Wow," says Cage. "That's deep stuff, Hamlet. So I gather from this line of thinking that you are experiencing a bit of existential angst, am I right?"

"Yeah," I say. "I guess you could say that."

"You know what's good for existential angst?"

"No," I say. "What?"

"Steamed dumplings."

"Really?"

"Yeah. Clinically proven. And spareribs are pretty good too. Also chicken wings, but not quite as good."

"I don't have any of those things with me," I say, shivering.

"Well, of course you don't, you silly depressed person. Chinese food doesn't just grow on trees. What do you think I am, some kind of ignoramus? You need to get your sorry self out of the aqueduct and down here to Panda Wok pronto. And you need to share a pupu platter with yours truly and you need to look at this gorgeous waitress named Maia who is talking with me right now, and you need to chat with your shit-faced advisor about literature and all things magnificent and then I promise you will be a happy camper once again. Depression gone. At least for the night. Money-back guarantee. Do you trust me?"

"Yes," I whisper. "I trust you."

"Foolish yet fabulous!"

"You'll wait for me?" I ask him.

"Will I wait for you? Max! My boy! My apprentice! My soul mate! It's only eight o'clock. I usually close this place. They know me here. This business would fall apart without me sitting like a manatee on this very stool ordering tropical beverages night after glorious night. You think you're depressed? You ain't seen nothing yet. So come find me, my

253

confused little dude. I'll be the fat mammal at the bar with the big fruity drink."

"Okay," I say. "I'll be there in about ten minutes."

"If you're not, I'm coming out there to find you. No funny business before you get here, understand? No hanging yourself from a tree or jumping off a cliff before I get some good Chinese medicine inside you. Is it a deal?"

"It's a deal," I say, feeling myself smile. "See you in ten minutes."

"I will count the seconds," says Cage. "One one hundred. Two one hundred. Three one hund—" And then he hangs up.

I plunge my freezing hands into my jacket pockets and trudge out of the aqueduct and into the center of town. Every once in a while, a truck drives by, windshield wipers going, as the snowflakes are falling down, and my heart quickens because I think it's going to be Dad coming to take me home, *Come save me from myself, Dad. Tonight I need to be saved,* but it is never him so I keep on walking. I pass the library and the ice cream parlor, and then I pass the Episcopal church, the boutique clothing shop, the bank and the juice bar, and then finally there is Panda Wok, all lit up, windows fogged from the cold, smelling heavenly, and inside there is a fat mammal at the bar with a fruity drink in his hand waiting to give me fried food and bad advice that may not change the world, but will make me feel better for long enough to make it through the night.

SCORPION BOWL

THE ELDERLY WOMAN AT THE COUNTER GREETS ME very enthusiastically, and gives me a choice of where to sit among the leagues of empty tables, scattered families picking absently and unenthusiastically at their food. In the back of the room, there is a well-dressed family, fully coiffed, manicured, way too fine for this shabby establishment, chatting to one another in low voices, much too refined for the way I'm feeling tonight. I need to be as far away from them as possible.

My phone buzzes in my pocket. It's Dad. I hit decline.

My eyes are drawn to the bar where two guys with swollen bellies are drinking, watching basketball, and shamelessly flirting with the pretty waitress. Cage is wearing an undershirt and suspenders. He has a big, fruity drink in his hand. The waitress wears a white silk top with two buttons open in the front. Every time she bends down to get something, which she does frequently, the men pretend not to look down her shirt. They clink their drinks and sing the national anthem. There is nothing like a low-cut shirt to make a guy feel patriotic.

"I'll sit at the bar," I say.

"How old are you?" asks the elderly woman.

"I'm twenty-two," I lie.

She frowns at me and looks as though she is about to ask for identification, but Cage gestures to me with his drink.

"Hey," he says, "I can vouch for this gentleman. Come over and join me, Mr. Friedman. Tell me all about graduate school. This first round is on me."

The old woman shrugs, obviously not convinced, but nonetheless leads me to the bar to sit with Cage and the bald guy. "It's a slow night," she says.

The waitress smiles at me from behind the bar.

I slide in next to Cage.

"What'll you have?" he asks.

"I've always wanted to try a scorpion bowl," I tell him.

He pounds me on the back and laughs. "Nice try, kid. No can do. Besides, guys usually share those drinks with a woman. Where's your woman, Friedman?"

"If I had a woman, do you think I'd be here with you?" I ask him.

"Touché. Still quick on his feet after all these years," says Cage, loud enough so the old woman behind the counter can hear. "That MFA has really sharpened your sense of humor. It was a good career choice. Led to all those published novels and the tenure-track position and whatnot. But I could tell you had talent when you were in my class. The stories you used to write impressed me. And if you remember, I am not easily impressed. I'll tell you what. I'll order you a virgin piña colada and me a scorpion bowl. If you're a good boy I'll let you have one sip. We can pretend I'm a woman. Maybe you'll write about it in your next bestseller."

"You're a writer?" the waitress asks me.

"One of the best," says Cage, thumping me on the back. "And he was my student, so I am taking credit. See me take credit? Yes. That's me. Taking credit. Can we order this man a virgin colada? He just won his first Pulitzer. This calls for a celebration. He's in the big time now."

"One virgin colada and one scorpion bowl coming right up," says the waitress. We sit and watch the game in silence.

"So?" says Cage finally. "What's with all the despair tonight?"

"Something bad happened."

"What?" says Cage.

"Well," I say taking a deep breath, "I caught my dad kissing Ms. Grossman."

Cage slams the counter with the palm of his hand.

"Lucky bastard," he says. But then when he sees me frowning, he changes his tune. "What I mean to say is, are you sure it was a real kiss? People greet each other with platonic kisses all the time and it means nothing at all. Sometimes they just grab each other. Look. I'll demonstrate."

Cage grabs the guy sitting next to him and kisses him roughly on the cheek.

"Was it that kind of thing?"

"Hey," says the guy, pushing him away. "Cut it out, asshole."

"No. It wasn't anything like that," I tell Cage. "It was romantic. Like they couldn't stop themselves."

"I know that kind of kiss," says Cage, sighing.

"Please don't demonstrate on me," says the guy next to Cage.

"No problem," says Cage. "To be honest, you smell like socks. A kiss on the cheek is all you're getting tonight, honey."

"Good," says the bald guy. He takes another swig of beer and turns back to the game.

The waitress comes with my piña colada and Cage's scorpion bowl.

She bends down to find two paper umbrellas, two cherries on plastic swords, and two straws. I have a perfect view down her shirt. I don't even pretend not to look.

Cage pokes me in the ribs. "Icarus!" he whispers sharply. "Don't fly too close to the sun. You'll burn your wings."

"Sorry," I whisper back.

"I'm only kidding," mutters Cage. "You don't know me very well. But next time don't make it so obvious."

"So," says the waitress, rising, "you want some food tonight, or just the drinks?"

"Want to share a pupu platter?" I ask Cage. "My treat." I pull a twenty out of my dad's jacket pocket.

"Is that from the Pulitzer?" he asks.

"Yeah," I say sarcastically. "This year they paid in cash."

"Weird," says Cage. "The first time I won the Pulitzer they gave me a lifetime supply of piña coladas. The second time they gave me a heart condition and quadruple-bypass surgery. Times have changed, Mr. Friedman. Be glad you're coming of age now and not in the days when old farts like me and this guy were young."

He pounds the other man on the back. They toast each other and drink.

"You're a real asshole, you know that?" says the bald guy.

"Yeah," says Cage. "I know."

"So do you want a pupu platter, or don't you?" says the waitress.

"Oh, we want it," says Cage. "We want it like a hole in the head. And we want a hole in the head, in case you were wondering."

"One pupu platter coming up."

"And make sure it's pretty," says Cage. "I only like them when they're pretty."

"They're always pretty at Panda Wok," says the waitress.

"Yes they are," says Cage, winking.

She sighs and walks away again.

Cage watches her go.

While he isn't looking, I take a sip of the scorpion bowl. It tastes like trouble.

I put my hands around the virgin colada and stir the straw in circles.

Cage leans toward me.

"You want to hear a secret?" he says.

"Yeah," I say.

"I tried to kiss Ms. Grossman at a faculty party a few years back."

"No way," I say.

"Way," says Cage.

"What happened?"

"She slapped me across the face. And then she stormed out. And then she filed sexual harassment charges."

"Dissed," I say.

"Dissed," agrees Cage. "Big-time. Of course she was married then. And the twins were just babies. And the husband had just been diagnosed with stage-four colon cancer. So maybe it wasn't the best timing. I don't know. Or maybe I'm just not handsome enough for her. Is your dad a good-looking dude?"

"My mom thought so," I say.

"Ah," says Cage respectfully. "Well, that's all that matters."

One of the players makes a crazy half-court shot. Fans on the television go wild. The bald guy sitting next to Cage stands up and cheers in a broken voice. He toasts the television with his beer and takes a long sip, and then wipes his face with the back of his arm. Cage and I drink too.

My phone buzzes. It's my dad again. I hit decline.

"So when are you going home?" asks Cage.

"I don't know," I say.

"He's probably worried sick about you."

"Probably," I say. "But he should've thought about that before he went and kissed Lydie Grossman. He should've thought about how that was going to affect me."

"Well yeah," says Cage. "Clearly he should've thought about it beforehand. No question. He *should've* thought it

261

through. Looked at all the angles. It's just that sometimes in this life you gotta do things without thinking through every single detail, you know? You've gotta do what your *body* tells you to do. If your body says breathe deep, you gotta *breathe deep*. If your body says cry like a baby, you gotta cry like a baby. Maybe tonight your dad's body was telling him to kiss the heck out of Lydie Grossman. And for that one moment what his body was saying to him was more important than your feelings."

"Thanks a lot," I say.

"You are most welcome," says Cage. "Carpe diem." And he clinks his scorpion bowl against my piña colada.

I spear the cherry with the plastic sword. Then I plunge it into my mouth and eat it.

"Yes!" says Cage, pounding my back. "That's it, Max. Eat the cherry when you still have time! *Gather ye rosebuds while ye may!*"

"I'm only getting, like, half of your references," I tell him.

"Pity," says Cage. "I'm even funnier when you get me. And now, if you will excuse me, I need to see a man about a horse. That means I need to take a piss, in case you didn't get my reference."

"Thanks for translating," I tell him.

Cage heaves himself out of his chair, salutes me, and then wanders off toward the men's room.

I pick up his scorpion bowl and take another sip. The drink is strong and sweet and it makes my insides warm.

"You like?" asks the bald man.

"I like," I say.

The waitress comes through the kitchen with our pupu platter and I put my hands around the virgin colada like a good boy. There is a blue flame underneath the platter and a wonderful array of greasy fried things. Cage comes back from the bathroom looking chuffed. He hands me an egg roll, takes a chicken wing for himself, and bites in. Now there are flecks of chicken in his beard, and his fingers are glazed. He wipes his lips on the back of his arm.

When he sees the disgust on my face, Cage laughs and motions for me to move closer to him so he can whisper.

"You know the best thing about being a writer?" he asks rancidly.

"The money?"

"Ha-ha," says Cage. "No."

"The women?"

"I wish," says Cage. "No. Not that either."

"What then?"

Cage bites into a sparerib. Then he lifts up his scorpion bowl, takes a tremendous gulp, and belches. "The best thing about being a writer is that no one expects you to act like other people. It's like a big old get-out-of-jail-free card."

"Reasons to publish," I say. "Act like an asshole and no one cares."

"You got it," says Cage, pounding me on the back. "Look how much you've learned in a few short minutes. An hour ago you were thinking of ending it all. Now you have discovered the meaning of life. Egg rolls and being an asshole. And they said I would make a lousy advisor. Look at me. I'm gonna get Teacher of the Year."

"To Teacher of the Year," I say.

We clink glasses. I drink my virgin colada and he drinks his scorpion bowl. Then our team lays down a monster dunk and Cage and the bald guy rise to their feet to cheer and hug each other and say things that guys say when they care about who wins. While he's carrying on, I lean over to the scorpion bowl and I drink and drink until my head and the stratosphere are spinning and the lights are gleaming much more brightly than they ought to be. The tumor loves basketball. He is bouncing off the walls of my brain like an inebriated jock. My tumor is infinitely more masculine than I am. If he could, he would call me a fairy and beat the living shit out of me. I shake my head vigorously just to bother him. Then I close and open my eyes.

"So," says Cage, sitting down and staring at me. "When are you gonna tell me what's been going on in that crazy noggin of yours?"

I blink at him.

"I've got an idea," says Cage in a whisper. "You want to take a sip of my scorpion bowl? Maybe it will give you some courage."

"Okay," I whisper conspiratorially.

I grab the scorpion bowl and take another sip.

"Hey," says Cage. "Easy there, sailor. Now tell me. What's going on in there?" He knocks on my head.

My phone buzzes.

"Hang on a second," I say.

It's a text from Fish.

Fishface1: Im so glad u texted. RU okay?

Maximus: Im having a very strange night.

Fishface1: Me too. Sorry I didnt answer before. Was talking things over with The Monk. Should we come get u?

Maximus: Is he mad at me?

Fishface1: A little. But hell get over it. Heading to rock quarry. Should I tell The Monk to come get u? I want to see u.

Maximus: I want to see u too.

Fishface1: Where r u?

Maximus: Panda Wok. With Cage. Drinking scorpion bowl.

Fishface1: Why please?

Maximus: Long story.

Fishface1: U can tell me about it when I see u.

Maximus: Come soon.

Fishface1: Thats what she said.

"Was that your dad?" asks Cage.

"No," I say, still flushed from her words. "It was Fish. My friends are coming to pick me up."

"Well, you better hurry up and tell me the truth then," says Cage.

My phone buzzes again.

It's a text from my dad.

I don't even read it. I turn my phone off and put it in my pocket.

"These are the most messages I've ever gotten in my entire life," I tell Cage.

"You should run away more often."

"That is excellent advice," I say. "Quick, give me more."

"Eat more crab Rangoon."

"Is this your plan for my eventual happiness?" I ask him.

"Part of it," says Cage.

"What's the rest?"

"Find a girl and kiss her the way you saw your father kiss Lydie," says Cage.

"I like this plan," I say.

We drink to that.

"And then go see a psychotherapist. You could use a good shrink."

"You should have stopped while you were ahead," I tell him.

By nine thirty, between Cage's trips to the bathroom, I have almost but not quite finished the scorpion bowl and the piña colada. Cage stirs the ice and licks his straw. "Aw jeez," says Cage, "can't believe I'm done already." I shrug and put my chin in my hands. The game is over, the well-coiffed family has gone home, the bald man is slumped over and snoring with his head on the bar, and Cage has his arm around me. He is giving me all the intimate details of his quadruple-bypass surgery. He lifts up his shirt and shows me his scar. He wants me to touch it, but I decline because he is my teacher and it's creepy. The waitress has turned off the television and has started sponging off the bar. The old woman at the counter is counting dollar bills. She calls to the waitress in Chinese.

"We close in half an hour," says the waitress.

"He'll have another scorpion bowl," I say, reaching in my dad's pocket for another twenty.

"I think it's time to call it quits," says the waitress.

I rest my head on my hand and watch her. "Did I tell you I just won the Pulitzer?"

"Yeah," she says. "And I said I believed you. Guess that makes both of us liars."

"Want to go out with me sometime?" I ask her.

"Nah," she says. "You're too old for me."

I dig around in the pupu platter for something I haven't chewed on yet. There are heaps of chicken bones and denuded spareribs, and crumbled bits of egg rolls. I select a chicken bone and gnaw on it like a dog.

"Keep chewing," says Cage, hugging me even closer so that the world smells like scorpion bowls and armpits. "Suck the marrow out. Suck it dry. And then when you're done, raise your face to the sky and howl. *Moloch! Moloch!*"

"Is that another reference, or have you totally lost it?"

"I have totally lost it. *And* it's a reference. Who said it?"

"No idea."

"Come on," says Cage. "Who said it? Who said it? You call yourself a Baldwin man? You need to know these things."

The bell above the door rings.

A breath of cold air.

"Who said, *Moloch! Moloch! Nightmare of Moloch! Moloch the loveless! Mental Moloch! Moloch the heavy judger of men?*"

"Ginsberg," says The Monk in a low voice, all six and a half feet of him suddenly blocking the entrance. Something about the way he is looking at me makes me uneasy.

He strides over to us in his Doc Martens, hands in the pockets of his black leather jacket. "Allen Ginsberg," he says. "From 'Howl.' I love that poem. I was totally born in the wrong era."

"That means I was born in the right one," says Cage. "Marched so hard my ticker gave out. Want to see my bypass scar?"

"While that is very tempting, we really need to be going," says The Monk.

Cage looks disappointed. "It's smooth," he says, "silky. You'd think it would be knotted and hard. But it isn't. They broke me open and left a part of me silky and nice. Me. The least silky person in the world."

I reach toward him. "I want to see it again," I say.

The Monk grabs my wrist and then yanks me onto my feet. "Come with me," he says.

The room tilts. My head is spinning. It could be the tumor. It could be the scorpion bowl. It could be the tumor is sitting at a table drinking the scorpion bowl with a bendy straw made of neurons.

"All writers need to break the rules at least once," says Cage. "Push the boundaries. Stick it to The Man. Go get 'em, tiger."

"Sage advice," says The Monk. "From a teacher who just spent his Friday night getting shit-faced with his underage student."

"That does sound bad," says Cage, "but I only gave him

one sip. Listen. You're not gonna tell anyone about this, are you?"

"Why?" says The Monk. "You think it will tarnish your angelic reputation?"

"That's funny," says Cage. "But also kind of ironic coming from you."

The Monk glares at him and then heads out of the restaurant and into the storm.

I pound my chest, kiss my fist, and point at Cage. Then I trip over my own foot.

"Don't forget to kiss the girl," says Cage sadly.

The bald man next to him raises his face for a moment and then sinks back down like a sleeping dormouse in a pot of tea.

TARDIS

I LURCH OUT OF PANDA WOK, EYES WILD, HAIR outrageously unkempt (devilishly handsome, of course), the world spinning with snow coming down falling against the streetlights, the tumor swearing like a sailor, and there, waiting on the street, is my trusty TARDIS in the form of a rusty orange Microbus, waiting to zoom me into some other dimension. All my attractive friends are inside. Ravi is in the middle seat, sitting next to Fish. I climb in and slide next to him and he punches me in the arm.

"Hey," says Ravi, "look who the cat dragged in."

I punch him in the shoulder. He punches me in the gut. I slap him across the face. He slaps me harder. It hurts but I don't care. The Monk swings into his seat, slams the door to the driver's side, and off we go, Smitty sitting shotgun with the Dead Kennedys screaming from his phone, Griswald in the way back, bobbing his head to the music, The Monk at the wheel dark and silent, his eyes on the road, windshield wipers going, and my face stinging from Ravi's blessed handprint. Cue Moog synthesizer.

I reach over Ravi and take Fish's hand. She is wearing a white winter coat with a hood lined with fur. She is also wearing huge white mittens so I slide my hand into her mitten and touch her fingers. Her hand is small and warm and the feeling of her skin floods me with something that has nothing to do with the scorpion bowl.

"Excuse me," says Ravi, "I am here, between the two of you, in case you haven't noticed."

"Switch with me," I tell Ravi.

"No," he says.

Fish has one long lock of pink hair falling down over her eyes. I reach over Ravi with my other hand and gently push the lock behind her ear inside her hood. Then I touch her cheek with the back of my hand.

"You can stop this now," says Ravi.

"Switch with me," I say again.

"No," says Ravi. "I don't want you to be happy."

"Shut up back there, will you?" says The Monk. "You're all making me sick."

The Monk floors it out of town and onto the highway. Soon, he turns down the narrow dirt road. We are going to the quarry. The wheels of Lady J. rumble over the uneven surface. Pine trees line either side. Smitty turns around from the front seat and winks at me. Then he cranks up the music. Now Rage Against the Machine shakes the walls of the bus, pulsing around us. Behind me, Griswald begins thrashing his head, his Mohawk bobbing in time with the bass guitar.

Then, The Monk slams on the brakes and Lady J. jerks to a halt. "Hurry, we don't have much time," he says.

Smitty turns off the music. We all tumble out, a barrel of monkeys. The snow is even deeper than the last time we were here, and it's falling harder now, lashing our cheeks. We have to lift our legs high to make our way, our boots making deep prints in the white tundra. The Monk strides toward the ice-covered footpath, barely visible in the dark. We make our way from the rim of the quarry, between the jutting rocks, and down toward the frozen water.

Fish reaches back for my hand and I take it. I slide my hand into her mitten and I look for the scar with my fingertips, but I can't find it. Her skin is on fire. She reaches for my other hand. Now I am pressed against her from behind, wrapping my arms around her belly, holding both her hands inside her mittens. We walk forward, slowly, slowly, with our bodies pressed together, one step at a time. Every movement is heaven. She stumbles and I pull her closer.

"Way to go, Skywalker," says Smitty.

"If he falls, he is going to crush you," says Ravi, from behind. "You will slip from the edge and you both will plummet to your deaths."

"Sounds good," says Fish. "Especially if he lands on top of me."

"Or if *you* land on top of *me*," I say, hugging her from behind. I pull her against me and she stumbles deliciously.

"You two are disgusting," says Ravi. "Get a room." And then he scoots by us to walk with The Monk, his red fro a halo around his head even in the dark.

I wish Fish would take her hood off so I could touch her hair. Maybe it's the scorpion bowl, but I am feeling so good, suddenly I can barely stand myself. The tumor is too dizzy to notice. Maybe it has fallen asleep like the bald man at the bar, its head drooping, its tendrils wrapped around itself, snoring for a blessed moment, taking a break from metastasizing for just a blessed quiet heartbeat, while I stumble down the path. Glory glory glory, say my footsteps.

"Careful," says Fish. "I don't want you to fall."

"I have already fallen," I whisper.

Behind us, Griswald snickers. The snicker grows into a barking laugh and then a howl so loud the sound of it echoes from one wall of the quarry to the other, a strange, crowing, howling, startling sound that fills the night with something both wonderful and unsettling.

The swimming hole is completely blanketed in white. So are the cliffs surrounding it, each rock hooded, monochromatic, the sky, the ground, the swimming hole, the snow coming down like a veil over the face of a frozen world.

Griswald is the first one onto the ice. He rushes past The Monk and Ravi, pushing them out of the way, screeching like a banshee, and then sliding on his knees across the snow-powdered ice until his momentum dies and he flops onto his back and begins making snow angels. The Monk packs hard little snowballs and starts pelting them full force, his eyes wild like he's out for blood. One snowball hits Ravi in the head. Now it's an all-out war, snowballs flying like expletives hurled through the air. Griswald sneaks up behind Smitty and puts snow down his back. Ravi throws a snowball at The Monk's crotch. The Monk screams and then charges after Ravi like some kind of crazed bull.

I look at Fish. "They're gonna kill each other," I say.

A snowball flies through the air and hits me on the shoulder.

"Hey," I say, "want to get out of here?"

"Yeah," says Fish. "Let's take a walk."

I loosen my grip on her waist and she twirls away from me, moving from my side. Then I pull her back to me and we slide together past the group, the feathery snow making deep powdery tracks as we wander away from the snowball fight and out onto the snow-covered expanse, our footsteps inviting us farther and farther away from the others until it feels like we are alone, the white sky above us, the white snow all around, and the two of us, tiny, electric, holding hands.

She takes my other hand, and all at once we are spinning, leaning back, whipping each other around and around. Everything is a blur except for her face. Her hood falls back and even in the dark I can see her pink hair tumble down, cascading, the scorpion bowl blushing through me, pulling me closer to her because I am going to kiss this girl and it will be my first kiss. We stop swirling and now we are just facing each other, holding each other's arms. Looking at each other's faces.

"Hi," she says.

"Hi," I say.

She takes her mittens off and touches my face with her fingers.

"You are so beautiful," she says.

"No," I say. "I'm not."

"You are," says Fish. "Every single part of you."

"I'm skinny," I tell her. "I look like a Holocaust survivor."

"You are perfect," says Fish.

I hold her hands.

"You're perfect too," I say.

We start to slow dance.

I lean my cheek on her head.

She looks up at me, her lips parting just a little. She closes her eyes. Her breath is warm against my cheek. I lean forward and close my eyes, and then, just as I lean in to kiss her, just as I bow my face, and tilt my head perfectly, and gather her body in my hungry arms, we are completely and rudely interrupted by the war cry of four hooting thespians, arms outstretched, dive-bombing us with snowballs, all of them laughing like crazy except The Monk, whose eyes are dark and whose snowballs hit their mark every single time.

The tumor is pissing on the walls and scratching his armpits. A white-hot wire behind my eyes. *Fight*, he says. *Fight fight fight.*

I grab handfuls of snow and roll it into a ball. "You are going down, Moniker. Say goodbye to this world."

The world spins.

"I'm scared," says The Monk.

I rush at The Monk with my snowball, screeching.

I hit him right in the face.

He staggers back, grabs more snow, packs it into a ball, hurls it at me.

Then Fish is at my side and we are an army of two, hurling snowballs at The Monk blindly as the rest of them come closer, and before I know it we are enveloped, snowballs bombarding the air from every direction, thwacking into my back, my face, my side, my ear, and I am stumbling,

stumbling with my head down like a bull, and so is The Monk, and we are heading toward each other at top speed, scorpion bowl and tumor cheering at the sidelines, thespians screeching our names, the world tilting and tilting and then I try to take a glorious side step like a toreador leaping out of the way, but the bull swerves, barreling into me anyway, knocking my feet out from under me so that I stagger and fall forward into the ice, the scorpion bowl and the tumor chanting, *Max Max Max,* and then there is the sound of my forehead hitting the ice and then there is the cold and then there is nothing.

CONCUSSION WITH EXTRA CHEESE

THE GOOD NEWS ABOUT HITTING YOUR HEAD IS THAT it proves, once and for all, that the walrus likes pizza. Don't ask me why. There are no clear answers for some things.

Bud ump bump.

His favorite bill of fare is pepperoni with extra cheese, but he tolerates sausage and hamburger with an occasional helping of ham and bacon for good measure.

And then, of course, there are the anchovies.

I like that word. *Anch. O. Vees.*

They remind him of his home at the North Pole or wherever walruses go to live their blubbery lives: Chicago. Topeka. Winnipeg. Scranton. Blustery places. With icebergs.

So he looks at me, and he has a slice of meat pizza in his hand. Meat pizza. Meatza.

I like that.

I will say it again. Meatza-meatza.

Like a little troll. Saying meatza.

Which is adorable.

This pleases me because I am rarely adorable, but suddenly I seem capable of thinking adorable thoughts, a step in the right direction by any standard, Mr. Walrus, sir. So eat your meatza and stop complaining.

Walruses, as you may well know, are not vegetarians.

Hence the tusks.

He carries me back up the path to the top of the iceberg, arfing to me the way they do, with their walrusy voices.

Arf. Arf. Max. Arf.

I have always been good with languages, which is why I suddenly understand his walrusing, and I know I am supposed to say whether or not I am okay.

Are you okay, Max? Are you okay? Talk to us.

Which strikes me as

funny.

Sorry. I fell asleep for a minute.

I keep on falling asleep.

Because it's so comfy mumfy here in your arms, Mr. Walrus. I will suckle at your teat.

Oh man.

No one with flippers has ever carried me so gently before.

O walrus dear.

I like the blinding whiteness of your tusks.

Colgate is a good toothpaste, case in point your smile, Mr. Walrus.

He says *ARF* and shines a flashlight in my eyes.

Jesus. Cut it out.

Oh shit, says one of his walrusy minions. *One pupil is bigger than the other one.*

Which pleases me although the walruses are obviously unhappy about it.

You know why it pleases me?

Because asymmetry is infinitely more interesting than its opposite. That's why. Mr. Tumor thinks so too. Hence the one bulging eye. Stick that in a pipe and

and

Then I am in the bus and we are driving fast and everyone is arfing and touching me with their flippers, which is lovely because no one usually touches me and today I have been touched. A lot. By walruses. And a fat man. And a girl with pink hair. The walrus and his friends are looking into my eyes. They are trying to keep me from falling asleep. *Stay with us, Max. Stay with us.*

Which is hard to do because I am so comfy mumfy, dear Mr. Walrus, inside your carpeted belly, all curled up like a bumblebee.

Buzz. Buzzzzz, I say when I finally fall asleep with all the little *zzz*s rising up out of my breath like snores.

No. Wake up. WAKE UP. Someone slap him on the cheeks or something, will you? Keep him from falling asleep.

Jeesh. Lighten up. Live a little. Carpe diem, man. Eat the cherry.

Max? Can you hear me?

So comfy. And I don't even have earbuds to suck.

Comfy. Like a sippy cup. Squishy and good.

The walrus drives down the road and I am curled up in his belly. I am aware that he is driving very fast.

Let me sleep.

Just.

Yeah. Just

      let me

WALRUS

Oh my God. I've been looking for him all night
long. Oh my God, what happened to him?
I'm so sorry, Mr. Friedman. He fell.
He hit his head on the ice. He had been
drinking. He's acting so strange. I brought him
back as soon as I could.
Mr. Friedman. Do you think one of his pupils is
bigger than the other. This one? Do you think
it's bigger? Do you think it's bigger?

>Oh my God, Joe. Look at him.
>Max. Max. Can you hear me?

———————————

Mr. Friedman, is one of his pupils bigger than the other?
It looks like one of his pupils looks bigger than the other.

Stop it. Stop saying that.

I think we need to get him to an emergency room.

Dial 911. Please, Lydie.

Beep. Boop. Boop.

Oh my God. We have an emergency. My friend's son.
He hit his head on the ice. Please come right away. It's 62
Assabet Lane. Please hurry.

I'm sorry. This is my fault.

Please take care of him.

We will.

This is my fault.

Please take care of him.

A kiss on your cheek. Soft.

Lifted.
Strapped.
Doors slamming.
Lights.

Do you hear me? Hang on. Please.

Sirens.

Hang on there, buddy. We're almost there.

Once upon a ghost the world rushed through your ears
and you could feel buildings and cars and schools and
streetlights trickle in one side and then out the other like
spinal fluid, like sap like pus like old men singing in the
streets.

His name?

    Max Friedman.

Age?

    Sixteen.

And you are his father?

    Yes. Yes. Joe Friedman. His father.

What happened, Mr. Friedman?

    I guess he had been drinking. He went out on the ice.
He fell and hit his head. Max. Max. Why aren't you
answering? Why isn't he answering?

    That's what we're trying to find out. Any medications?

No.

Any changes in his behavior until now?

No, not really.

And how much did you say he had to drink tonight?

I don't know. A lot, I think. I wasn't there. If I had been there, this never would have happened. This is my fault.

Try to calm down, sir. And he fell and hit his head, is that right?

Yeah. Pretty hard. Right on the forehead. That's what they told me.

Max? Can you talk to me? Can you tell us what's happening to you?

Why isn't he answering?

How many fingers am I holding up?

Why isn't he answering? Could you look at his eyes, please? Please look at his eyes for a minute. His friend was worried that one of his pupils is bigger than the other. Scared me half to death. Do you think that's true? Take a look at his eyes.

       Hmmm.

       Take a look. This one. Does it seem bigger than that one?

       Might indicate some sort of brain trauma

       Brain trauma

       Brain trauma

       Brain trauma

It could indicate some sort of brain trauma or it could just be an optical illusion. Hard to say what's happening, between the alcohol and the fall. Could be some bleeding in there, or some swelling maybe. His blood alcohol level is .25. That's high. But still, it's hard to say. We're going to need to check it out. Okay? Run a few tests. Quick. Non-invasive. Just hang tight, Mr. Friedman. I know this is scary but we're doing everything we can. They'll be down to get him soon. We'll figure this out.

This is called a CT scan. It should tell us what is going on in there.

Just lie back, Max. This machine is going to take pictures of your br. This machine is going to take pictures of your br your br. This machine is going to take pictures of your b b b

just lie back and let

It's still too early to tell. The doctor needs to see the scan. But he'll speak to you as soon as he is available, okay? Blood pressure looks good. Oxygen and heart rate look good. Alcohol level going down. He's on the IV getting nice and hydrated. I'd say he's on the mend. We'll know better when he sobers up. Max, how are you feeling? Want a drink of water or something? Still too soon to tell, Mr. Friedman. But try not to worry. The doctor will come by as soon as she can, to talk with you. For now, try to get some sleep.

You hear sounds and see things. Nurses back and forth outside the curtain. An old woman talking about what hurts. A little girl crying and they are trying to calm her down, shhhh shhhh, it's okay, Katie, just look at the bubbles, just look at all those pretty bubbles, that's a brave girl, we're almost done now, televisions on in different cubicles. You hear these things, and you know you should say something to show them you can hear them, but something in you is too hazy, something in you is too chicken-soup hazy, all swirly and steamy, so instead of answering them you just look at the ceiling until it is hard to keep your eyes open and you drift drift you drift you drift you drift to sleep.

EARLY-MORNING SINGING SONG

*One morning, as Gregor Samsa was waking up from
anxious dreams, he discovered that in bed he had
been changed into a monstrous vermin.*

THE SKY OUTSIDE THE WINDOW IS STILL DARK.

My dad is sleeping in a chair, a jacket thrown over him
like a blanket.

"I'm thirsty," I whisper. My voice sounds strange.

"Oh thank God," says my dad, waking up immediately.

He gets up from the chair, brings me a cup of water in a
pink-and-brown Dixie cup.

He holds the cup against my lips. I take a sip. His hand
is shaking.

My head feels like it's being squeezed in a vise.

"I don't feel so good," I say.

"Just lean back," says my dad. "You've been through a lot. The doctor says it's going to take a while for things to go back to normal."

"Where am I?" I ask him.

"We're in the hospital, Max."

"Hospital?"

"We've been here since last night. Do you remember any of it? The tests? The doctors? You had a lot of people worried about you."

"I don't know," I say. "I think I remember a little."

"What's the last thing you remember?"

I stare at him and try. It starts to come back, like a veil lifting slowly. Dad kissing Lydie. Sneaking sips of Cage's scorpion bowl. Sitting in Lady J. Putting my hand into Fish's mitten. Feeling her fingers. Walking down the path to the quarry with Fish leaning against me. Then spinning and spinning and being just about to kiss her. And snowballs and screaming and running on the ice, my hand around a snowball and The Monk heading toward me like a bull with his head down—and nothing else.

"Did I fall on the ice?" I ask.

"You did," says my dad. "Your friends brought you home and you were in pretty awful shape. And then that boy Ravi started going on and on about one of your pupils being bigger than the other one and it completely freaked us out. We were so scared, Max."

"I'm sorry,"

"Don't be sorry," he says. "I'm the one who's sorry."

"You kissed Lydie."

"Yes," says Dad. "I am so sorry you saw that."

He looks at me like he wants to tell me something, but instead he looks out the window at the winter sunrise.

"It's cold," I say.

He finds an extra blanket in the tiny white closet. He brings it over and tucks it around me. I can't remember the last time he tucked me in. He pats the blanket in place and pulls it up to my chin.

"Is that better?"

I can't answer him. Tears come all at once.

Dad sits on the edge of my bed. When the tears come harder, he curls up beside me on the pillow and holds me.

"There's something I haven't told you," I say to him.

"What is it?"

I take a deep breath. "I have brain cancer."

"Shhh," says Dad. "You don't have brain cancer."

"I'm dying."

"You're not dying," says Dad. "You're going to be fine."

"I want to be buried next to Mom."

"Stop talking that way," says Dad.

I turn my face to the wall.

Sometimes I am asleep. Sometimes I am awake. Sometimes I am both.

The sky begins to lighten.

Dad stays with me. He turns on the television with a remote control and flips through the channels with the sound turned off. Images flit by: each moment a different shot, a different angle, a different take, the surrealistic broadcasting of very early morning. Cut. Cut. Cut. News program. Infomercial. Talk show. Celebrity interview. TV evangelist. A bald head and a red face. Arms moving. Fire and brimstone. Glory hallelujah. We don't need to hear him to know what he is saying. The lord giveth and the lord taketh away. He looks directly at the screen and shouts at us, silently. My dad turns the television off and looks out the window at the dawn breaking like he did our first morning without her.

LAUGHTER AND TEARS

IT TOOK ALL DAY AND ALL NIGHT. THE DYING. THE
throes of it, as my father remarked later in a rare moment of poetry, reminded him so much of her labor with
me that at times he was tempted to say things like *Any
time now*, and *Almost there*, or to breathe with her, *hoo hoo
haa haa*, as though the end could possibly produce something precious that would live with us after she was gone.
So strange, he told me, that Lamaze teaches the husband
to take part in the birth process: to sit behind the woman,
rub her back, and remind her to breathe and push, but
there is no Lamaze for death. No matter how hard we tried
to help her, this was something my mother was going to do
all on her own.

The plan was that we would be around her bedside the entire time, being strong, holding her hands, telling her how much we loved her, how proud of her we were, how much we would miss her, how it was okay for her to leave us whenever she was ready to go. We wanted to make sure she would feel our presence around her the entire time. We didn't take into account our need to take breaks. How Dad and I, since we were the ones not dying, would need to occasionally stretch our legs, go to the bathroom, have a drink of water, take a walk outside in the sun for a moment, look up at the sky and breathe. Nor did we take into account that one of us or both of us might fall asleep during the night and that Mom, in her infinite wisdom, would choose this time, the very moment when we were not paying attention to her, when we were not holding her hand or speaking softly to her, to leave us for good.

I don't know what time it was. No clocks stopped ticking to mark her passing. No watch hands mysteriously froze. She wanted to hold on to us as long as we were awake. As long as we were touching her, talking to her, focusing on her, needing her, she couldn't allow herself to go. I moved from her bed to the chair after three in the morning. I wanted to rest my eyes for just a minute.

"Don't worry," said my father. "I'll wake you up if anything changes."

He was kneeling by her bed, his forehead on her hand,

watching the uneven scarcity of her breath. One and then nothing. Another and then nothing.

At some point I fell asleep.

At some point my father fell asleep too, his head still resting against her hand.

And then, at some point, when both of us were asleep, she let go.

I imagine that she had clarity for a few seconds, maybe in darkness, maybe just before the sun came up, when the world was orange and gray, maybe she opened her eyes and saw us in the room, me in the chair, Dad by the bed, both sleeping because our bodies needed to sleep and she knew that it was time for her to sleep too. So she turned her face toward the window and before she had the chance to pray or call out to us, or even to breathe one last time, it was over just like that.

When I opened my eyes, dawn was breaking.

Dad was standing by the window looking out.

The room was quiet.

I didn't have to look at her to know what had happened.

The silence was heartbreaking.

And then I looked, because some curiosity in me made me look, and I was shocked at how my mother had already changed. How her eyes and her cheeks had sunken in, her face white and still.

A sound came out of me. An animal sound. Like howling.

"She didn't want us to cry," my father said, his back still to me.

I couldn't help it. I fell across her body and wept.

My face brushed against one cold hand.

"Hey," said my father, stronger this time.

He picked me up and held me.

He wiped my tears.

"Stop," he said again, more firmly, into my hair. "She didn't want us to cry."

He held me hard and we breathed in and out, our breath wanting to moan but not moaning, wanting to screech but not screeching, wanting to cry but forbidding ourselves to cry. Just holding each other still. Stopping each other from breaking. Our heads on each other's shoulders, and my mother behind us on the bed, eyes wide open, but seeing nothing.

SLINGS AND ARROWS OF OUTRAGEOUS FORTUNE

AT EIGHT THIRTY, THE ATTENDING DOCTOR COMES IN to talk with us. Dad pulls himself out of the chair to shake her hand. He looks ragged. His face is gray.

"How's he doing?" asks the doctor.

"Better," says my dad. "He woke up a few hours ago and asked for water and a blanket. He's not quite himself yet, still kind of shaky, but he's a heck of a lot better than he was last night."

"That's great news," says the doctor. "Hi Max. I'm Dr. Keene. We met in the emergency room last night, but you probably don't remember. How do you feel?"

"Okay," I say.

"Any dizziness?"

"A little," I say. "When I sit up."

"Headache?"

"Yeah," I say, and now I am sobbing again.

"He's scared," my dad explains.

Shoulders shaking, I stare at the ceiling and the tears roll down the sides of my face. Dad comes back to my bed and pulls me toward him.

"His mother died of cancer," he tells the doctor. "He's worried he has it too."

"What kind of cancer was it?" the doctor asks.

"Sorry?" Dad asks. He has been looking at my face and has become lost and overwhelmed by my tears.

"Your wife," says the doctor. "What kind of cancer was it that she died from?"

"Oh," says Dad. "They told me it was HER2. Does that sound right? It started out as breast cancer. She was in remission for ten years, and when it came back it was in her brain. There were only nine months between her second diagnosis and her death. It was horrible. But she wanted us to be strong. So we were."

Everything is silent except my sobbing.

Dad sits next to me on the bed and puts his arm around me.

"You don't have cancer," says the doctor.

My heart stops beating.

"How do you know?" I whisper.

"Well, for one, HER2 is not a genetic form of cancer. You

can't inherit it. If your mom had this form, even though it was devastating for her, there is really no way on earth that she has passed it on to you. Not now. Not ever. Do you hear me? Max. Stop crying. Listen. This is not a trait that can be inherited. You are not going to get this from her. You might have her eyes or her temper or her hair color, but you are not going to get her cancer."

Dad wipes my eyes. "Are you hearing her?" he asks.

"You don't have cancer," repeats Dr. Keene. "You do, however, have a concussion. And a hangover. You may also have some depression and anxiety because of what happened to your mom. But I can tell you with great confidence— and I would not say this to a patient unless I was sure about it—that you do not have brain cancer. You. Do. Not. Have. Brain Cancer."

"But what if I got it some other way?" I ask. "I can still feel something pushing against my eye. Right here. Do you think there might be some kind of tumor in there?"

"No," says the doctor. "There is nothing pushing against your eye."

"Are you sure?"

"I am completely sure. I had a chance to take a careful look at the CT scan. If there was a tumor big enough to push against your eye, I would have seen it. You're a lucky guy, Max Friedman. You knocked yourself pretty hard right on your frontal lobe. But besides confirming that there are

299

no tumors in there, the scan shows there is no internal bleeding. No swelling around the frontal lobe or any other parts of the brain. No fracture of the cranium. You, my extremely lucky friend, are going to be okay."

"Thank God," says Dad.

Dr. Keene opens up her iPad. She types quickly, swipes a few times, and then looks at me with a sly smile. "Ever look inside your brain?" she asks.

I hesitate. "No," I say. Although this is a metaphorical lie because of how much cranium gazing I have been doing lately.

"Well, I want to show you what a healthy brain looks like. Come closer, Mr. Friedman, if you want to take a look at the scan too. So here we are. This space here is your sinus cavity. Your temporal lobe is here. That's the part that retains memory. And back down here are your medulla oblongata and cerebellum. Can you see that?"

Dad and I lean forward. We gaze at my brain.

"It looks like a butterfly," says my Dad.

"Yes," says Dr. Keene. "It kind of does with the lobes spreading out on either side. But mostly what it looks like to me is a perfectly healthy brain with no tumors, no swelling, and no bleeding. This is the brain of someone who is going to be okay."

"That is wonderful news," says my dad.

Dr. Keene closes her iPad. "You may have some symptoms

over the next few days. Headaches, dizziness, nausea, irritability, maybe even sleepiness, confusion, trouble concentrating. All of these things are normal after a moderate concussion. But they will subside if you take care of yourself. Rest. No school until you're feeling better. No television. No computers. No reading. No heavy concentration." She looks at my father. "Schedule an appointment with his pediatrician to make sure things are moving in the right direction. And if the pain increases or his mental state deteriorates, make sure to bring him in right away.

"And one more thing," says Dr. Keene. "Be careful with alcohol. Your blood alcohol level was .25 last night. That is extremely high. Especially for a thin guy like yourself. Do you drink frequently?"

"No," I say. "This was my first time."

"They all say that," she says, winking at my dad. "Anyway, besides the fact that you are underage, which makes it illegal, you had about two hundred times more alcohol than someone of your weight should ever consume. It could have been very dangerous for you."

"Okay," I say.

"We're printing out the discharge papers now, and they have specific information you need about caring for a concussion. You're going home, my friend. What do you think about that?"

"I don't know," I say.

For some reason that I can't understand, I feel unspeakably sad.

"Well, I think it's wonderful," says Dad. "Thank you, Dr. Keene. Thank you so much."

The doctor shakes my dad's hand again. Then she shakes my hand, puts her hand on my shoulder, and leaves.

The nurse comes in to disconnect my IV and help me out of bed.

She gives my dad the discharge papers, goes over the details, and tells him that whenever we are ready we can be on our way.

I look out the window so my dad doesn't have to see me crying again.

He finds my plastic bag of clothes and starts laying them out for me. T-shirt. Sweatshirt. Skinny jeans. Red Converse All Stars. He comes up behind me and places both his hands on my shoulders.

For a moment or two, I lean back against him and we look out the window at the world below us: the cars, the snow, the heavy sky, the hurrying mortals on the sidewalks who are not even thinking about their mothers and fathers and grandparents and great-grandparents who have been gone all these years, all these generations. They hunch into their winter coats, trying to keep themselves warm despite their losses. They keep trudging on, their hearts still beating inside their chests, their blood still coursing through their veins, their eyes straight ahead, never looking back at the empty footsteps they have made in the snow.

"Come on, Max," says my dad. "Let's get out of here."

LONG ROAD HOME

LYDIE PULLS HER CAR UP TO THE HOSPITAL ENTRANCE
so we don't have to walk through the snow. We move slowly,
through the revolving glass door, Dad's arm around me. It
feels strange to have this sudden gust of winter on my face
after so many hours in the sealed climate of the hospital. I
hunch my shoulders against the cold.

Lydie rushes out to hug us with tears in her eyes.

"I was so worried," she says.

"Thanks," I say.

"Lydie and the twins spent the night at home with
Grandma," says Dad.

"Oh Max," says Lydie, putting her arm around me. "I'm
so sorry about what happened. About what you saw. I am
just so sorry. I don't even know what to say."

"It's okay," I tell her. "You don't need to say anything."

"I want you to know, that was the first time," says Lydie.

"Please," I say. "I don't need to talk about this."

"Maybe later," says Dad.

"Okay," says Lydie. "Later when things calm down. If you want. Or not at all. What's important is you're okay. Hey. You know what? It's so cold today. Let's not stand out here and freeze. I want to get you home to your grandma, where you belong. The girls are in the car. We stopped by Whole Foods on our way and I'm going to make us all some organic carrot-ginger soup. And then I'll take the twins home. We've all had a long night."

We get in the car, my dad and Lydie in the front and me in the back with the twins. They throw their arms around me and bury their faces in my sides. Lydie pulls away from the curb and I watch through the rear window as the hospital's red letters and white brick dissolve behind us like a bad dream. We head down the street toward the center of town, where normal people are doing what they always do on a snowy day: a store owner is shoveling his walk, a scruffy guy is clearing off his car. I watch them go about their business while my dad tells Lydie about all the things that happened to us in the hospital, some that I remember and some that I don't.

I look out the window at the world going by and I feel like a speck, like a comma on a page, so tiny and voiceless,

I could almost disappear and the world would go on, a never-ending sentence without pause.

Lydie pulls up outside our house.

She slings a cloth bag of vegetables over her shoulder, comes to the back, and opens the car door for me and the twins.

They walk me up the snowy path to the porch, my dad and Luna on one side and Lydie and Soleil on the other. Dad hands his keys to Lydie and she lets us in. The door opens and we are warm before we even step inside. I am enveloped by the familiarity of this intimate space, filled with our breath and our sweat and the cells of our skin. But at the same time, this feeling of complete familiarity makes me want to cry.

Grandma comes to the door.

"Max," she says. "I was so scared."

"I was scared too," I tell her.

We sit at the kitchen table and watch Lydie make us soup.

We don't say anything. We are too exhausted. The twins pull their chairs close and lean against me on both sides, two small, blond heads. I put my arms around their limp, warm bodies. Lydie doesn't seem to mind the silence. She's busy cooking for us: Carrots. Coconut milk. Ginger. Pepper. She finds our blender in the cabinet under the sink and sets it on puree. For a full minute, our kitchen is filled with whirring blades, and that horrible sound like bones grinding. Then she finds a saucepan. She lights the burner on the stove and puts up the soup. Lydie stirs and bustles around our kitchen, finding spoons and soup bowls, tidying up the counter and table while we watch, silently, too overwhelmed to speak or move. The soup warms. She adds butter and more ginger. Soon the kitchen smells orange and spicy. She pours soup into our bowls and joins us at the table.

"Drink up," she says. "It's good for you. Here's a fun fact. Most people know that carrots are good for eyesight, but did you know that carrots are also an amazing natural brain food? It's true. Perfect for concussions."

"Huh," says my dad. "That's good to know."

He takes a sip and his entire body melts.

"It's wonderful," he says, sighing.

Grandma takes a sip. Then she looks up and smiles at Lydie.

I take a sip in spite of myself. It is heavenly. I pick up the bowl with both hands and drink and drink until I am warm and orange on the inside, and I can't help but close my eyes so I can taste it better, the way all things taste better with your eyes closed, buttery and thick going down.

Dad raises the bowl to his lips and drinks until his bowl is empty.

"Thanks," he says when he is finished, and I know that he is thanking Lydie for more than the soup.

"You're welcome," says Lydie. She washes the dishes and puts them in the drainer to dry. Then she comes back to the table and kisses me on the head. I don't stiffen or move away. I let her do it. I don't know why. Her lips are warm from the soup.

"Get some rest," she says.

We nod, too exhausted to say anything. Dad starts to get up from his chair to walk her to the door, but Lydie pushes him down gently. "Don't," she says. "I'll let us out. I'll call you tonight to see how you're doing, okay? Take it easy. And take care of each other."

She takes Luna by one hand and Soleil by the other.

"Take care of each other," says Luna.

Lydie kisses Luna on the top of her head, smiles at us, and walks with the twins over to the front door. The door closes behind her, a soft, careful thump, much too soft to be final. Soon, I can hear the engine turn over, the sound of her car pulling off down the road.

PAPER CRANES

THE FIRST HOURS GO BY QUIET AS A CLOUD. DAD falls asleep on the couch. Grandma covers him with a quilt. He holds it to his cheek and curls toward the wall. Then she sits down in the armchair and falls asleep too. The discharge sheet says I'm supposed to rest my brain. No reading. No screens. I break the rules once, texting Fish that I'm home and okay, and then I wander through the house like a ghost, passing through one room after another, picking things up, holding them, and then putting them back. I do not feel tethered to the world. I have seen the inside of my brain and it is empty.

Do you miss me? whispers the tumor, his voice still sarcastic but more distant now, an echo of smoke and shadows. I squeeze my eyes shut and try to block out his voice. *I was the only thing left of her. Now that I'm gone you have noth-ing.* And then a wisp of laughter. The last note, the tail end of it, rises and curls into the air so that it sounds like a sob, broken, plaintive, and desperate.

I wander into my dad's bedroom. An empty bed with one pillow. A photograph of Mom on the dresser. I start open-ing drawers. Here are Dad's white socks, rolled into tight balls. Here is a drawer filled with black T-shirts from vari-ous epic heavy metal rock concerts. Then I open one more drawer. Inside, there is a jewelry box. I lift the lid with trem-bling fingers. I find things Mom used to wear, a turquoise pendant, a charm bracelet. And then I see what I realize I've been looking for this entire time, tucked away. A small folded piece of paper with my name printed across the bottom in capital letters, the scrawl of a five-year-old boy. M A X.

Carefully, I unfold the paper. I know what I will find there, but even so, my hands are shaking because I haven't seen this since that first day when Mom came home from the hospital. I unfold it again and there is the picture of an orange boy riding on a purple dragon. I am flooded with the hopefulness and fear of that drawing, the heartbreaking promise of crayons and imagination, the blessing of tears, Grandma hugging me: *It will be okay, it will be okay, Max,* because we needed it to be okay even if it was only for a moment.

I find a lighter in Dad's sock drawer. It is exactly what I

need. I come downstairs with the lighter and the drawing of the dragon in my pocket. Dad and Grandma are still asleep, Grandma in the chair and Dad on the couch, but Dad is facing outward now, the quilt crumpled in a heap on the floor beside him. I pick it up and cover him again. His hair is rumpled and his face is filled with shadows. He opens his eyes with a start.

"Are you feeling all right?" he asks. "Does your head hurt?"

"It doesn't hurt anymore," I say.

I don't tell him that what hurts now is the emptiness.

I swing on Dad's plaid jacket. I put the lighter and the picture of the purple dragon in my pocket. I know what I need to do.

"Where are you going?" asks Dad.

"Just into the backyard to get some air," I say.

"Don't be long," says Dad.

"I won't."

Outside, the sun glances off bare trees, shining through icicles. I watch the sky until the silence is broken by the sudden sound of a car engine and Smashing Pumpkins blaring from an open window. The rusted car swerves back and forth along our street and then lurches to a halt in front of my house. Oh my lord. It's Fish.

She shuts off the engine, leaves the keys in the ignition, leaps out the door, and runs into my arms.

"I stole my mom's keys," she says. "She's sleeping, so she doesn't even know I'm gone, but I had to see you. I got here in one piece. No one pulled me over. It's a minor miracle."

"You're crazy." I sigh, wrapping my arms around her. We hug for an eternity.

"Tell me about your head," she says finally.

"I have a concussion," I say. "I'm staying home from school for a few days, but I'm going to be okay."

"I was worried," says Fish. "You kept talking about walruses."

"I thought I had brain cancer," I tell her.

Fish throws back her head and laughs, but then stops when she realizes I'm not joking.

"You thought you had brain cancer?"

"Yeah," I say. "Since the funeral. I accidentally invited the tumor to move in and it was a terrible tenant. A total pig. Peed on the walls. Broke a window. I couldn't think about anything else."

"That's weird," says Fish.

"Isn't it? All this time, I've been worrying about dying instead of living. And then the doctor showed me the CT scan, and it turns out there's nothing in there at all."

Fish reaches up and puts her hands on either side of my face. "Nothing but straw," she says, pretending to pull a piece from my ear.

"Maybe the great and powerful Oz can fix me."

"I think he did already," says Fish. "He fixed you so good, you ended up in the emergency room with a concussion. Which proves that while you may not have a tumor, you do have a nice juicy brain. And a heart. And courage. All we need are some ruby slippers and I'll click my heels three times and everything will go back to normal. Mom will be sober and Dad will be home and everything will be peachy."

"But it doesn't ever work out that way, does it?" I say.

"Nope," says Fish. "When I get home, Mom will still be drunk as a skunk and the house will still be a holy mess."

"At least we've got each other," I tell her.

"That's a pretty good *at least*," says Fish.

Inside my pocket, the blue woman is kneeling on her shard, whispering to the orange boy, stroking his head. I put my arm around Fish and we walk together into the backyard. The sun slants through the bare branches, casting long shadows on the snow. I clear snow off the bench in the fallow garden. We sit side by side. A crow lands in the stone birdbath and then takes off, screeching. I reach into my pocket. Fish puts her head on my shoulder.

"Remember I told you I used to have a sketchbook filled with dragons?" I say.

"And I told you mine was filled with unicorns."

I kiss her head. "That's how I knew I was going to like you. Well, today I found a drawing I hadn't seen in eleven years."

"What was it?" says Fish.

I take the drawing out of my pocket and Fish and I unfold it on our laps like a map. We peer at it together. It feels right, somehow, looking at it with her, as though doing this now throws me back in time to comfort myself when I was five. Here is the purple dragon. Here is the orange boy. Here are the letters M A X scrawled across the bottom, the long hard marks of a desperate hand.

"Oh, Max," says Fish. "This is who you were."

"Yeah," I say.

"Hello, little Max," says Fish.

"Hello," I say.

She runs her fingers across the face of the orange boy, across the back of the dragon, and then she traces each letter: M A X.

"She had just come home from the hospital after a double mastectomy. This picture was supposed to make her feel better."

"I bet it did," says Fish.

"I found it in her jewelry box."

"It must have been precious to her," says Fish.

"I've always wondered where it went."

"What are you going to do with it?" Fish asks me.

"Burn it," I say.

"But then you won't have it anymore," says Fish.

"I know," I say. "But it belongs to her and she should have it."

"You're brave," says Fish.

"No I'm not. I'm scared of everything."

"It takes bravery to let things go. Can I burn a picture too?"

"Sure. We can help each other."

"But what if mine gets mixed up with yours and your mother ends up with both of them? I don't think she would like me very much if she saw what I've been drawing."

"She would love you," I say.

"Are you sure?" asks Fish.

I'm sure, says the blue woman standing on her tiptoes and spreading her arms wide.

"I'm sure," I say.

Fish takes her sketchbook out of her shoulder bag and opens to the page with that horrible drawing of herself and The Monk, the one with the handcuffs. "We were no good together," says Fish. "We played head games. On again. Off again. Never exactly boyfriend and girlfriend, but not just friends either. He comes on strong. I pull away. He gets jealous. I get mad. He gets hurt. I feel guilty. We get back together, and then it starts all over again. But I'm done with all that. I'm ready for something real. Do you really think your mom's going to like this picture?"

"She'll like that you're being brave," I say.

Fish puts our drawings together and folds them into a single paper crane. We each hold one wing. I flick the lighter. The flame is blue and bright. The purple dragon and the orange boy smile at me. So do the twisted Fish and the twisted Monk and all their pain, the blue flame coming out of the dragon's mouth. They wave to us. Goodbye goodbye. I let the paper crane catch fire. Then I shove the lighter back into my pocket and we wait together. There it goes. The pictures burn together and curl and turn to ash. They blend and blur. Orange boy. Handcuffs. Dragon. It doesn't take long. We blow out the flame before it burns our fingers and all that's left are two charred corners, which we blow into the air. There is a breath of wind. The trees wave goodbye. The last shards of paper rise into the perfectly blue sky. They swirl in the air and vanish.

SHARD

ON MONDAY I STAY HOME FROM SCHOOL WHILE DAD IS
at work. I follow the doctor's advice: no reading, no screens,
and no stress allowed. Instead I do quiet things with
Grandma. We play gin rummy. We make rubber-band balls.
We water the plants. When we're tired, we take naps on the
couch.

Just before dinner, the dean of students calls and says
he wants to speak to both Dad and me. Dad puts it on
speakerphone so we can hear together. The dean's voice is
low and serious. He says he didn't call over the weekend
because of the accident, but someone in the community saw
me drinking downtown with a member of the faculty. Administration also knows that I was out late with several
boarding students who were caught breaking curfew.

The dean tells Dad how serious this all is because they need to be able to trust their students to represent the school both on and off campus.

The review board has taken actions to make certain that none of the individuals involved in this event will repeat their mistakes.

Dr. Cage has been fired.

The boarding students who broke curfew have been issued demerits.

I will be issued a behavioral warning.

If I ever break the code of conduct again, my financial aid package will be revoked.

Dad assures the dean that this will never happen again. He explains how important Baldwin is to both of us. Then he thanks the dean for calling, apologizes again, and hangs up.

Dad exhales and looks at me for a very long time.

My stomach feels like lead.

"I'm sorry," I say.

"Yeah," says Dad. "I know."

"I got everyone in trouble. I got my favorite teacher fired. This is horrible."

"It is," says Dad. "It's horrible." And then, instead of telling me how disappointed he is, he grabs me and hugs me hard.

Later that night I call Fish on the phone and tell her about what the dean said, how if I break one more rule they might take away my scholarship. Fish fills me in on what happened to our friends. The Monk dropped her off before they headed back to campus so no one knows she was involved, but the others were caught coming in late. This morning the dean called them into his office one at a time and doled out the punishments. Ravi, Smitty, and Griswald all got warnings for breaking curfew, and since he was the one driving, The Monk was put on probation, which means they are going to watch him like a hawk and from now on, no more driving on or off campus. "Can you believe that?" she says. "No more Lady J. No more late-night adventures. It's the end of an era."

I ask her why she didn't tell me sooner.

"I didn't want to stress you out," she says, "and I figured bad news could wait."

When I ask about Cage, she sighs and says he's gone already. Just like that. They replaced him with this young guy who doesn't believe in being critical. Who are they kidding? No one can replace Cage. I feel so terrible. I've ruined everything for everyone. But Fish tells me to stop worrying and try to get some sleep. "I'll call you tomorrow," she whispers into the phone, her voice soft as honey. "I'll call you every night." Fish recites my favorite lines from *Hamlet* into the phone. *"Good night, sweet prince, and flights of angels sing thee to thy rest."*

But how can I sleep when I feel so guilty?

At about midnight, Grandma wanders into the room and sits on my bed.

"Why aren't you sleeping?" she says.

"I'm thinking about what an idiot I am."

"Stop it," says Grandma. "You're not an idiot."

"I got my teacher fired. I got all my friends in trouble. How am I ever going to fix this?"

"You can't. But you can apologize. And hope they will forgive."

"How can I apologize to Dr. Cage? They fired him. He's gone."

Grandma smiles at me. "You'll find a way," she says. Then she tucks my blankets around me. "You should get some sleep," she whispers. "The doctor said that rest is the most important thing for you right now." She kisses my forehead and turns off my light.

The days pass. Fish keeps her word. She calls every night. Tuesday turns to Wednesday and Wednesday turns to Thursday. All I do at home is think about her face. I draw pictures in my sketchbook. I imagine how it would feel to touch her. Sometimes I touch the drawings instead. Finally it's Friday morning. Time for me to go back to school. I come down the stairs all dressed and ready. Dad is still in the shower. Grandma is waiting for me at the kitchen table, an angel with white hair and a white nightgown. She smiles when she sees me.

"Hey there, early bird," she says.

The kitchen smells like heaven. She has set a place for me with a glass of orange juice and a whole plate filled with matzo-meal latkes and grape jelly. It's been a long time since I was hungry. She watches me the way only a mother or grandmother can watch you eat, without wanting a bite for themselves, just watching you chew and swallow because they made it for you, and they want you to love it.

"There is something secret about this breakfast," says Grandma, smiling.

"You made it yourself," I say.

"That's not it!" says Grandma, and she is so pleased with herself, she looks like she is going to burst into blossom. "You have to finish your breakfast to know. You have to eat everything."

So I do. And as I eat (a little latke, a little jelly), I see it. The plate. Mom's favorite plate. Put back together.

"I gathered up all the pieces," she says.

"Oh, Grandma."

"The night it broke I came back downstairs after everyone was asleep and I picked the pieces off the floor and saved them. And then the night of your accident all the commotion woke me up. The ambulance came. Your dad went with you to the hospital. After Lydie got the twins settled down, she and I stayed up waiting for your dad to call and tell us you were okay. We got to talking. She brought up how Soleil had broken the plate and I told her how I'd kept the pieces for you. It was her idea to glue them back together."

"Oh Grandma," I say again.

"It wasn't so hard. Look how we did it. Can you see? It was like a puzzle."

I finish my last bites and hold the plate so I can see. It's amazing. Here is the bridge. Here are the mountains. Here is the pagoda. Here is the trail and the bird flying overhead. There are long scars that crisscross through the scene where she glued the pieces back into place, but with the exception of one missing spot, the plate looks almost whole again.

"There are some slivers missing. And there's a whole missing piece," says Grandma, apologetically. "One shard. Right in the middle. Just that one triangle."

"I know where it is," I say.

"Where?"

"I have it," I say. "I've been keeping it." I take the shard out of my back pocket. "I've been keeping it with me ever since."

"Oh, perfect!" says Grandma.

She shuffles to the odds-and-ends drawer and takes out the superglue.

Carefully, carefully, I spread glue on the edges of the shard with a butter knife.

Then I place the shard in its spot on the winding trail. I tap it into place with the tip of the knife.

"There," says Grandma.

The tiny blue woman stretches up on her toes. She lifts her arms as though they are wings and raises her face to the sun. All around her, tiny folded pieces of paper are falling like feathers. This one has the wing of a dragon. This one has a slender ankle. This one has the letter *M*. This one has the eye of a beautiful girl. The tiny blue woman twirls in circles until she catches each one like a child catching white butterflies.

Dad comes down. He has shaved and put on a brand-new shirt.

"You ready for school, Max?" he says.

"Yes, I am," I whisper.

"*Almost* ready," says Grandma. "There's one more thing. One more important thing we need to do." Grandma picks up a pencil.

"We need to go, Jean," says Dad, checking his watch.

"This will only take a second. Measure him. It's his first day back."

"Okay," says Dad. "Got your stuff ready?"

I lift my backpack to show him. Then I grab my jacket off the back of the chair. Grandma gives the pencil to Dad.

"Are you sure you want to?" Dad asks me.

"Yeah," I say. "I was too sad before. But now I'm ready."

Together, we walk to the wall where Mom used to measure my height. Kindergarten. Grade three, grade five. All the way up the wall. One for every year until this past year. Dad and I stop in front of the wall. We look at all the different years written in my mom's handwriting, letters and numbers that curl and twist, thin and slanted like tendrils. I stand against the wall, just like I have done every first day of school since I was in kindergarten.

"No tippy toes," says Grandma.

I drop down an inch or two. Dad draws a line.

I am towering above the last line we drew.

"Would you look at that?" says Grandma. "How can this be true?"

But it is true, Grandma. It is true.

AFTERMATH

EVEN THOUGH FISH MEETS ME IN TROWBRIDGE HALL just like she promised me she would, even though she welcomes me back with her classic, fabulous, full-body koala hug, even though she grabs my arm and skips me Yellow Brick Road–style all the way down the corridor to World Literature class, my stomach is still in knots. I'm worried about how The Monk will react to seeing me again. We take our seats. I look over and try to make eye contact with him. He doesn't even look at me. He spends the entire class taking notes and nodding at Dr. Austerlitz with great interest. I try to get The Monk's attention, but he looks through me as though I were a ghost.

At the end of class, I walk up to him.

"Hey," I say. "Can we talk a minute?"

"I don't have a minute," says The Monk. Then he pushes me aside and storms off to his next class.

———————

I get up the nerve to call Cage during my free period and arrange to meet him during lunch at the Salty Dog, a café. I have to admit, I have a real craving for an egg roll, but Cage makes a good point that meeting at Panda Wok would be like returning to the scene of the crime. And besides, they probably wouldn't be too happy to see us since they had to pay a fine for serving alcohol to a minor, even though it wasn't their fault.

The Salty Dog seems like the perfect hole-in-the-wall for two outlaws to meet for the last time. It's dark. The walls are covered in posters from old Ingmar Bergman and Woody Allen movies. There are people sitting in faded leather chairs with their feet up on scuffed tables drinking mugs of dark coffee and working on their computers; others are just browsing the Internet and trying to look intellectual while they hide away from the world for a while.

I spot Cage sitting on a couch in the back of the café and hurry over to him.

"I am so sorry," I say. "I am so sorry for what I did."

"Don't be," says Cage. "I had it coming. Sit down. You look completely freaked out. Jeez. I'm still the same guy. I'm gonna live. You want me to order you something?"

"No thanks," I say.

"Right. I get it. It didn't work out so well last time. Listen. Sit down. You're making me jumpy standing there. Or maybe it's the caffeine. Either way, please get over here and stop looking guilty."

I sit beside him.

Cage offers me his coffee. "Want a sip?"

"Um. No."

"Jeez, did you see that? I almost made the same mistake twice. Don't want them throwing me in the can for offering you a hazelnut double-dark macchiato, do we? No sir. Coffee is bad for kids. All those Minnesotans and Sicilians have got it wrong, my friend. Wouldn't want to lead you down the path toward evil, now, would we? Oh. Right. Too late. I have already tainted your brain. And the whole school board knows it."

"How did they find out?"

"You wouldn't believe it, but the entire Trowbridge family was dining at the Panda Wok the night we were there. I know. It's crazy, but it's true. I didn't see them, of course, squiffed as I was. But they saw me ordering the scorpion bowl. They saw you stagger out. The rest is history. They notified the school. They met with the review board. By Monday I was out on my ass."

"I can't believe it," I say. "It wasn't your fault."

"That's what I told them. But no matter how many times

I explained what happened, it didn't measure up. You had a virgin piña colada. I gave you one sip of the scorpion bowl. But somehow you got drunk. Just tell me one thing so I know I'm not crazy. You had way more than that one sip I gave you, didn't you?"

"Yeah," I say. "I had many, many sips."

"You think you had about half?"

"Probably," I say.

"That's what I figured," says Cage. "I can't believe I missed that."

"I should go to the administration and tell them you didn't know."

"It wouldn't do any good," says Cage.

"But I made you lose your job."

"*I* made me lose my job," says Cage. "If it wasn't this blunder, it would have been another. The administration's been on my back for years. And those Trowbridges never liked me. They've been looking for a reason to give me the ax since I started at this school. Remember I told you that the best thing about being a writer is that folks don't expect you to behave like everyone else? Get-out-of-jail-free card and all that?"

"Yeah," I say.

"That was bullshit," he says.

"I knew that already," I tell him.

"Good. You're a better man than I am, Gunga Din.

Listen. Before we say our tearful goodbyes, you owe me one thing that you should have given me a long time ago."

"What's that?"

"Tell me what the hell has been going on in that head of yours all these months. What's the big secret that's been twisting you up into pretzels?"

"You want the long version or the short version?" I ask him.

"Well, I want the long version of course, but I gather you need to head back to campus soon, and if I hear you got in trouble for skipping class and they kicked you out of paradise, the bad news will be a tad too rich for my diet at the moment, so the Reader's Digest version, please. No pun intended. And that pun, in case you weren't listening closely, was *diet* and *digest*."

"Okay," I say. "Reader's Digest version. At her funeral, instead of crying, I convinced myself that my mother's brain tumor had somehow gotten inside me."

"Kinky," says Cage, leaning forward.

"Yeah, isn't it? So when I was in class, even when I tried, I couldn't concentrate. I was imagining this tumor living inside my brain. Calling me a wuss. Listening to loud music at all hours of the night. Throwing epic keg parties. Scratching off the wallpaper. Peeing in the corners, etcetera."

"He was a very bad tenant," says Cage.

"The worst."

"And so you were convinced you were dying of brain cancer?"

"Pretty much. And I didn't tell anyone because I didn't want them to know what a mess I was."

"Big mistake," says Cage.

"Yeah. Then after I fell, I went to the emergency room and I was so blitzed out, they decided to give me a brain scan. They took pictures of every nook and cranny. And as you know, there are lots of nooks and crannies in the brain. Guess what they found?"

"No tumor?" says Cage.

"Yeah," I say. "No tumor. Not even a baby one. It turns out I'm going to live."

"Congratulations," says Cage.

"Thank you. And I should be congratulating you too."

"And why is that?"

"If you hadn't accidentally gotten me trashed, I wouldn't have hit my head and I wouldn't have gone to the ER, and I wouldn't have had a brain scan and I wouldn't have found out the truth."

"Which was?" asks Cage.

"Which was that besides being a total basket case, I am going to be okay."

"I was an accidental hero," says Cage.

"Yes, you were."

"Rescued you from yourself with my trusty scorpion

bowl. Even though I tried to be virtuous by ordering you a virgin piña colada."

"Are you sure you don't want me to tell the dean it was my fault?"

"Nah," says Cage. "Let's not press our luck. Listen. You need to get back to campus. It's time to say goodbye, young grasshopper. But first, one last piece of advice, however unwanted. I think you should consider talking to a professional about what's been going on. A shrink. A counselor. Someone who can help you sort through what's really in your head. Trust me. It'll be good for you. Tell me you'll consider it."

"Okay," I say. "I'll definitely consider it."

"Good," says Cage. "Freud is good people. And listen. They're gonna give you a new advisor. The one and only Mrs. Donna Pruitt. I've touched base with her already, and she is actually going to follow the handbook and meet with you at least once a week for the rest of the school year. Don't worry. You'll like her better than me."

"I don't think I could possibly like anyone better than you," I tell him.

"Aw," says Cage. "You're just saying that because I used to feed you egg rolls and booze. Give me a man-hug."

We stand up. Cage grabs me and pulls me in to him. He smells terrible.

"Thanks for everything," I say against his sweater.

"Keep on writing," says Cage.

"I will," I tell him.

"Dedicate your first novel to me."

"I will," I tell him.

He pushes me away and looks me right in the face.

"You're a good kid," he says. "I'll never forget you. Now get out of here quick before I start crying like a baby. Go live your life."

STEAMPUNK

FISH MEETS ME AFTER SCHOOL AND WE WALK through the auditorium doors together, down the aisle, onto the stage, and into another world. Everything is made of gears and metal pipes, as though the Kingdom of Denmark has been rebuilt inside a gigantic industrial clock. The castle looks like a factory belching steam and dirt into the sky. Everything is hard and angular and dark, but somehow at the same time it is beautiful too.

Donna Pruitt strides toward us. "Costumes," she says briskly. "Hurry up. Rehearsal starts in twenty minutes. Places in twenty!" she calls.

"PLACES IN TWENTY" screams the stage manager.

"Thank you! Twenty!" calls Fish, who grins and then bounds off backstage.

I stand still for a moment, gazing at the set and wondering how it's going to feel to be onstage with The Monk and all the others. Will they give me the cold shoulder? Will they pretend nothing ever happened? Was Fish telling the truth when she said the others weren't upset? I take a deep breath and try to work up the courage to go backstage.

Donna Pruitt puts her hand on my shoulder. "How are you feeling?" she asks.

"I'm okay," I say. "I'm just a little nervous, I guess."

"Don't be nervous," she says. "We all missed you. Everyone's going to be really glad you're back. We'll talk later about advisory stuff. For now get into your costume. It's a work of art."

Backstage, everyone is rushing to get ready. She is right. The costumes are amazing. Leather and silk. Lace and studs. Many of them include accessories. Belts. Boots. Vests. Smitty bounds over in his leather tunic and we bump fists. Ravi strides by with an armful of costumes and winks at me.

Griswald shuffles over, puts both of his hands on my shoulders, and touches his forehead against mine, very gently. "I'm glad you're back," he whispers.

"Thanks," I say. "Listen. I'm really sorry about all the trouble I caused."

"Hey," says Griswald. "I like a little trouble."

I find my costume hanging on the rack. It's a suit of armor made of gauze, leather, and pressed tin.

"What do you think?" asks Ravi at my elbow.

"I don't even know what to say," I tell him. "I've never seen anything like this in my life. You are amazing."

"Aren't I?"

"Truly," I say. "You're truly amazing. I had no idea how amazing you were."

"Because I have amazed you?"

"Yes," I say.

"Put you in a maze?"

"Yes."

"How does it feel? Being in a maze as you are?"

"Mazey," I say.

"And is that better or worse than having a concussion?"

"Much better," I say.

"Good," says Ravi. "Welcome back to the maze then."

The Monk is sitting by the bubble mirrors putting on makeup. He brushes the sponge in the brown base and begins covering his face, dabbing it across his forehead, down his nose, across his cheeks. Then he puts shadows under his eyes so that he looks as though he has been crying.

"Hey," I say.

He doesn't respond. He is still looking at his face in the mirror.

"So, I just wanted to let you know I'm really sorry about what happened."

The Monk shrugs.

"I was in pretty bad shape that night. And I'm not sure what I would have done if you weren't there to help me."

"Give me a break," says The Monk. "None of this would have happened if I hadn't been there. I frigging *attacked* you with snowballs, dude."

"But then you saved me."

"I used my head as a battering ram, and I frigging mowed you down. So don't you dare thank me. I don't want to be thanked."

"Okay," I say. "I won't thank you."

"See, that's what bugs me about you, Friedman," says The Monk, his eyes smoldering. "You're just too goddamned agreeable. Where's your edginess? You're turning into Trowbridge on me. Next thing I know you're going to be calling your mother, telling her I broke a rule."

"My mother is dead," I tell him.

We stare at each other. The Monk shuts his mouth and turns back to the mirror.

"PLACES IN FIVE!" screams the stage manager.

"Thank you! Five!" shouts Ravi.

"What the hell does that mean?"

Ravi grins at me. "That's what you say when you're *in the know*, as I am. You shout that. *Thank you! Five!* So they know you heard them. And also so that they know you are theatrically knowledgeable. Like a knowledgeable guy. As I am."

"Thank you! Five!" screams Smitty, grabbing his cape and jogging through the dressing room doors and onto the stage.

And now people are shouting, "Thank you! Five!" and running all over the place to get ready, buttoning each other's buttons, buckling each other's belts, spritzing hair-spray in each other's hair. Fixing each other's swords, breathing deeply.

"PLACES!" shouts Donna Pruitt from the stage.

"Thank you! Places!" everyone says, because that's what you say when you are *in the know*, as I now am.

We spill onstage and form a circle, Ophelia in her leather corset and skirts, Hamlet with leather and black doublet, Gertrude with wig and black leather gown, Laertes and Horatio and Claudius and Polonius and Rosencrantz and Guildenstern and Lords and Ladies and Attendants and all of us, all of us, transformed in front of this mag-nificent set rising behind us like some kind of dystopian metamorphosis.

We can feel each other's hands, and through our hands, the steady pulse of our hearts, the warmth of blood and life.

Donna Pruitt claps from the audience. *Let's go*, she says. *It's time to begin rehearsal*. And we do, each of us falling into our characters as though they were our own gleaming spirits, our words, Shakespeare's words, filling the auditorium like golden feathers on the wings of an angel.

READY TO FALL

WE ARRIVE IN THE AUDITORIUM HOURS BEFORE THE
curtain rises, hours before the magic begins. We shuffle som-
berly into two even rows before the stage as though we were
pallbearers carrying a coffin between us.

It feels strange to be so near the magnificent set in our
street clothes. The stage lights are off and the houselights
are on, and for now it's just us, the cast, together for one
last time before the show.

Donna Pruitt stands with us, feet flat on the floor,
breathing the possibility and impossibility of what we are
about to do. Together, we feel humbled, like supplicants ap-
proaching an altar with the great gears and chimneys of
Ravi's steampunk Denmark rising behind us in the dark.

"Are you ready?" she asks, her beautiful voice awed,

hallowed, hushed, as though we were about to give birth or die together.

We nod and assemble our arms so we can take each other's weight without dropping our most precious cargo, each one of us grabbing another one's wrist, a web of arms, waiting for the shock and impact of falling weight.

First we catch Donna Pruitt, her long, angular body falling backward without hesitation. Glorious.

Then we catch Griswald, who is so certain and so joyful in his falling, I think he would have leaped into our arms if we had let him.

Fish makes eye contact with every single one of us before falling.

Smitty falls screaming *Geronimo!*

Ravi falls after a perfect pirouette.

When The Monk falls, he falls with all his rage gathered in his bones, his body rigid and heavy. And all the others fall with all their beings as well, whatever they carry with them. Gertrude and Claudius and the Gravediggers and Rosencrantz and Guildenstern and the Lords and Ladies and Attendants. They all leave and then return to earth, one resurrection after another.

One by one, each kid goes up on the stage, turns their back to the group, and crosses their arms across their chest.

"Ready to fall," they say.

"Fall away," we say, our voices triumphant, because we know we will catch them whenever they choose to let go.

"Falling," they say, in various voices, strong, whispered, shaking, joyful, an entire rainbow of voices.

And then, one at a time, they let go of the earth and they fall backward into nothingness. It is a miracle. We catch them every time. We allow no harm to come to them. We cradle their bodies in our arms and we bring them safely into heaven.

And then, finally, it is my turn.

Fish squeezes one of my hands. Ravi squeezes the other.

I leave the group and take the long walk up the stairs and onto the stage. The set is dark. A marvelous sleeping metropolis. Then I turn and look down at my friends, who are assembled just below the apron of the stage in their two even rows, their faces calm and ready. The Monk nods imperceptibly. Fish has tears in her eyes.

I don't know who came up with the rule that a grave should be six feet deep. When you are standing at the edge with your father's arm around your shoulder, and they lower the casket slowly down, six feet seems like a fathom. The coffin is a ship sinking to the bottom of the ocean before it is allowed to settle. And then comes the first shovelful of earth, a sound so horrible that you look away because no one could possibly sleep through this kind of thunder, so it must be true. She is not coming back. I put my hands across my chest and feel my heart beating. I look down at my friends, who are waiting for me to speak my one line. The only one that matters. Then I take a deep breath and turn my back so I am facing the dark gears and factories rising up like the gates of heaven on earth.

"Ready to fall," I whisper.

"Fall away," they say.

I gather everything good that is inside me that came from her. I gather everything that is strong and everything that is courageous and everything that has a heart and that can trust that when I fall, the people I care about will be there to catch me.

"Falling," I say.

And then, because I am finally ready, I fall backward from the stage and into their arms.

THE FALL OF A SPARROW

ELECTRICITY. THE FEELING OF AN AUDIENCE ON THE other side of the curtain. The buzzing murmur of their voices fills the auditorium. Unseen. Expectant. There is the commotion of ticket sellers and ushers handing out programs. People settle into their seats. We can't see them, but we know they're out there, our families and friends taking off their coats and getting seated, looking for our names in the program and then finding us, smiling. Backstage, we get into our costumes and help one another with makeup and hair. Ravi spikes The Monk's hair so that it is standing straight up.

"I look like I just put my finger in a socket," says The Monk.

"Deal with it," Ravi says. "This is the way I want you."

"That's what she said," says The Monk.

"That's what *he* said," says Ravi, grinning.

"Places!" calls the stage manager.

"Thank you! Places!" everyone calls back.

And then the lights flicker and we are silent.

The curtain rises.

The audience gasps when they see Ravi's set. The gears. The clockwork. The factory chimneys spitting steam and smoke. Their delight is an electrifying sound, pure appreciation. Astonished. Like opening a present. Lifting the lid off a velvet box and seeing, for the first time, the diamond you have been waiting for your whole life. A promise of even better things to come. Engagement.

And then the show begins.

The Monk is phenomenal as Hamlet. He has always been wonderful in rehearsal, but now there's something wild and raw about him. His father, the king, is dead. Hamlet paces the stage, his eyes haunted and shining. He is alive in his grief, the way sometimes immense sadness can make a person seem even more human than they were before, the way we can sometimes see ourselves more clearly in another person's weeping and that is why we care so deeply.

I am the ghostly father of this confused, grieving boy. I know he loves me. He always loved me when I was alive. But when I haunt him, treading in his footsteps, folding into his shadow, he lashes out at me like a caged animal, uneasy and furious. In act 1, scene 2, when it is time for his first soliloquy—*O, that this too too solid flesh would melt*—Hamlet doubles over and rocks himself on the bare stage, crying so hard it seems that his insides are about to leap from his mouth or seep from his ears, his eyes, like blood.

I try to comfort him. I kneel behind him and try to stroke his tears away, as only a parent can, but he pushes me backward and screams. He wants to be alone in his sadness. *Angels and ministers of grace defend us!* His sadness is heartbreaking and familiar. I see myself in it. It swallows him the way it swallowed me. It tears at him the way it tore at me.

When I finally speak at the end of scene 5, revealing myself as the king come back from the dead—*I am thy father's spirit, doomed for a certain term to walk the night*—Hamlet falls on his knees, reaches out, embraces me, burying his face in my shoulder because until this moment I had been a memory, a nightmare, a worry gnawing at his brain for all these days and now, finally, I am real.

When I haunt Gertrude's bedchamber I am still real, even though she cannot see me standing there. She was my wife, but she has betrayed me by moving on to love another. Hamlet takes her chin and turns her face toward mine, pleading with her to recognize me. *Do you see nothing there?* he says, gesturing toward me. *Nothing at all,* she says. *Yet all that is I see.*

I am the Ghost, fabulously un-ghosted. Hamlet grabs his mother's bare shoulders and berates her. *O shame! Where is thy blush?* Gertrude pleads with him to stop. She tells him *These words like daggers enter in my ears,* and though invisible to her, I gaze at her familiar, beloved face, a face I will never touch again for as long as I live.

And this is where something extraordinary and unexpected happens onstage.

I begin to cry.

At first it is not noticeable. I try to hold back my tears. But then I climb into the bed with Hamlet and Gertrude. I wrap my arms around them and hold them as they break each other's hearts the way only a parent and child can do: *O Hamlet, thou has cleft my heart in twain.* I rock them in my arms as if to say *It's okay, I love you both, this is who we were.*

It is only a brief moment onstage. Even though Gertrude can't see me anymore, even though our lives on this earth have changed forever. We still are who we were: the mother, the father, and the son. I realize that the tears are perfect. They rise from inside me (both Max and the Ghost), silent at first, but then powerful, the sound of my own raw grief coming and coming from the bottom of my gut, from a

346

wordless, animal place, unhindered, like a wolf raising his face to the moon.

Gertrude still doesn't see me. She sees only what is there. But when I reach out to touch her hair with my fingertips, when I blow on the back of her neck with my ghost's breath, she feels me. Her hand reaches toward me blindly, and I reach toward her with my hand, so close you can feel the electricity. *Be thou assured, if words be made of breath, and breath of life, I have no life to breathe what thou hast said to me.*

I feel the audience leaning in to listen. They are present in each breath as my sobs subside and I move back into the shadows, leaving them to live without me. Act 3 folds into act 4. Act 4 bleeds into act 5. When Ophelia walks onstage, we are a triangle just as Donna Pruitt said we should be. I see Ophelia through Hamlet's eyes. How lovely she is. And how impossibly out of reach. And when Ophelia dies offstage, I am there, suspended in Hamlet's grief. Grief resonates through his words, masquerading as madness. By the end of the play, grief has wrapped its pale hands around the throat of every character: Polonius, Ophelia, Gertrude, Claudius, Laertes, and finally, finally, Hamlet himself. *Good night, sweet prince, and flights of angels sing thee to thy rest.*

In the last moments of the play, I step out of the shadows one last time. I watch the Soldiers carry Hamlet's body from the stage, my face full of grief, and compassion and wisdom. Because I know what comes next. I know the impossibility of picking up the pieces. I know the impossibility of moving on. Now, there is a death march. Each body is carried by four Soldiers. They walk, stiffly, their eyes downcast. A dirge. The long, low notes of the death knell rise from beneath the stage and fill the entire auditorium until every member of the audience mourns, some of them weeping, some of them clutching their hearts, the living carrying the dead, a somber parade of corpses and lovers trying to find their way on this earth. And then there is me. The Ghost. Walking slowly behind the line, following them, one step at a time, until there is no one left onstage.

ENCORE

THE CURTAIN FALLS. THE AUDIENCE BREAKS INTO uproarious applause.

The curtain rises again.

They are on their feet still calling for us. They clap and stamp their feet.

We come out onstage one at a time.

They shout for each of us in turn, me and Smitty and Griswald and Ravi and Fish, getting progressively louder and more boisterous until The Monk finally walks out, exhausted, humbled, and then they scream *Bravo! Bravo!*, the entire auditorium ringing with appreciation. The Monk bows. Someone throws a bouquet of flowers onto the stage. He picks it up and holds it in the air, triumphant. Then he gestures back to the stage manager, who walks out from backstage, bows, and then runs back behind the curtain; he gestures to the person doing the lights. He gestures to Ravi, our costume designer extraordinaire. Ravi twirls and curtsies. He gestures to Donna Pruitt, who is sitting in the front row clapping so hard it looks like she is going to rise into the air.

And now we all take a bow together. The whole cast. *One, two, three, bow,* and when we come up, the audience is still shouting, amazed by their own joy in us, astonished by how completely they have fallen in love. They stomp and scream and we drink it like ambrosia.

I peer over the footlights and into the auditorium. I see Dr. Austerlitz. I see Dad and Grandma and Lydie and the twins standing together, screaming at the tops of their lungs. Soleil is holding Grandma's hand and leaping in crazy circles, her pigtails flying. Dad is whistling and clapping so hard, I can almost hear it from the stage. Way back near the entrance, I see a familiar-looking man with a beard and dark sunglasses and a baseball cap and a trench coat with the collar up to his ears. He is smiling with crooked yellow teeth. When he sees me looking at him, he gives me a thumbs-up.

Then the curtain falls and we run backstage to leap around and hug each other and scream at the tops of our lungs.

The Monk grabs me in a headlock, screaming, "I love you, man."

And then, because my whole being wants to do it even though it's awkward, I hug him hard, and he hugs me and now we're pounding each other on the back and laughing and crying and Ravi comes bounding up to us, and then Griswald and Smitty, and we are all shouting and spinning, a huge, whirling "Hava Nagila" circle, a gypsy ring, raucous, triumphant, elated. But Fish is nowhere to be seen.

When the spinning finally dies down, and most of the cast has retired to the dressing rooms to get back into their street clothes, I look for Fish. She's not backstage.

I jog down to the dressing room and get changed out of my costume. The place is full of commotion, people talking in loud voices about what went well, what didn't, they are shouting their favorite lines in outrageous accents, throwing discarded costumes around, wigs, duffel bags, shoes. Lots of actors are at the bubble mirrors taking off their makeup but I don't see Fish anywhere.

I run out to the foyer where the ushers and the ticket sellers are closing up shop.

There are Baldwin students standing around the bulletin board with all our head shots, trying to figure out who was who. There are parents waiting for their sons or daughters to come out so they can congratulate them.

351

Groups of people snapping pictures and giving bouquets, but Fish is nowhere to be seen.

Dad and Lydie and Grandma and the twins are standing by the door, waiting for me. Lydie hands me a bouquet of yellow roses.

"You were outstanding," she says.

"Thanks," I say.

My dad pulls me in for a hug.

"You were amazing," he says. "You brought out so much in that character that I didn't even know was there."

Some of the other girls who played ladies and townspeople head out the doors together. Fish isn't with them.

"I've seen Hamlet onstage before," says Dad. "I watched the old Laurence Olivier film, I studied the play in school. But Max, you brought things to that character that just seemed so much more . . . more . . ."

"More personal?" supplies Lydie.

"Yes," says Dad. "More personal. And more real. And much, much more sad. I don't know how you did it. I don't know if Shakespeare meant for it to be this way. But you were just outstanding."

"Your dad was crying through most of it," says Grandma.

"You were?" I ask, surprised.

"I was," says Dad. "Seeing you up there made me think about Mom. It made me think about how much you've grown. How far you've come."

And now he is crying again, smiling foolishly at his own lack of control, tears flowing completely free. He points at himself and smiles and cries and doesn't even try to stop himself. Luna and Soleil put their arms around him and lean their blond heads against him. Grandma strokes Luna's hair, and Soleil purrs like a cat.

"Come here," says Lydie to me. She holds her arms open, and I step in for a hug.

"I'm proud of you," she says. At first I remain rigid, letting her do all the hugging. Her hair smells like peppermint. I relax into the hug. I put my arms around her shoulders. Then I put my head in her hair because this is the part I miss the most. Then everyone is hugging, Luna and Soleil and Grandma still gathered around Dad. Lydie holding me and stroking my head.

"Enough of this!" hoots Grandma, finally. "How about we go get ice cream?"

"Ice cream, ice cream," chants Luna.

"There's a great place around the corner," says Lydie, wiping her eyes. "Let's take Max out to celebrate."

Everyone seems very happy about this idea, especially Grandma, who is swinging Luna's hand and singing, "I scream, you scream, we all scream for ice cream."

All around us there are actors leaving the auditorium with their parents, heading toward the dorms to get their things for spring break. I spot The Monk with his parents, who are not surprisingly both over six feet tall, and there is Griswald with his parents and Smitty and Ravi with theirs, all my new friends looking young suddenly next to the adults who love them. But I don't see Fish and her mom anywhere and suddenly I realize what must have happened. Her mother didn't come. She didn't manage to get out of the house to see Fish onstage.

"You guys go," I tell them. "I have something I need to do here first. I'll meet you there, okay?"

"Sounds good," says Dad. "But don't wait too long. It's getting late."

"Hey," I say, elbowing him. "Live a little."

"Touché, young man," says Dad. And then he opens the door for the rest of them and they all wander out into the surprisingly warm night, a breath of almost spring.

CURTAIN CALL

I FIND HER BACKSTAGE, WRAPPED UP IN THE BLACK velvet curtain. Somehow, she has pulled it around herself like a fort so I can't see her, but I know she's there because I can hear her sniffling and I can see a rounded bulge in the curtain where she is sitting with the very tips of her toes showing because the fabric does not quite hit the floor of the stage.

"Can I come in?" I ask.

"Okay," says Fish. "But don't unwrap me."

"I won't unwrap you," I say. "I promise." I lift the curtain and climb inside. I can barely see her in the dark, but I know she's sitting there with her knees drawn up to her chin, hugging herself, and I know that she's been crying because her breath is uneven the way it gets when you've been crying hard and for a very long time. Without seeing it, I know her face is red and her eyes are puffy. I move closer so I am facing her and my knees are touching her knees.

"My mom didn't come," she says in a tiny voice.

I reach out and stroke her legs.

She is still wearing her costume. I feel silk and leather in the dark.

"I just thought maybe tonight she would get it together. Get herself out of the house for *me*, you know? Just do something for *me* just this one time. I was so stupid. How could I have been so stupid?"

"You're not stupid," I tell her. "She should have been here."

There is silence for a while. Fish holds her knees. I touch Fish in the dark. I find the side of her face. Her hair. Her hands clasping her knees. I take one hand away from her knees and run my fingers up and down the inside of her arm.

"I never told you about my scar," says Fish in the dark.

I find it with my fingers. It rises above her skin, more pronounced in the dark, a raised line, down the inside of her arm to her wrist and then across her wrist and around her thumb. I kiss her hand and hold it against my cheek.

"Sometimes things get so hard, you know?" she says. "People think I'm happy all the time. People think I'm just always jumping around and smiling and being silly all the time. But sometimes things get so hard it just feels like I can't do it, Max. I just can't do it anymore. That's what happened. I just got so tired of pretending."

"You don't have to pretend with me," I say. "You don't have to pretend to be happy when you're not. What happened? You can tell me. How did you get the scar?"

"I tried one time," she whispers into the dark. "When I was eleven. I broke a window and I took a piece of glass and I tried. But it didn't work."

I move closer to her. I gather her in to my body and hold her and rock her and kiss her hair. "I am so glad it didn't work."

"Me too," she says, her lips close to my ear. "Because if it had worked, I wouldn't have met you. I wouldn't be about to kiss you."

I turn my face and find her mouth in the dark. We kiss for an eternity, all enveloped in velvet darkness. We kiss each other's faces. Each other's hands. Each other's mouths, we find each other over and over and over again. Fish leans close and pushes in my nose. "Beep," she says. Then she pulls on both of my earlobes. "Bong."

We uncurl the curtain and step out onto the stage together. I feel like I am glowing. My whole body is alive, every pore, every cell, my face flushed. I bring her to the edge of the stage, bend her back, and kiss her. We must present an interesting picture alone on the empty stage, me in my black skinny jeans and my red Converse All Stars and Fish in her gown. I take her hand and spin her. She throws back her head and laughs her wonderful, contagious, raucous laugh. Then she wraps her arms around my neck and I am spinning too, both of us together, and we're laughing so loud that our laughter fills the auditorium.

"To be," whispers Fish into my ear. "That is the answer."

"Definitely," I say.

"I want to celebrate," says Fish.

"How about some ice cream?"

"Great idea," says Fish. "Let's go. Right now."

"Do you think you should change out of your costume?"

Fish looks down at her gown. "What," she says, "this old thing?"

"Ravi's gonna kill you if you get ice cream on it."

"Come on," says Fish deviously. "Live a little."

She takes my hand and we jump together off the stage and run like crazy people up the aisle of the auditorium, through the double swinging doors, and into the empty foyer, where the janitor is pushing his tired broom across the floor. When he spots me and Fish holding hands, he winks at me, tips his baseball cap, and continues on down the hall, whistling.

I hold the door for her and she spins into the night, her gown floating around her like white mist. Most of the snow

358

has melted. You can smell spring under the ground, stirring in the earth, pulsing like a heartbeat. I stop in my tracks and look at the sky. I can't remember the last time I looked at the stars. Mom knew the names of all the constellations. When I was little she would help me connect the dots, as though all things had meaning and purpose and order. *Look at this one, Max,* she would say. *Can you see it? Can you see it?* I would gasp, because gasping seemed like the right thing to do. *I see it, Mommy. I see it up there.* But I never did.

They gleam above me now. Beautiful and chaotic. I take Fish's hand and stride, straight-backed and smiling, toward the ice cream parlor around the corner, where I know Dad and Grandma and Lydie and the twins are waiting for us. They will order us a double-fudge ice cream sundae and we will eat it with two spoons. They will make room for Fish to sit at the table with us and they will tell us both how proud they are. I will close my eyes and feel all that pride and love on my head like a blessing, like sunshine coming down, like two soft angel's lips kissing my hair.

ACKNOWLEDGMENTS

I am deeply grateful for the wisdom and eagle-eyes of my editor, Margaret Ferguson, who offered me the gift of her time, her critique, and her superhuman patience draft after draft. I am grateful for the positive spirit of my agent, Victoria Wells Arms, who talked me down from the ceiling when I thought I would never get it right. Thanks to my good friend Esther Ehrlich, who reminded me to find the love in every scene, and whose beautiful book, *Nest*, gave me the courage to keep writing. Thanks to the librarians at the J.V. Fletcher Library, who always smiled when I stayed late, and to the baristas at Pleasant Street Tea Company in Gloucester, Massachusetts, who supplied endless green-tea smoothies and the perfect funky ambiance for long summer days of writing by the sea. Finally, I owe a tremendous debt to my three gorgeous muses: Stephen, Joshua, and Benjamin Pixley, who gave me the gifts of their ears and their hearts when I read pages out loud during our beloved cross-country road trips. I could never have done it without your support. This novel is for you.

TEEN AND YA FICTION FROM PUSHKIN PRESS

THE RED ABBEY CHRONICLES

MARESI

NAONDEL

Maria Turtschaninoff

Translated by Annie Prime

'Combines a flavour of The Handmaid's Tale with bursts of excitement reminiscent of Harry Potter's magic duels'

Observer

THE BEGINNING WOODS

Malcolm McNeill

'I loved every word and was envious of quite a few…
A modern classic – rich, funny and terrifying'

Eoin Colfer

THE RECKLESS SERIES

1. THE PETRIFIED FLESH

2. LIVING SHADOWS

3. THE GOLDEN YARN

Cornelia Funke

'A wonderful storyteller'

Sunday Times

PIGLETTES

Clémentine Beauvais

Translated by Clémentine Beauvais

'A triumph of a book; so funny, so original, so sharp, so warm'
Katherine Rundell, author of *Rooftoppers*

THE DISAPPEARANCES

Emily Bain Murphy

'The Disappearances is a wonder of a book. I lost
myself in this world where reflections, scents and
stars go missing, and revelled in its reveal'
Kiran Millwood Hargrave, author of *The Girl of Ink & Stars*

THE WILDINGS

Nilanjana Roy

'A stylish, bloody, literary addition, set in India and
already a considerable critical success there. Rich
in cat telepathy and shuddery feral madness'
Guardian

THE OKSA POLLOCK SERIES

I. THE LAST HOPE
2. THE FOREST OF LOST SOULS
3. THE HEART OF TWO WORLDS
4. TAINTED BONDS

Anne Plichota and Cendrine Wolf

Translated by Sue Rose

'A feisty heroine, lots of sparky tricks and evil opponents
could fill a gap left by the end of the Harry Potter series'
Daily Mail